HAZE

Rebecca Crunden

ISBN-10: 198536428X
ISBN-13: 978-1985364288

Edited by Daniela Tarlton-Rees
Cover Art by Garrett Leigh @ Black Jazz
Design

For Dani, Meredith and Heather.

INTRODUCTION
Dirt

The tome weighed more than all of their schoolbooks combined and smelled musty, like a shop filled with things much older than themselves. Each page looked one breath away from breaking, and the boys took great pains not to damage the book. Given the fact that both had used their schoolbooks for batting practice more than once, the care they took not to tear the pages only emphasised just how nervous they were.

Erik and Miles had come to the cabin first thing after school, jumping out of their seats the second the bell rang. Neither had been able to focus all day and twice their teachers caught them passing each other notes.

Luckily, none of their teachers knew what to make of the odd questions scrawled in their nearly illegible handwriting:

Did you get what you needed?
Yeah. Dirt.

And, equally as perplexing:

Latin? Are you sure? Not Hebrew?
Nope. Latin, bro. Definitely Latin.

When their English teacher asked what they were discussing, Miles flashed a winning smile and said they were comparing their favourite versions of the Bible. How he'd kept a straight face, Erik couldn't fathom, but they'd somehow managed to avoid detention.

As Erik began leafing through the pages, turning each over with bated breath, Miles unpacked his bag and placed several odd-looking items on the table. Each one was more confusing than the last. Bones, sticks, a rabbit's foot. A very large jar of dirt.

Erik picked up the jar of dirt with a dubious expression. 'Why do we need dirt from the cemetery?' he asked, turning it over in his hands. The insides clinked together, rocks and twigs and leaves mixing with the dirt. There were a few bugs. He eyed the worm, feeling slightly bad. At least the plan wouldn't involve killing any of them.

Erik still vividly remembered seeing his father tear the wings off a dragonfly. A knot twisted in the pit of his stomach and he ran his finger over the glass where the worm was, making a silent promise to set it free later.

'I don't know,' said Miles, tearing Erik from his thoughts. 'I'm just doing what the book says to do. You said you wanted to talk to your ma. This is how we do it.'

Whether or not it was wise to attempt summoning the dead never occurred to either of them. At ten years old, they spared little thought to consequences. And both had already agreed that the consequences were worth it.

Miles stuck a stubby finger at the page where a large, confusing symbol was inked. 'We draw this one.'

Erik followed his gaze, still not wholly convinced but wanting so badly to believe. 'Are you sure Henry's right about this?'

'He's a priest,' said Miles with an air of authority. As if he himself was a priest. 'Priests are smart.'

'But I'm not religious,' said Erik. 'How does it even apply to me?'

Miles waved a hand. 'The dead don't care if you're religious.'

'How can the dead not care when the living do?'

'Because they don't,' said Miles simply. 'Religion's for before you die, not after. And your ma really won't care.'

Something inside Erik constricted painfully at those words. But before he could voice any further misgivings, Miles carried on. 'Besides, they wouldn't put someone stupid in charge of souls. I mean, I was gonna ask Rabbi Jacob, but he's out of town. And I don't know anyone else with knowledge of dead people and the afterlife. Do you?'

Erik's brow furrowed as he thought of the few adults who might be of use. 'We could ask the morgue?'

'You think the morgue is going to know more about souls than a priest?'

'I guess not.'

Miles gagged dramatically. 'And Paterson is so creepy.'

The apt description of the doctor they met in the morgue months before made Erik snort. 'Paterson is creepy,' he agreed.

'He looks like he bathes in the stuff they put on dead people.'

'*Gross*, Miles.' But Erik agreed all the same. The thought of going to a place filled with bodies was more than enough reason to concede Miles' point that priests had to be smart – after all, they were in charge, weren't they? People wouldn't entrust their souls to just anyone. That would be silly.

The boys drew the symbol along the floor of the abandoned house with far more meticulousness than they'd ever displayed in art class. Even still, their chalk kept snapping in the old floorboards and they had to remake several of the lines.

'Should have bought paint,' said Miles at one point when the piece of chalk he was holding snapped in half for the second time, leaving only a nub between his fingers.

Everything about the cabin was old and crumbling and mouldy. They'd found it when they were eight and had spent the last two years making it their fort. No one else ever came there and it had been a good meeting place when Erik used to crawl out his window each night, back when his mother was alive. Back when life didn't involve death.

In the months since, the cabin remained the one solid, steady thing in Erik's young life after Miles, and he hoped that doing the spell in the cabin would bring them some luck. He'd told his mother about the cabin. She would know where it was. She would know how to find him.

He hoped.

He hoped so badly that his stomach hurt and his hands shook and he wanted to cry. But he held it in and kept drawing. He didn't want Miles to see him cry again. At this point it was just embarrassing.

'Dude,' said Miles when they finished, staring at the page with wide eyes. 'I just realised I don't know how to pronounce anything in Latin.'

Erik glared at the words. He didn't, either. 'Is it phonetic?'

'What's *frenetic*?'

'*Pho-ne-tic*. Like, it's said how it's spelled.'

'Oh. Maybe.' Miles held the book out to him. 'You phonetic it.'

Rolling his eyes, Erik took the book. He tried to say the words as best he could, but they sounded odd and jarring and not like anything anyone – even the dead – would respond to.

Nothing happened.

He glanced at Miles, feeling sick with fear that it wasn't going to work. That his mother wasn't out there, watching over him, just waiting to be asked to come home. But Henry had said at the funeral that she would be listening. *She* had even said so before she died. 'Death is watching, Erik.' That's what she'd always said. 'Death is a friend who greets us at the end.'

So where was she?

'Now what?' he asked as the silence dragged on. He felt somewhat stupid.

'Try again?'

Erik repeated the spell. Still nothing happened.

Miles scratched the back of his head. 'Maybe Henry doesn't know what he's talking about.'

'Or maybe there's no way to bring someone back from the dead,' said Erik, closing the book with a snap.

He kicked out and his foot connected with the jar of grave dirt. Glass and dirt sprayed everywhere. A piece cut his cheek.

He didn't even feel it.

'We can try –'

'I don't want to,' said Erik, close to tears. His eyes found the worm on the ground. Had it died, too? Something else dead that didn't deserve it.

He forced a breath that felt like it was drawn through a plastic bag and turned away from the symbol, the dirt, the worm, and wiped furiously at his eyes. 'Let's just go.'

'Okay.' Miles offered up a smile of solidarity and put a hand on Erik's shoulder. 'Let's go to town. We'll get pizza. Dad gave me some money.'

With a last, hateful look at the symbol on the ground, Erik let Miles steer him out of the cabin and into the cold winter evening. The blood continued to drip down his cheek.

Hope was for idiots.

NINE YEARS LATER

CHAPTER ONE
She's Dead

The rain lashed down upon the town of Riverside with relentless gusto, flooding the gardens and streets, and filling the boots of anyone caught outside. This time of year, rain was an enduring companion and dealing with it was something of an art form for the residents of the small town. Wind screamed as it blew past the windows of Maplebrook, a small house that was far sturdier than it appeared and had seen its share of maelstroms.

Curled up on her bed, cast in a dim orange glow from the apple spice candles on the windowsill burning merrily away, Eliza Owens found the sounds oddly soothing. It was a chaotic orchestra that could not be stamped down or quieted, and yet somehow the madness outside always settled her racing thoughts. Like the night had a presence and reminded any and all listening that they were not alone. But where most nights the sounds eased her mind when it raced with anxiety, tonight her mind was spinning from giddy shock.

She rotated the ring slowly around her finger, a smile on her face. There was something decidedly odd about having a ring. Never one for jewellery, the feeling of it was as strange as the sight. A blue stone instead of a diamond. The type of ring that spoke of a far-removed generation.

She'd finished work early that day due to the rain and Erik, who had worked as a stable hand ever since he quit working for Wyatt Irons, had suggested they go for a hike instead of going home. The rain only increased on the drive. But then, so did their excitement.

Sam, Eliza's older sister, often called them insane for hiking in thunderstorms. But Eliza loved the lashing rain, the shrieking wind, the way the lightning painted its way across the darkening sky in the briefest of flashes, and Erik found her love of it deeply amusing.

They left his car at the trailhead and made their way up the muddy trail, squelching and sliding, laughing all the while as the rain soaked them to the bone.

They stopped by the lookout to admire the view. And it was then that Erik wrapped an arm around her stomach and held the ring up with his other hand.

'It was my mother's,' he'd whispered. 'And she'd love you as much as I do.'

Such simple words and yet they meant everything. The idea that Stacey Stern would have liked her made Eliza's stomach tighten; in happiness, and in sadness, for she would never get to meet her.

The sudden vibration of her phone jolted Eliza out of her musings, and she picked it up.

Unknown.

Not in the habit of answering unknown phone calls, she put it down.

The ringing ended a few seconds later. And then started up anew.

She bit her lip. The worry that it was Erik from an unknown number made her decision for her and she slid the green arrow to the other side of the screen.

'Hello?'

'Is this Eliza Owens?'

'Yeah,' said Eliza, heart hammering. At least it wasn't Erik. Even now, after he'd parted ways with Wyatt Irons, she worried.

'Who is this?' she prompted after the silence dragged on too long. Her gaze went up to the cracks in her ceiling that splintered around the glow-in-the-dark stars she put up with Sam when she was four. They still somehow worked.

'My name's Paige,' said the caller. 'Paige Osbourne.'

Eliza shrugged, still staring at the stars. It wasn't a name she recognised from school, but perhaps it was someone on a committee of some kind.

'*Okay?*' she said. 'What can I do for you, Paige?'

'I used to date Erik Stern.'

'You used to date Erik,' Eliza echoed, completely baffled and now thoroughly distracted. She sat up and crossed her legs, suddenly tense even if she had no reason to be. 'And that has what to do with me?'

'I have something to tell you,' said Paige. Her voice was strange. Almost too quiet. And not in a reassuring way. 'Will you meet me?'

'Just tell me now,' said Eliza, trying to keep herself from snapping. It was by far the strangest phone call she had ever received and she regretted answering at all. 'I'm not driving out in the rain to meet someone I don't know.'

'Please.'

'Why?'

This question was followed by a bizarrely long pause. So long that Eliza half-thought Paige had hung up. But then —

'It's important.'

'If you have something to tell me about Erik, say it, or I'm hanging up.'

There was a second long pause.

'Please.' Paige sounded ... scared. 'It won't take long.'

Now alarmed as well as curious, Eliza found herself unable to decline. 'Where?' she asked after several seconds.

Better to find out, surely?

Paige let out a rattling sound of relief. 'Do you know the Roadside Diner?'

It sounded vaguely familiar, but Eliza had no idea where it was. 'Is that in town?'

'It's on the main road heading west out of town,' said Paige. 'About twenty minutes. Past Briar's Hill.'

After another moment's deliberation, Eliza rolled off the bed and looked around for her coat. 'I swear to God, if you're full of shit, I'll kick your ass,' she warned.

'I'm not,' said Paige. 'Hurry.'

Eliza heaved a sigh. 'Fine. I'll be there in half an hour.'

The line went dead.

Not sure what to make of the phone call, Eliza donned her still-wet coat and sodden shoes with a grimace. They were cold and squelched with every step.

In the corridor, the low hum of sounds from the television downstairs in the sitting room told her that her father was home, but her mother wasn't. Likely Mira was working another night shift and wouldn't be home for hours yet.

Her parents were planning a holiday soon and both were working overtime to save extra money so that they could, according to Mira, 'Have fun without checking our bank accounts.'

Eliza was halfway down the stairs when she heard her sister call her name. She stilled on the landing and looked back.

'You going out?' asked Sam, stepping out of her bedroom. The soft chords of a folk song on her laptop followed her through the open door. She'd clearly just come home and looked exhausted from work. Her clothes were rumpled and her hair had mostly come out of its ponytail. Pink strands fell messily around her heart-shaped face.

Eliza nodded and gestured over her shoulder at the door. 'Meeting Erik. I won't be long.'

She wasn't sure why she was lying, but explaining the call would be too complicated and would raise questions she didn't yet have answers to.

Sam leaned against the stair railing, lips pursed in thought. She looked more exhausted than usual, with deep circles under her eyes; a strain in them that wasn't normally there.

'Everything okay?' asked Eliza, eyeing her curiously. They'd both been so busy of late there hadn't been much time to catch up with each other. After Erik, Sam was her best friend, but in recent weeks, Eliza spent all of her time with Erik and Sam spent all of her time with Maya, her girlfriend of four years.

Sam nodded. 'How are things with you two?'

'Perfect,' said Eliza, happy butterflies in her stomach. 'I'll be back in a bit. Tell you then?'

'Yeah, okay.'

Eliza didn't miss the odd expression on her sister's face. 'Something wrong?'

'No.'

'Sam, what?'

After an oddly long pause, her sister made a face and said, 'Are you being safe?'

Thoroughly taken aback, Eliza's eyebrows shot up. 'Nosy, much?'

The laugh that escaped Sam's lips was oddly strained. 'Just be careful, okay? Erik's great, but sometimes I think you two are moving too fast. I worry about you doing something you'll regret.'

Beyond perplexed by the rapid change in conversation, Eliza crossed her arms. 'We've had sex, Sam. You know that. We're safe.'

'Every time?'

'*Yes*. God. What's up with you?'

'You're nineteen, Eliza.'

'Thanks for the update,' she retorted. 'Any other enlightening bits of information?'

Sam sighed heavily and held out her hands. It was almost condescending, and Eliza's irritation spiked. 'I'm just saying, take it slow,' she said. 'Especially with him.'

'Why *especially* with him?'

'You know why.'

Eliza glared at her sister reproachfully. Of all the people she'd had to defend Erik to, her sister had never been one of them. 'It's not enough that he gets shit from literally everyone in town?' she snapped back. 'Now he gets shit from you? I thought you liked him.'

'I do like him,' said Sam vehemently. She walked around the railing and joined Eliza on the landing.

There was a strange urgency in Sam's bright green eyes that Eliza rarely saw there. Her sister was usually the calmer of the two, the one who took a step back before acting. Eliza had always admired that about her. And now Sam was jumping on the bandwagon. Just like everyone else. From schoolyard bullies to the elderly locals, Eliza had witnessed some truly revolting behaviour on behalf of the townspeople. More than a handful held Logan's heinousness against his only child. Never mind the fact that Erik had been in his aunt's custody since Stacey Stern was murdered.

'Erik's a good person,' she hissed at her sister. 'It's not his fault Logan's his father.'

Sam's next words were like salt on a wound: 'Yes, and it's not like we don't know what Wyatt Irons does.'

Eliza knocked her fist against the wall. 'Erik quit working for Wyatt *before* we got together.'

'How do you know?'

'Because he told me.'

'People lie. Guys lie.'

'He doesn't lie to *me.*'

'Don't be that idiot who believes the guy just because he's cute.'

Angrier than she could put into words, Eliza turned and darted down the steps, ignoring the apology Sam called after her.

She was near the door when her father waved her into the sitting room. 'Elle? You okay?'

Heart still pounding from the fight, Eliza pulled her sleeves down over her hands, in no mood to tell her father she was engaged and wandered into the sitting room. He was on the sofa folding laundry. There was a pot of tea on the table beside an empty box of cookies. It made her smile despite everything. Her father always seemed to be home, at the ready, there to comfort her and make her fights with her sister seem silly only a minute after they'd occurred.

Sure enough, he gave her a knowing, fatherly look over the rim of his glasses. 'You and Sam fighting?'

Eliza crossed her arms. 'She's decided she doesn't like Erik.'

Ryan's eyebrows shot up. 'Why's that?'

'Because it's the theme of this town, I guess.'

He tossed aside the socks he'd just balled and walked over. Wrapping his arms around her, he kissed the top of her head and said, 'Erik's got one of the saddest stories I've ever heard, but you know what?'

She leaned against him, inhaling the comforting smell of his aftershave. At least her dad was still on Erik's side.

'What?' she grunted.

'As a father who'll kick anyone's butt who hurts his daughters, I've never once doubted how much that boy loves you.'

A lump in her throat, Eliza stood on her tiptoes and kissed his cheek. 'Thanks, Dad.'

'And give Sammy a break,' he told her, ruffling her hair. 'She's known her share of shitheads. She's just worried about you. That's sort of her job.'

Eliza drew back and gave him a resolute nod. He was right. Sam had always been protective. That wasn't new. Likely someone at work was dealing with relationship drama and she was projecting it onto Eliza and Erik. She'd apologise later, and they'd forget the whole thing.

Almost instantly, the nauseated feeling diminished and Eliza nodded to herself. 'Yeah, okay,' she agreed begrudgingly. 'I'll forgive her stupid face.'

Ryan chuckled. 'Good woman. You heading out?'

'Just going to meet a friend for notes,' she said. 'I won't be long.'

'Okay,' he said, cupping her cheek and smiling. 'Drive safe. Call me if the rain gets too bad and you want me to come get you.'

'I will, I promise.'

It was raining steadily when she stepped outside, and the night was cold and off-putting, but she was still too intrigued by the phone call to not show up. She could name just about everyone in their fishbowl of a town and it bothered her immensely not to know who Paige was or why Erik had failed to mention her.

Before she could even start the engine, her phone vibrated again and this time it was Erik's name which appeared.

'Hi, babe,' she answered, starting the car and heading out onto the main road just as thunder rumbled in the distance and the rain fell with renewed fury.

'Hey,' he replied, and she could hear the smile in his voice. 'Wanted to say goodnight.'

She glanced at the clock. 'Since when do you go to bed before midnight?'

'Since I proposed to my girlfriend.' A low chuckle resonated from his throat. 'Well, fiancée, now.'

She smiled. 'Sounds weird.'

'Get used to it.'

'I intend to.'

'If I go to sleep now,' he continued, 'I'll be awake faster. And then I'll be able to see you.'

'Sounds like a plan.'

'Still want me to come for breakfast?'

The exit for the motorway appeared, distracting her temporarily. It had been a while since she'd come this direction and she took a second to orientate herself before remembering to respond to Erik.

'Ma's making muffins or something,' she said. 'She'll take it personally if you don't come.'

'That's because I compliment her cooking more than you three combined.'

'That's because you eat *all* her cooking.'

'Growing boys need food, babe.'

'Growing boys need two pies?'

'Absolutely.'

They laughed in unison, but Eliza couldn't maintain it.

'You're quiet,' he noted after the pause dragged on. 'And you seem distracted. What's on your mind, babe?'

She took a deep, somewhat stilted breath. 'Nothing,' she muttered, tapping her thumb anxiously on the steering wheel. 'Had a fight with Sam, that's all.'

'Oh. I'm sorry. What happened?'

'Nothing.'

'Babe,' he said softly. 'What is it?'

She propped her elbow against the window and bit the edge of her pinkie nail. There was no reason not to tell him, and answers from him might explain at least some of what was going on. After a moment's hesitation, she asked, 'Do you know anyone named Paige?'

Erik was quiet for a second and then he said, 'Yeah, my ex-girlfriend. And Paige Krieger at school. That's it, though. Why?'

'I got a phone call earlier,' she mumbled, relieved he hadn't lied and then getting annoyed at herself for letting Sam's doubt crawl under her skin. She added, 'From Paige.'

'Paige Krieger?'

'No, your ex.'

He made a small noise and she heard him sit up. 'Eliza, Paige is dead.'

Eliza's hand slipped on the wheel and she pulled over to the side of the road before she crashed into a tree. 'What?'

'We started dating when we were twelve and she killed herself when we were fourteen,' he said. He sounded more wretched than she'd ever heard him. 'Why do you think I don't talk about her?'

Eliza shook her head in confusion. 'Then who called me?'

'I don't know,' he said. 'What did she say?'

'That she wanted to meet me.'

His breath caught. 'Eliza, where are you?'

She made a face at the window. 'I'm going to meet her.'

'What? Why? Some girl calls you in the middle of the night and asks you to meet her and you agree? That's crazy, babe!'

It was hard to disagree with him, but she tried to justify it regardless. 'She sounded scared, Erik.'

'Paige Osbourne died five years ago. Whoever called you isn't Paige.'

'Why would someone lie about that?' she asked, totally perplexed.

'I don't know.'

'Well, I want to know.'

'Whoever you spoke to wasn't Paige. I don't know who it was, but that's so creepy and weird.'

She held out a hand. 'Why don't I just meet this person and see what her deal is?'

'Because we don't meet strangers in the middle of the night. Especially when they pretend to be a dead person.' She heard him leaving his house and he raised his voice over the wind. 'Eliza, do you remember my father's fans? The ones who used to show up? Fucking psychos. This is a really bad idea, babe.'

Despite the twisting in her stomach, Eliza felt stupidly curious. 'She might be crazy, but isn't that all the more reason to meet her? Get her help? She could be, I don't know, like a danger to herself.'

'What if it's not someone crazy?' he countered. The background noise around him died down as he got into his car. 'What if it's someone messing with you?'

She scowled at her reflection. 'Then they're getting a punch on the nose.'

'Fine,' he said, and she heard his engine start. 'Do you mind if I join you?'

'Of course not.' Relief seeped through her. She very much did not want to confront a crazy woman alone.

'Where are you going?'

'The Roadside Diner.'

'Where is that?'

'On the main road heading south. Past Briar's Hill.'

'Okay, I'm on my way. Just ... wait for me, okay?' he added. 'I love you.'

'I love you, too,' she told him before ending the call and pulling back onto the road. The rain continued to lash down from the heavens and cold crept into the car, chilling her to the bone. When at last the diner came into view, Eliza's stomach was churning.

She got soaked jogging into the diner, but the warm blast of coffee-scented air that hit her upon entry was somewhat calming.

She brushed wet hair out of her face and looked around as discreetly as possible. There were only two customers inside: an elderly couple drinking coffee in the corner, speaking in low tones. No sign of a young woman.

Eliza took a seat by the window and glared out into the night. The rain was still coming down hard and it was difficult to see anyone outside.

She jiggled her foot with increasing nervousness. Now that she was here, she had no idea what to expect.

The door jingled behind her and she glanced around.

To her surprise and horror, Logan Stern stepped inside. He looked nothing like his son. Out of prison on a technicality, no one in Riverside felt safe when he was around. Only Wyatt Irons was openly cocky about it, but Wyatt had thugs to back up his boldness. It was why Erik had joined in the first place and why Logan had mostly left him alone. But Eliza didn't know what the story was since Erik quit.

Logan caught sight of her instantly and walked over to her booth. ''Evening, Eliza,' he said, sliding into the seat across from her.

'Hi,' she said, sitting back and shifting uncomfortably. 'What are you doing here?'

'I wanted to talk to you,' he said. 'I'm glad we now have the chance.'

'Erik's on his way.'

Logan waved a hand airily. 'This won't take long.'

'What do you want?'

'That ring belongs to me. Erik had no right taking it from the safe.'

A cold realisation crept up her spine and she had to resist the urge to shiver. 'How did you know I was here?'

The smile which spread across his face was catlike and spine-chilling. 'I saw you drive up.'

But he hadn't been there when she walked in. Only the waiters and the elderly couple. Which meant he'd either followed her, or known she was going to arrive.

The bizarre events of the night suddenly felt even more suspicious, and she got out of the booth, trying not to shake with rising fear.

He caught her arm and her stomach flipped.

'You're a creep, Logan,' she said through gritted teeth. 'Let go of me.'

A few of the waitresses looked over and one raised an eyebrow, silently asking if she needed help.

Eliza shook her head and smiled in gratitude before looking back at him. 'Touch me again and I'm telling my father,' she promised, wrenching her arm out of his grip. 'And won't *that* be fun for you?'

It wasn't much of a threat. She wasn't even sure her father knew how to punch anyone. He was a quiet, reserved sort of man, one who preferred offices and theatres. One who wouldn't cross paths with someone like Logan in a million years. Regardless, the threat made her feel better. If nothing else, her father knew more than a few good lawyers and he gave investment advice to half the town. Where everyone counted the days until Logan left or died, and hated Erik for being related to him, everyone loved her father for helping them with their good fortune, and Eliza and Sam were beloved as a result.

She left the diner without a backward glance and headed to her car, shaking so badly it was a miracle she didn't trip.

Less than a second later, she heard the door open behind her and moved faster. She could hear his footsteps even over the sounds of the wind and rain. Before she could unlock her car door, he put a hand on the window.

His proximity meant she could smell the beer and smoke he'd been consuming and the sick aftershave that failed to cover it, which instead added a noxious, chemical edge to his odour.

'Give me my ring, Eliza, and we'll call it a night.'

'You need to go,' she said, voice rising as her panic did. 'Right now.'

Eliza yanked on the door handle, but he didn't remove his hand and she couldn't force it open. Panic tightened her throat; if she moved an inch, they'd be touching. It was much, much too close for her comfort.

'Move,' she said, fingers tightening around her keys.

'Give me my ring.'

'Logan!'

She almost cried with relief and whirled around to see Erik sprinting towards them. He hadn't even turned off his car or closed the door. A second later he had his father by the coat and yanked him away. She'd seen Erik angry a few times, but never as furious as he looked in that instant.

Logan snorted, and suddenly there was a gun in Erik's hand.

Eliza went cold all over.

'Back the *fuck* off,' he spat at his father. Then, to her, 'Babe, get in your car and lock the door.'

With zero hesitation, Eliza yanked open her car door and got inside. She watched, heart hammering.

She couldn't make out what they were saying over the rain, but Erik kept the gun aimed at Logan as he backed towards his own car.

But Logan held her gaze until she averted her eyes and drove onto the road, the diner being swallowed by the night.

When she pulled up outside of her house twenty minutes later, Erik parked and got out of his car only to join her.

Erik ran a hand through his black hair and looked over at her. 'Are you okay?'

'Not really,' she admitted. 'I feel sick.'

He reached out and wrapped an arm around her, drawing her close. 'I'm so sorry, babe.'

She buried her face in his neck and breathed in the smell of him. 'Why can't he just leave you alone?'

'Because he's psychotic.' Erik sat back. Even half-shrouded in darkness, the fear in his eyes was apparent. 'Can I stay tonight? I'll sleep in the guestroom. I just –'

'Erik,' she interrupted. Her heartrate picked up with anticipation of whatever answer she was going to get to her question. 'Where did you get a gun?'

He scratched his cheek, clearly uncomfortable. 'I got it out of his safe when I took the ring.'

'Why?'

'I feel better having it on me.'

She didn't know how to take that, so she asked, 'Do you even know how to shoot a gun?'

'Yes,' he said.

Eliza didn't know what to say to that, either, so she pressed her head against the steering wheel and closed her eyes.

'Babe?'

'What?'

'Are you mad at me?'

She looked over at him. She suddenly felt bone-tired and defeated. Heaving a sigh, she slipped off the ring and held it out. 'Give it back. You can get me another one.'

'No,' he said, almost sharply. Like the mere suggestion insulted him. 'That ring was given to my mother by my grandmother. It's mine. Not his.'

Eliza shook her head and offered it again. 'Babe, he's insane. I don't care what ring I have. It doesn't matter to me.'

'Well, it matters to me!' Erik slammed his fist against the window. He didn't break it, but it sounded like it hurt; he shook his hand, hard. 'He's taken enough, Eliza! He's taken too much.'

She could see him start to disintegrate and got out of the car. Walking around to his side, she opened the door and held out her hand.

Where she panicked continuously about losing the ones she loved, Erik was forever angry about all that he had lost already. Neither were good, but she knew how to make his mind quiet down. At least long enough to breathe.

They went into the house quietly and she led him up to her bedroom. Slipping inside and closing the door, she steered him over to the bed. Before she could move to sit beside him, he wrapped his arms around her and pressed his head against her stomach.

'I love you,' he whispered, tightening his grip. 'I love you so much, babe.'

She ran a hand over his head in soothing motions. When at last he sounded steady, she asked her next question.

'Why did you never tell me about Paige?'

Erik shook his head, as if he didn't even know the answer himself. 'I was just a kid when we were together,' he muttered. 'She'd always been unhappy, but it just got worse and worse.'

'How so?'

'I met her when she was twelve; she'd already started cutting herself when she was eleven.'

'Christ.'

Erik nodded, and his face scrunched up with memory. When next he spoke, he sounded painfully detached. 'At the time it made no sense to me. I'm not sure it even makes sense to me now, to be honest. But as a kid I couldn't fathom how someone could be so unhappy in such a happy home.'

It broke Eliza's heart. 'Was she sick?'

'Had to be, no?' He shrugged and moved back across the bed until he was sitting against the wall. Kicking off his shoes, he crossed his arms and tucked his fists into his armpits.

Eliza sat across from him and drew her legs into her chest. Half of her wasn't sure she wanted to know, but the whole event had left her achingly curious.

'I mean, that's not normal,' he surmised. 'Kids don't want to die unless there's something very, very wrong. But at that age, it frustrated me. It was too much for me. Not even childhood infatuation and love made me strong enough to handle all of her pain.' He looked disgusted with himself and she reached out and put her hand over his.

'It's not your fault.'

'Does that make it better?'

'No,' she agreed. 'I guess not.'

'I got a frantic phone call from her one day after school begging me to come over. I got two buses up to see her. Her parents weren't home. I had to break the downstairs window just to get in. I found her on the bathroom floor covered in blood, half-dead.'

'Oh my God.'

He blinked tears from his eyes and his hand tightened around hers. 'I think she tried to hang herself first. Her neck was so bruised. But by the time I got there, she'd cut her wrists. And … And all I could think when I saw her was how much she looked like my mother … just lying there …

'I held a towel around her wrists until the responders arrived. They drove me home and a few days later she asked me to come see her. I couldn't. I cared about her, but I just didn't know what to do. I was fourteen and so scared and freaked out.' He let out a shaking breath and knocked his head back against the wall. 'She killed herself a few days later. After, her mother asked me to come to the funeral to say goodbye. We keep in touch. Even now.'

For a while, neither spoke. Erik's sad story filled the space between them, but Eliza was still confused as to how it was at all relevant to *her*.

'Why would Logan get someone to pretend to be Paige just to get the ring back?'

Erik held out a hand and snorted. 'I have no clue.'

'What if the two have nothing to do with each other?'

'Who else could have known about Paige?' he wondered aloud. 'My father met her.'

Eliza's eyebrows shot up. 'How? I thought Gloria got custody.'

He shook his head slowly. 'I lived with her just after Ma died and Logan was in prison. But when he got out, she had to fight him for custody. There were a few months there where I lived with him.'

'I didn't know that.'

'Only Miles knew.'

She moved to his side and rested her head on his shoulder. In his arms, she felt warm and safe and content. 'You deserved better,' she murmured.

He kissed the top of her head and hugged her close. 'I got you. You're proof the universe gives you good for all the bad.'

She looked up at him, smiling stupidly. 'You're kind of wonderful, you know?'

'And you're perfect,' he replied, and he leaned in to kiss her.

The day could not have had more ups and downs, and both passed out from exhaustion soon thereafter.

Neither slept well and come morning, Erik suggested they do nothing at all but eat and watch movies, to which Eliza wholeheartedly concurred.

It was late afternoon when Sam came in with Maya. From the flush in their cheeks and their gasping breaths, both were in high spirits.

Maya had a box of beer under her arm. 'I'm being promoted!' she announced, raising her free arm into the air in a fist pump. 'Who's up for celebrating?'

Eliza disentangled herself from Erik to give Maya a hug. 'Congratulations.'

'Not bad, dude,' said Erik, walking over and clapping her on the back. 'Getting a raise?'

'Barely!'

'The best kind of raise,' said Eliza with a laugh.

Erik nudged Maya. 'All in the title, none in the bank.'

Maya ruffled his hair affectionately and the small, simple act sent a wave of relief through Eliza. After years of dating Sam, the four of them constantly together, Maya treated Erik like the little brother she didn't have. Whatever Sam's issues with Erik, it was clear Maya had no reservations.

'So?' she prompted, grinning from ear to ear. 'We celebrating or what?'

'Of course,' said Erik, winking at her. 'Where to?'

'The mountains! Get your coats!'

Eliza caught Sam's eye and smiled tentatively. After a beat, Sam returned the gesture.

It was a cheerful drive, and Erik held Eliza's hand, his finger playing absently with the engagement ring. Every time they caught each other's eye, they'd smile and laugh, the shroud of the night before all but gone.

When they reached the trailhead, Maya parked, and everyone clambered out.

The late spring air was warm and within minutes they removed their coats. Bugs flitted about, brought out by the rain the night before, happy to dance in the damp air.

'So,' said Erik as they moseyed along. 'Does this pay raise mean you're buying us all beer from now on? Because I approve.'

Maya shoved him. 'Not on your life, Stern!'

Everyone laughed.

Halfway up the hill, Maya called them to a stop and began passing around beer cans. When she handed one to Eliza, she did a doubletake and caught her hand.

'Hang on,' she said, looking up and grinning broadly. 'Is that an engagement ring I see?'

Sam, who had been staring into the trees, clearly lost in thought, whirled around. 'What?'

Eliza smiled as Erik slung his arm around her shoulders. 'Yeah,' she said happily. 'As of yesterday.'

Maya held up her beer. 'That's amazing, guys. Congrats!'

But Sam's face had gone whiter than the snow which capped the mountains in the distance and Eliza's heart sank.

'You can't,' she murmured. The words were barely more than a whisper, but Sam still managed to draw everyone's attention.

Eliza raised her eyebrow at her sister, all hope that Sam would be supportive vanishing. 'Can't what?'

'You can't get married.'

Beside Eliza, Erik looked more than a little surprised and more than a little hurt. It was apparent he had not expected Sam's reaction to be negative. Nor, it seemed, had Maya, who seemed equally as taken aback.

'I'm sorry,' Sam continued, setting her beer on the ground and walking over to them. 'But you're both too young. It won't last. You don't even know each other well enough yet.'

'Not all of us have the attention span of a gnat,' said Eliza acidly.

'Hey,' said Maya, always the peacekeeper. 'That's not fair. She's looking out for you.'

'Clearly.'

'I am!' Sam reached out and took her hand. 'Look, let's just discuss this at home. Alone.'

Eliza wrenched her arm out of her sister's grip. 'Anything you say I'm just going to tell Erik.'

'Eliza —'

'No,' said Erik. 'I want to hear whatever it is you've got to say. It's obviously about me.'

Sam clammed up, clearly disinclined to share whatever it was in front of him. She crossed her arms and looked pointedly at Eliza.

Maya raised her hands, one still holding a can of beer. 'Why don't we all calm down, all right? It's been such a good night. Let's not ruin it.'

'No,' said Eliza. She glared at her sister, who was still wavering. 'What is your problem?'

'Eliza —'

'Just tell me!'

Sam reached out and grabbed her by the arm again. She pulled Eliza a few paces away until they were by the river's rushing edge. She leaned in and pitched her voice low. 'Erik's too much like his father at times, okay? It scares me. It's *been* scaring me.'

Eliza stared at her. 'He's nothing like Logan.'

'Isn't he? He's not safe, Eliza. One of these days he's going to lose his temper and you'll be in the middle. You should hear some of the stories going around about him.'

'I have!'

'Where there's smoke, there's fire, Elle.'

'Bullshit.'

'Is that really what you think of me?'

Eliza and Sam glanced up to see Erik and Maya within earshot. Maya looked shocked; Erik looked stricken and betrayed.

'I thought we were friends, Sam,' he croaked.

Frustration coming off her in waves, Sam stamped her foot. 'I want to think you're a good person, Erik. But good people can have bad tempers and I don't want Eliza around that. I don't want to see her get hurt.'

His eyes widened, his mouth twisting in disbelief. 'You think I would hurt her.'

'Maybe not intentionally,' she allowed. 'But you're erratic, Erik. It's a little worrying.'

A ragged noise tore out of him. 'You honestly think I could do that? You think I could hurt – you think I could do something to Eliza?'

Despite the heated outrage in the words, Erik no longer looked angry. The confrontation had transformed him from tall and forbidding to someone so small, so fragile, a gust of wind could have knocked him over. It made Eliza's blood boil and she wasn't sure she'd ever been more furious at her sister. They all knew what Logan was like. They all knew why Erik had so many scars and had gone to the doctor so often as a child. He deserved their compassion, not suspicion.

Sam sighed unhappily. 'I didn't want to have this conversation now.'

'You brought it up!' he roared. 'I thought we were friends!'

Maya put a hand on his shoulder and offered him a small smile. 'Let's everyone just calm down.'

Erik stepped back, dark eyes narrowed angrily. 'Why? You think I'm going to attack your girlfriend? You think I'll do to her what my father did to my mother? You think I'm like that?'

'I never said that,' said Maya. She held up both hands pacifyingly. 'I said nothing. I'm just trying to help.'

'So you agree with Sam or not?'

A horrible silence followed, filled only by the matching sounds of gasping, unsteady breaths coming from all four. When it became clear Sam wasn't talking, Erik turned to Eliza. There was a beseeching glint in his eyes.

'Babe —'

'Of course I don't think you would hurt me,' she said, cutting him off. 'You're nothing like your father.'

She reached out and took his hand and, without a word to her sister, she led Erik down the path away from them.

It had been a warm night to start with, but at that point the world felt frozen. There was no sound in the surrounding forest, not even crickets. It was as if the fight had sucked the warmth from the world.

They were halfway around the bend when Sam caught up to them.

Maya trailed behind, an incredibly uncomfortable expression on her face.

'Erik, wait!'

He stilled. There was an edge to his stance, but it was clear he hoped Sam had changed her tune.

'I didn't mean it to come out like that,' said Sam sincerely. 'I just worry about my sister. Is that so unreasonable?'

'I worry, too,' he whispered, and Eliza squeezed his hand.

'It's not the same.'

'What it is you think I'm going to do to her?'

Sam made a face.

'What is it? What have I ever done to you?' He looked beyond confused and hurt. As if Sam was his sister, not Eliza's, and she was taking one of his last vestiges of family. 'For fuck's sake, Sam, I *helped* you!'

Maya looked at her girlfriend. 'What is he talking about?'

Before Sam could answer, Erik added, 'He roofied you and I put him in a hospital bed for it!'

Eliza looked from one to the other in astonishment. She felt dizzy and ill. 'What?'

Maya, too, was staring at Sam in horrified bewilderment. 'How didn't I know about this?'

'It was years ago,' said Sam quietly. She tucked a stray strand of pink hair behind her ear before crossing her arms protectively over her chest. 'Before he and Eliza were even dating. An awful house party.'

Erik's scowl only deepened. 'And have I ever given you *any* reason to think badly of me? How can you compare me to that *murderer*?'

Sam bit her lip, clearly not wanting to say more.

Now Eliza's interest was piqued. The anger she had initially felt dissipated as confusion set in. 'Sam, what is it? Come on.'

'Can we please just go home and discuss this in private?'

Erik snorted in hysterical derision. 'Oh good, so you can try and convince her to leave me?'

'That's not going to happen,' Eliza assured him. 'Come on, you know me better than that.'

He didn't look away from Sam. 'Just say it. We're all dying to hear what your reasoning is for suddenly hating me.'

Sam nodded, suddenly looking resolute. 'Fine. You really want to know? I talked to Paige Osbourne.'

Where Maya appeared utterly lost, Eliza and Erik both let out sounds of disbelief.

'Oh my God,' said Eliza irritably. 'That's what this is about?'

Sam did a doubletake. 'You know?'

'Paige is dead, Sam. It's just Logan being a dick.'

'I spoke to her a couple of weeks ago,' said Sam. 'She's not dead.'

Cold confusion set into Eliza's bones and her hands went to her head. 'What the fuck is going on?'

'She's dead,' said Erik adamantly.

'No, she's not,' said Sam. 'I had coffee with her.'

'Maybe it was just some sick joke,' Maya suggested, hands in her pockets. 'A rotten prank.'

'It wasn't,' said Sam firmly.

Erik had had enough. 'Paige is *dead*!' he bellowed. 'I went to her funeral!'

'I saw her bruises!' shouted Sam. 'She told me about the cabin!'

The colour drained from his face. 'What?'

'Don't play dumb.'

'I'm not playing dumb. What are you talking about?'

'You're not the first one in your family to —'

Eliza lunged at her sister, slapping her so hard across the face that Sam stumbled backwards. Pain shot through Eliza's hand and up to her elbow as a red print appeared on her sister's face. Remorse cascaded through her, but before she could utter an apology, Sam shoved Eliza back just as hard.

'Enough!' said Maya, catching Sam's arm. 'This is ridiculous!'

It was clear Sam wasn't listening. She wrenched out of Maya's grip and Erik stepped in front of her.

'Don't,' he warned.

'Move, Erik.'

'I'm serious,' he said, voice low and filled with warning. 'Don't touch her again.'

For a second, Eliza thought that would be the end of it.

And then Sam socked him in the jaw.

He shoved her away on instinct.

It ought to have sent her only a step back; there was little force to it. Instead, it sent her flying.

Sam collided with a tree on the other side of the path and dropped to the ground; the same way a rag doll would fall if flung across a room by a child.

Eliza's whole world became fog.

Fragments.

Erik running to Sam's side and begging her to wake up.

Maya screaming and sobbing.

Sam, unmoving.

Dead.

FIVE YEARS LATER

CHAPTER TWO
Look Who's Back

It was a cool, slightly humid Tuesday, rain on the horizon, skies grey and grim, when a familiar car pulled up into an empty space on Main Street. Anyone who saw it knew instantly who was back and few were polite enough to pretend not to notice.

Erik stepped out, donning his jacket, stomach in sickening knots.

He tried to ignore the other pedestrians, although it was hard not to wonder what they were thinking. At twenty-four, his beard had stopped growing in patches, his body had caught up with itself, and he no longer flinched or quickened his pace when people stared at him. It helped to look more intimidating than he felt, because at that moment he felt about as welcome as wet dog shit.

But unwanted attention had followed him his whole life and he was used to it. In Riverside, his father's reputation coloured everyone's opinion; in Silverlake, the reputation that had hung over him had been of his own making. One he was less than proud of.

Not bothering to lock his car, he walked towards the town dentistry where his aunt had worked for almost twenty years.

Business appeared to be good; the building had been redone since last he had seen it, updated and freshened. Flowers grew in abundance out front. Everything was tidy and manicured.

The little bell over the door chimed as he walked inside, and Gloria looked up. With greying hair and an ageless smile, she was a comforting sight and he knew instantly that coming home was the right choice.

'Erik!' She hurried over to him and pulled him into a tight embrace. 'Oh, darling! How have you been?'

He stepped back after a beat. 'Miles told me about Logan. I came to sort out the house.'

Gloria was still appraising him with concerned confusion. 'You didn't have to come all the way down for that, honey.'

'I did,' he said. 'And I came for you.'

She smiled gratefully. Perhaps more gratefully than she meant to show, for a second later she hesitated. 'You sure —'

'I am.'

'Erik —'

'*Auntie.*'

She smiled in defeat. 'Thank you, sweetheart. Where are you staying?'

'With Miles.'

'Do you have a phone I can reach you at?'

Erik nodded and leaned down on the receptionist's desk. He scrawled a number on the notepad and tore it off to hand to her.

'I'm going to the house later to sort through his crap,' he said. 'Key's still the same?'

She nodded. 'I'll meet you there.'

Erik kissed her cheek and left the office without another word. He felt ill just talking about his father, but he waited until he was halfway down the street before stopping and lighting a cigarette in a desperate attempt to quell the shaking of his hands. He had to smoke about half before he could source enough calm to carry on.

Pulling his phone out of his pocket, he sat on an empty bench and waited for Miles to answer.

After several rings, Miles grunted a 'hello'.

'It's me,' said Erik.

'You back yet?'

'Yeah. In town. Where're you?'

'Finishing a sale. Wanna meet at Joanie's?'

'Sure,' said Erik, blowing out a cloud of smoke. His blood was thrumming with anxiety and he couldn't stop bouncing his leg. 'Ten, twenty?'

'Give me about twenty,' said Miles. 'I'm going out to Calico.'

'See you then.'

Erik put the phone back into his pocket and stuck the cigarette between his lips, glancing around the street.

It hadn't changed at all. In truth, Riverside had probably looked the same since 1860 and was unlikely to change much in the future. Aside from the electrical lines and parked cars, it could have been in another century altogether. He'd loved that about it once. Now he wished it wasn't so familiar. Every shadow felt sinister, every gust of wind ill. He felt like the very air of the town was watching him.

'Erik? Erik Stern is that you?'

He looked around, startled, and then dearly wished he hadn't.

Behind him, holding two bags of shopping, was Mira Owens. It was hard to be surprised — there were only so many shops in town, he was bound to run into someone he didn't want to see — but he still felt like kicking himself for not waiting in his car.

She looked decades older than she had the last time he had seen her. The spark was long extinguished from her eyes and she had more wrinkles than she ought to in her early fifties.

Heart pounding with guilt and remorse, Erik stood and walked over to her. Not sure whether he should embrace her or back off, he nodded uncomfortably.

'Hello, Mira,' he mumbled. 'Long time.'

'You look wonderful,' she said with a motherly smile that set off pangs in his chest. 'Time away has done you a world of good, sweetheart.'

It was not the reaction he had been expecting.

'Thanks,' he said stupidly. 'How are you?'

Her smile didn't reach her dark eyes and the small attempt threatened to shatter him. 'We're hanging in there. Things are difficult, but ...'

Erik had to clear his throat to force away the worry and guilt before he could respond. 'How's Ryan?'

'A bit under the weather,' she said quietly. 'But you should come by for dinner if you're here for a while. I know he would love to see you. I would, too. We've missed you around here.'

For so long – and even now – he'd wanted to be part of their family. Entertaining the idea, even for a second, felt like opening an old, barely-healed hole in his chest. It was Mira who taught him how to make cheesecake from scratch, how to write a school paper; Ryan taught him how to tie a tie, maintain a garden and fix the engine in his car on his own. Erik had wanted them as parents almost as much as he'd wanted Eliza to be his wife.

He shifted back and forth on the balls of his feet, discomfort mounting. 'Yeah ... I'm here to help my aunt with Logan's things, you know? If I have time, though ... yeah, that'd be nice.' He winced at his utter lack of tact.

'How are you handling everything, sweetheart?'

He shrugged. 'It's not like anyone's going to mourn him.'

She put a hand on his arm. 'He was still your father, Erik.'

'No, he wasn't.'

He felt like he was being judged by his own mother and put his sunglasses on so that he had an excuse to break eye contact. Not wanting to linger longer than necessary, he lit another cigarette and stepped back. 'I ought to go,' he said stiffly. 'I'm meeting Miles at Joanie's.'

'Sure,' she said with an understanding smile. 'You'll drop by if you can?'

'If I can,' he said, very much hoping he couldn't. 'It was lovely to see you, Mira. Give Ryan my love.'

'And Eliza?'

Erik said nothing, only nodded and walked away. By that point his hands were shaking too badly to hold the cigarette, and he stamped it out with his foot.

He wanted to punch something, but fortunately there was nothing nearby, and he carried on down the road.

Joanie's was a café that had been around since Erik's parents were children. It was filled with cracked, worn chairs and benches, and made truly terrible coffee that everyone loved for some reason unfathomable to anyone who was not from Riverside.

After he'd ordered, the manager, Ciaran, who had worked there for over a decade, asked Erik how he was and where he'd been; Erik gave a noncommittal answer and took his coffee outside. Ciaran let him be and didn't follow him out. Ciaran, unlike most, didn't care about anyone's personal life.

Erik was halfway through his second cup of coffee and on his fourth cigarette when Miles arrived.

Short, blonde hair in a messy disarray, stubble all over his cheeks, and smelling strongly of cannabis, Miles was one of the few familiar things in Erik's life which brought him any comfort.

He stood and Miles yanked him close, clapping him on the back.

'Welcome home, brother.'

'Thanks.'

When they parted, Miles dropped down into the empty chair across from him and leaned back. 'So, Riverside's wayward son returns.'

'Front page news,' said Erik with a grimace. 'Christ, I hope not.'

Miles wiggled his eyebrows as he lit a cigarette. 'Baby, I wrote your name all over my calendar and counted down the days.'

Erik threw a napkin at him with a laugh. It felt good to laugh and he was suddenly glad to have come back. If only to see Miles.

'Gone to Gloria yet?'

'First thing.'

'How's she doing?'

'Seems all right.'

'That's good. I had dinner with her two nights ago.'

Erik smiled at that. 'Thanks, man.'

Miles waved off his gratitude. 'Anyone else?'

'Mira.'

Miles raised both eyebrows and let out a low whistle that was accompanied by a billow of smoke. 'That's rather unfortunate timing. How'd that go?'

'Wonderful,' said Erik dryly. 'Not uncomfortable at all.'

Miles leaned back in his chair, flicking his lighter open and shut. When the sunlight caught the zippo, Erik noticed with a small smile that it was the one he'd given Miles for his sixteenth birthday.

'She didn't chase you down with a pitchfork, did she?'

'No,' said Erik. 'She was delighted to see me.'

For a second, Miles eyed him. When it became clear Erik didn't feel like enlightening him, he nudged him under the table and prompted, 'And you look like someone pissed in your coffee because?'

Erik shrugged and took one of the cigarettes. The guilt left him shaky and weak. 'What am I supposed to say to her? I have nothing to say that is remotely good enough.'

Miles looked up as Ciaran appeared and placed a cup of coffee down in front of him. 'Cheers,' he said. 'Another one for EJ, here.'

Ciaran nodded and looked between them. 'Anything else?'

Miles glanced at Erik with a thoughtful expression. He took food very seriously and ate whenever the option was presented to him. 'Bagels? Bagels. Blueberry? Everything? Cranberry? Chocolate? No? Definitely blueberry.'

Ciaran rolled his eyes and Erik had to stifle a laugh. Miles was exactly the sort of person who had waiters repeat the specials at least twice.

'And for you?' said Ciaran.

'Same,' said Erik quickly.

'With jam,' said Miles.

Ciaran nodded. 'Cream cheese?'

The suggestion made Miles gag. 'I'd rather eat smegma,' he said tartly.

Erik choked on his coffee and Ciaran turned on his heel, lip curled in distaste, and walked back inside.

'Trust you to ruin my appetite,' said Erik. 'Christ, Miles.'

Miles' lips turned down pompously. 'Cream cheese ruins all appetites.'

'You have a real problem with such an innocuous spread.'

'It's the little things that ruin a day, my friend. Now,' said Miles, leaning back in his chair and putting his hands behind his head. 'Tell me about your adventures.'

Erik shrugged. 'Not really one for adventures.'

'My. Foot.'

With a rueful chuckle, Erik ran a hand through his hair before holding it out in question. 'What do you want to know?'

'Last we talked you said you were finishing up a job for Wyatt.'

'I did,' said Erik. 'Finished. Told him I wanted out. Again.'

'How'd he take that?'

'He wants me to think about it. Gave me a month.'

'That's worrisome.'

Erik shook his head. 'Wyatt wouldn't touch me.'

'Yeah,' said Miles with a small scoff. 'Maybe.'

Erik stamped out the end of his cigarette and scratched the side of his face as he tried to formulate an answer.

Wyatt had been good to him for years, but Erik was more than done making money with him. It left an acrid taste on his tongue and a twist behind his heart he couldn't untangle.

What he said was, 'I'm not bringing that shit back here. I told him that.'

Ciaran returned then with their bagels and they paused their conversation to thank him. When he disappeared, Erik tore off a piece of the bagel and ate a bite, not feeling very hungry at all, but glad to have something to do with his hands.

'You coming back?' asked Miles, piling strawberry jam in thick globs over his bagel. 'I was going to say that I could use a roommate.'

'You hate living with people.'

'You're not people. You're just a little shithead.'

They grinned at each other, but then Erik shook his head. 'I'm not staying. I appreciate the offer, though.'

'Because you have so many other places to be,' said Miles, kicking him affectionately under the table. 'Why ditch Wyatt if you're not staying?'

Erik made a face and downed the rest of his coffee. When the silence dragged on, a noise of exasperation left Miles.

'Eliza?' He snapped his fingers in front of Erik's face. 'It's because of Eliza, isn't it?'

Erik had to pause just to figure out where his voice had gone. 'Have you seen her?' he enquired at length.

'I see her all the time,' said Miles mildly. 'She buys off me almost every week.'

Erik's heartbeat hurt his ears. 'Is that right?'

He did not sound as calm as he'd hoped.

'Yeah.' Miles finished his bagel before prompting, 'Ask if you're going to ask. You're practically foaming at the mouth.'

'How's she doing?'

For a second, Miles said nothing. Then, 'She's alive. That's a fairly big deal for her.'

Erik's whole body suddenly felt like it was rushing towards something, only to be slammed into a wall.

'What happened?' he finally managed to croak.

It was clear Miles wasn't entirely comfortable having to be the one to relay this bit of information, but he didn't hold back. He never had.

'Yeah, she's not been shiny. I mean, better now all things considered. She crashed with me for a while. And then one day she just didn't come home. I found her at Roger's.'

A wave of icy horror passed through Erik. Horror and hatred.

'Roger Kray?'

'There aren't any other Rogers in Riverside.' Miles shook his head and drank more coffee before continuing. 'I've tried to get her to stop. You know I don't hold with chemical, laboratory, back-of-a-van crap. It's not natural. The green? That's natural. Grows in the ground. You don't inject it into your veins. And if you did, it sure wouldn't rot you from the inside the way some of Roger's stuff will. But she's too ... blank, I guess. She won't listen to me.'

Erik was glad that his sunglasses were hiding his expression. 'And Roger?'

Miles held out his hands. 'He's still around.'

'He shouldn't be.'

'He's my cousin, EJ.'

'He's lowlife scum.'

'So are we,' said Miles pointedly. 'But I get ya.'

On the other side of the patio, another customer appeared and took a seat. Miles waved, temporarily distracting Erik from his downward spiral.

'One of yours?'

'Hell yeah.' Miles winked at him. 'Business is booming.'

Erik nodded slowly at that. His heart had stopped trying to slam its way out of his chest and his stomach had ceased threatening to revolt. 'Is she ... okay?' he asked.

'How much do you want to know?'

'Nothing she wouldn't want you to share,' he said. Eliza would hate him if he pried too deep.

With a grimace and a nod, Miles said, 'She got worse and worse, bro. She started doing more and more shit. Got really bad. Eventually I got her to take a job at the ranch. It seemed to help. She's been living out there since. I think they appreciate the company since their folks died and Mitch moved home. But she's different. Quiet. Haunted, you know?'

Self-hatred had become something of a refined art form for Erik, but he had never hated himself quite so much as he did in that moment. He'd hoped leaving would help. He'd hoped she'd be happier without him around.

'Eliza's not quiet,' was all he managed to say.

Miles leaned in and pitched his voice low. 'Are you going to see her?'

'No,' said Erik. 'It'll make everything worse.'

'But you want to.'

'Of *course* I want to.'

'Self-imposed exile isn't cute in real life, EJ.'

Erik glared at him, even though he secretly agreed. 'I killed her sister. This entire situation is my fault.'

'You're not that powerful.'

'I'm not saying I am. I'm stating the facts.'

'Maybe. Maybe you're just being a coward.'

'Thank you,' he grumbled. 'That really helps.'

A cold breeze picked up, teasing the autumn, and Erik downed the rest of his coffee as a shiver went up his spine. He hated this time of year. He felt restless, uncomfortable in his own skin, antsy.

In an effort to distract himself, Erik went and got another round of coffee, drumming his fingers on every surface he passed as anxiety-fuelled adrenaline thrummed through his bloodstream.

By the time he returned to the table outside, Miles had finished the rest of his cigarette and was twiddling his thumbs. He gave Erik a small, knowing smile and took the coffee with a wink.

'Tell me about work,' said Erik. 'How's Eirin getting on these days?'

To his relief, Miles took the bait, and they passed another couple of hours accumulating empty cups of coffee and filling two ashtrays to the brim.

Come sundown, hoarse and tired, Erik left Miles outside Joanie's and drove to his childhood home on the other side of town.

When Logan was released from prison, Gloria and Erik moved to an estate with a gate. One that had a guard and locked at night. He hadn't been back to Logan's house since the night he broke in and stole his mother's ring from the safe. It was, however, the only thing he stole from his father. The gun had already been in his possession.

He'd brought it along when Eliza called him and hadn't known what to say when she looked at him with such fear. Telling her he'd had it since Wyatt brought him on when he was eleven hadn't seemed the best choice.

Light was shining from within when he drove up, and through the parted curtains he could see Gloria bustling about inside.

Gritting his teeth, he killed the engine and stared at the dilapidated house. The lawn was overgrown and poorly kept, the fence falling down; paint was cracked and peeling all over and the shutters were hanging by a few bent and rusting nails. All signs of an unhappy, neglected home.

With a heavy sigh, he stepped out of the car and walked up the crumbling drive, past a rusted bike now covered in weeds, and on into the house.

Everything smelled strongly of mould, beer and waste. No surface was clean, the carpet was black with grime, and he could smell the toilet from the hallway.

'Wonderful,' he muttered. 'Home sweet Hell.'

'Erik? Is that you?'

'It's me,' he called.

'I'm in the kitchen!'

By in the kitchen, Gloria meant she was elbow deep in dishes, bulging bags of rubbish all around her. The smell in the kitchen was even worse and he almost vomited.

'Christ,' said Erik, wrinkling his nose and stepping over mouldy trays of food. His shoes made sticking sounds on the linoleum. 'He really did run this place into the ground, didn't he?'

'I'm trying to salvage what I can for selling or giving away,' she said, looking over her shoulder. 'To be honest, I am not entirely sure it's worth the effort.'

'It's not,' said Erik, kicking a beer can out of the way. 'If we can't set fire to the damn place, let's do second best and get rid of it all.'

Gloria leaned back against the counter, her lips pursed. 'Nothing you want?'

'He was a wife-beating murderer,' said Erik bluntly. 'Let's just put everything in bags. I'll find someone to come by and collect it in the morning. Jerry can fix the lawn. Kennedy will do up the house for a high price, but she'll make it sell faster. Done and dusted. Let's not be here a second longer than we have to be.'

Gloria bit her lip. 'I was going to do all that. Cheaper.'

'You don't have the time and it isn't your responsibility. I have money. I'll pay for it.'

'Erik —'

'I came back for you, not for him,' he said with a pointed look. 'Let's get this done so you can rest. I know you have to be up at six for work.'

Gloria's eyes filled with tears and he turned away quickly, picking up the extra pair of yellow gloves and pulling them on.

Over the next hour they piled the dirty clothes, broken shoes, crumpled papers, empty bottles, stained glasses, torn books, rusted cutlery, mouldy food, cigarette butts, and Logan's sticky pile of magazines that made both Erik and Gloria dry heave with revulsion, into large black bags.

They opened the windows and scrubbed down the worktops, shelves, and floors until everything smelled strongly of pine, bleach, and stomach-churning floral soap. But even that sickening combination was a marked improvement.

The bags they piled on the curb, and beside those they brought out the broken chairs, scratched table, and creaky sofa with questionable stains; the yellowing mattress and once-suede armchair went next, and then the wardrobe, bookshelves and busted television.

There was nothing worth saving.

It was well past midnight when they finished, soaked in sweat and exhausted. Erik had never wanted a shower so badly in his life.

'I'll make sure this is picked up in the morning,' he said, peeling the gloves off and tossing them onto the last open bag. 'Go get some rest.'

Gloria placed a hand on his shoulder and smiled gratefully at him. 'It means a lot that you came down.'

Erik kissed her forehead and pulled her into a hug. 'I'll sort out the debt collectors tomorrow.'

Gloria shook her head. 'You have your own problems to worry about, sweetheart. I can handle it.'

'We both know you don't make that kind of money,' he said. 'I do. It's not a problem.'

'Erik —'

'Don't fight me on this, Auntie. You know I'll win. I'm much more stubborn than you.'

Gloria laughed. 'You are stubborn.'

'Runs in the family.'

'Will you have dinner with me tomorrow? Before you leave?'

Erik agreed and they said goodnight. Minutes later, he was back in his car, following Gloria down the road.

He flashed his lights once in farewell before turning and making for Miles' apartment. But halfway down Florence Junction, he turned onto Old Oak Road without even thinking about it.

The frail light from the town disappeared as he drove past field after field. Most of the animals were in their pens or stalls for the night, but a few looked up in irritation as his car startled them.

The quiet of Riverside was unlike any place in the world and he felt homesick before he'd even left. Even with so much to hate about his childhood, he'd wanted to make Riverside his home.

It wasn't until he drove under the large arch of Calico Ranch that he even realised where he was going.

He parked at the end of the road and stepped out. It was foolish, what he was doing. He ought to turn around and go straight to Miles' and not taunt himself with things he had worked so desperately to leave behind, but his feet would not listen to his mind, and he continued up the road toward the lights.

He did not even need to walk the full way. In the upper window of the farmhouse, he caught sight of her.

The lights in her room were on and she was leaning against the windowsill, smoking. Music filtered from a hidden stereo, but it was too far away for him to make out the sounds clearly.

He stopped short and gazed up at her.

Her long black hair was pulled into a ponytail, her face obscured by dark makeup. She was smaller – much smaller – than last he'd seen her, and he wondered worriedly if she was eating. Her cheek bones were sunken, her collarbone noticeable even from so far away.

His stomach twisted with guilt.

Everything up to now had just been ideas and imaginings. Seeing the evidence of what he left behind made it so much worse.

He wondered what their life would have been like if they had been able to have the future they both wanted.

They would have been happily married now, perhaps with a few dogs, maybe a horse for Eliza. Sam and Maya would likely live nearby.

It was the dream of a life that had vanished in the span of seconds.

One that had left none of them unscathed.

Eliza finished her smoke and began to undress. Looking away quickly, Erik walked back to his car, wishing he could make any of it better.

But if the night's events hadn't made sense then, they made even less sense now. And five years had served only to drive him mad with unanswered questions.

CHAPTER THREE
Unfinished Business

The cacophonous mixture of rain, wind, thunder and crackling lightning woke Eliza far earlier than she had intended, but she was never able to go back to sleep once she was awake.

She rolled out of bed, her head spinning, and stumbled into the bathroom. Maggie and Mitch were still sound asleep, and she tried not to make much noise as she showered, dressed, and crept down the stairs.

In the gloom of the kitchen, she pulled her work boots on and opened the window over the sink. Cool air that smelled of grass and damp filtered in as she put the kettle on. The wind seemed to be speaking as it whistled through the trees, and Eliza often wondered, if she listened hard enough, whether words would form from the noises. But at least it wasn't silent. She needed to hear something, or all the world seemed dead.

As the coffee brewed, she moved about aimlessly. She felt strange. Something was different, but she didn't know what.

With a shake of her head, she grabbed a mug from the press and filled it to the brim. The vet was coming at nine o'clock and the animals scheduled to be checked out had to be ready. Mitch was off for a weeklong trip that afternoon, leaving the farm in her and Maggie's care. It wasn't the first – or tenth – time, but Eliza always worried something would go wrong in his absence.

When she finished her coffee, she donned her raincoat and stepped out into the thunderstorm. Mud suctioned her boots into the ground and every step took effort. But the effort also took all of her attention and kept her mind from wandering to the dark, grim places it so often went.

Inside the barn, all of the animals were uneasy. Stamping, snorting, bleating, neighing and clucking greeted her upon entry.

She busied herself for the next while mucking the pens and stalls. After an hour, Mitch joined her, rubbing sleep from his eyes and nursing a cup of coffee. Together they got the animals fed and finished cleaning the barn. When it looked tidy enough, they went through the stalls and pens one by one to reassure the animals and calm them down. None of them would go out in the pastures or pens in the rain, as it was a sure way for one of them to go lame and the footing would be obliterated, but as they spent most days outside, the animals grew antsy if cooped up indoors for too long, so they had to be kept entertained on rainy days. Despite the tediousness, Eliza didn't mind the fussiness of animals. It was humans which made her crazy.

Around eight, Maggie called them inside for breakfast, and Eliza and Mitch trudged in, drenched and dirty, stamping their feet on the doorstep to remove as much muck as possible before entering.

'Breakfast is almost ready,' Maggie called from the kitchen. 'Go put on dry clothes and toss everything that's wet into the machine.'

'Might as well toss ourselves in,' said Mitch as he peeled off his shirt. His skin was red with cold and Eliza could hear his teeth chattering.

'My hands are completely pruned,' she said, examining her stark-white palms. She opened and closed them with a grimace.

'Aching yet?'

'Getting there.' She pulled off her shirt and jeans and tossed them into the machine, before taking a pair of dry trousers and a worn shirt from Mitch.

In the dining room, Maggie had set the table and the heady smells of freshly brewed coffee, pancakes, fried eggs, turkey bacon and hash browns made Eliza's stomach growl with anticipation.

She tied her wet hair up into a messy knot and sat down. Drinking deeply from the cup in front of her, she gave Maggie a thumbs-up.

Where the loss of Sam had left a rotting crater in her chest, Eliza felt like Maggie's sisterhood was something of a balm. A little sister to watch out for as opposed to a big sister to take care of her. She liked to think Sam would be proud.

She hoped.

'It smells amazing,' she said to Maggie, praying neither of them noticed the way her hands trembled. 'Thank you.'

'It smells like heaven,' Mitch concurred, eyes on the skillet. 'Best sister ever.'

Eliza swallowed hard.

'There was a call for you this morning,' said Maggie, nodding to her. 'Your mother was hoping you could stop by.'

Eliza raised her eyebrows. 'Did she say why?'

Maggie shrugged. 'She's your mother.'

'That doesn't answer my question.'

'One would presume she didn't think she needed a reason.'

Eliza rolled her eyes. 'You're a terrible secretary.'

'Precisely why I am not one,' said Maggie, jabbing the spatula in her direction. 'Don't be a brat. Go see her after lunch.'

'*You're* not my mother.'

Mitch chuckled and threw a piece of toast at Eliza. 'You know she thinks she is. Go in once we've sorted things out with Casey. Should be fast enough. Routine shots and check-ups. Done after lunch.'

Eliza was spared answering as Maggie announced that the food was ready.

Throughout breakfast, Eliza picked at a pancake and touched little on her plate. It was a terrible thing to admit that she hated going to see her parents, but it was true. Her father had become a shell of his former self, a pitiful echo of the lively man he had once been. The man she went to for everything. He spent his days and nights drinking.

Her mother, on the other hand, looked more frail and exhausted by the day. Mira seemed to be holding herself together for Eliza and Ryan, and sometimes it hurt too much to see.

Not wanting to sit still, not wanting to think, Eliza left the table and headed back out to the barn.

The rest of the afternoon passed too quickly, and by three o'clock, Eliza had no more excuses not to go into town.

She borrowed Mitch's car and drove the familiar route up to her parents' house. They lived just outside the centre of town, in the same house Eliza's grandparents had lived in before they died.

Three generations of their family had lived in the house, and once upon a time Maplebrook felt like a safe haven. She and Sam agreed early on that Sam and Maya could have it when their parents retired. Eliza had dreamed of Willow Lane, the long-abandoned house Erik had shown her when she was sixteen.

Her chest clenched, and she redirected her thoughts. The very worst thing she could do was dwell on the past and reopen old wounds. Especially where it concerned Erik.

Her eyes flicked automatically to the scars on her arm and her hands tightened around the steering wheel.

She forced herself to stare straight ahead as Miles' words came floating back to her.

Nothing is worth your life, baby girl. Not Sammy. Not EJ.

He'd said it to her in the hospital room, an incongruously stern look on his mild and amiable face.

Miles became one of her favourite people following that day, and he was the closest thing she had to a best friend. He never missed one of their meetings and answered the phone no matter the hour.

That in mind, she pulled out her phone and sent him a quick message: *Morning dickhead.*

A few seconds later his reply appeared: *Morning bitchface.*

She grinned, feeling instantly better, and put the phone back in her pocket. Miles was like bottled sunshine.

But the slight uplift in her mood dampened when she caught sight of her childhood home.

After nearly a minute of deliberation, she cut the engine and got out. Flowers dotted the whole garden, untended and wild. She ghosted her fingers over a large rose bush with bright white flowers, trying to gather her courage, before she trudged down the path to the door.

She knocked twice, her stomach in knots. She still had her keys, and she doubted it was even locked, but since Sam died, she always knocked before entering. The same way a stranger would.

It only took a moment for her mother to answer and usher her inside. Mira looked tired and drained. There were obvious circles under her eyes and she was thinner than ever. And her cheery smile never quite reached her eyes as she waved Eliza into the kitchen.

'Tea?'

'I'm fine,' said Eliza. 'Maggie said you wanted to see me.'

Mira poured her a cup of tea, ignoring her protests, and pushed the cup towards her. 'I wanted to check in on my daughter. Is that a crime?'

Eliza glared down at the contents of her cup. 'I'm sorry,' she said quietly, guilt flaring like a wound which would never fully heal. 'How are you?'

'I'm fine,' said Mira, although her tone of voice wasn't convincing. 'It's your father I'm worried about.'

Eliza glanced around, feeling sick with foreboding. 'Where is Dad?'

Mira sighed.

'What?'

'He didn't come home last night.'

Fear burned through Eliza's chest like toxic whiskey. 'Where is he?'

'My guess would be the pub,' said Mira softly. She looked away, blinking back tears.

There was something truly awful about watching her mother cry, and Eliza walked over and wrapped an arm awkwardly around her shoulders. They had once been so close. The four of them. All of Eliza's friends in school had been so jealous of how close and open their family were with each other. It seemed like a laughably distant dream now.

'The Weaver or Finnegan's?' she asked, already resigned to going.

'Probably Finnegan's,' said Mira.

Eliza took her keys back out of her pocket, heart slamming so hard in her chest it hurt.

She struggled to get air into her lungs and she thought she might choke on the attempt.

'I'll go fetch him,' she managed to croak.

'Thank you, sweetheart.' Mira squeezed her hand. 'Should I make us something to eat for when you get back?'

Not wanting to tell her mother that she'd rather eat dirt than sit through an awkward family luncheon while her father slept off a drunken stupor in the next room, Eliza forced herself to smile and nod before heading back out into the rainy, humid afternoon.

So late in the day, the pub was already open again for the drunks and day-drinkers and lost souls.

Inside, everything smelled of salt. Salt from stale beer, salt from sweat, salt from the sticky finger foods. It was a heavy, wretched environment that she wanted to be as far away from as possible.

Cameron Mahon, the owner, waved at her from behind the bar as she entered and nodded to one of the booths in the back.

There, in the corner, messy and with vomit down his front, was her father. His clothes were wrinkled and had days-old stains on them. Normally clean shaven, Ryan had long pokey hairs sticking out like white blades of grass all over his face.

It was a heartbreaking sight, but she couldn't propel herself toward him.

'Do you want some help? He might be a bit heavy for you.'

Roger had appeared at her side. He was tucking his black ledger into his coat pocket and behind him three men were heading towards the bathroom about as subtly as a herd of hippopotamuses, small bags with white powder no doubt in hand.

Eliza hesitated. She cared little for what Roger thought of her or her father, but he always seemed to be there when Ryan was at his worst and she wasn't delighted about it. Not that Roger would ever tease or mock her, but she didn't want anyone seeing her father like this.

She didn't want herself seeing her father like this.

Likely guessing her reservations, he held up his hands and offered a smile. 'Just an honest good deed, baby.'

And it was clear he meant that, too. Roger was an odd duck; somehow genuine and slimy in equal measure.

She let out a resigned breath and nodded. 'Fuck it. Yeah, please.'

Between the two of them, they managed to lug Ryan out of the pub and into the backseat of Mitch's car. It was raining a little less heavily by that point, but it was continuous, and droplets quickly coated them.

She brushed the damp tendrils of hair from her face as she closed the passenger door and turned to Roger.

'Thanks,' she muttered.

He leaned in. 'Anything for you, baby. You know that.'

'I should go.'

'Okay.'

Before she could move, he kissed her.

Not a second later, someone called her name from across the street, startling both of them, and she pulled back to see Miles jogging towards her, his face stormy.

Miles openly hated Roger, although he was one of the few people in town brave enough to do so. If they hadn't been cousins, one of them would likely have wound up in a ditch at some point.

'Hey, baby girl,' he said before turning his glare towards Roger. 'What do you want, Kray?'

Roger shrugged and crossed his arms. 'Just doing my good deed for the day, Hennessey. Is that a problem?'

Miles raised an eyebrow and his gaze went to Ryan's unconscious form in the back of the car. His scowl deepened, and worry flared in his eyes. With a small breath, he looked away and squeezed Eliza's arm before turning his attention to Roger once more. 'Well you've done it.'

'I'm allowed to talk to anyone I want.' Roger sneered at him. 'I don't have to run it past you.'

Thunder boomed in the distance and the rain began falling harder, but neither man seemed to notice. Eliza, on the other hand, desperately wanted to leave.

'See, that's where you're wrong,' said Miles, stepping towards Roger with a menacing edge that was incongruous to his cheery self. 'I think I made myself perfectly clear last time that you needed to stay away from my people.'

Roger scoffed. 'Your people?'

'Yes,' said Miles.

Ignoring him, Roger smirked at Eliza. One eye on Miles, he kissed her pointedly before leaning back and, with a wink, added, 'You need anything else, baby?'

'I've got it,' she said, rolling her eyes at the obvious attempt to goad Miles.

Roger, however, was no longer looking at her. He was looking at something over her shoulder, his expression one of shock and outrage. There were about a million things which could make Roger's face twist so horribly, and Eliza followed his gaze without thought.

She went cold all over.

Six feet tall, slightly crooked features now more striking than awkward, his body finally caught up with itself, the sight of Erik struck Eliza like a blow to the stomach.

Gone were his leather jacket and Converse. Instead he wore denim jeans and boots, and a fine black coat. And if Miles looked angry, it was nothing compared to how Erik looked. His face was drawn and tight, his mouth a thin line. His black eyes were filled with hatred, and Eliza was silently glad she was not on the receiving end of his ire.

He reached them within seconds. 'What are you doing here, Kray?' he asked Roger.

'He was just leaving,' said Miles.

Roger heaved a put-upon sigh and looked at Erik with unmasked dislike. 'When did you get back, Stern?'

'Apparently not soon enough.'

'No, you've got that backwards. You should have stayed a memory.'

'Leave, Kray.'

'Are you going to make me?'

'Yes.'

Eliza had had enough. Grabbing Erik's coat, she shoved him backwards, catching him completely by surprise.

She walked around the three of them, climbed into the car and slammed the door, wanting nothing more than to be in a hole in the ground, dead to the world and away from everything.

'Looks like she didn't want you, either,' she heard Roger say as she drove away.

In the mirror, she saw Erik lunge for him just as she rounded the corner.

She hoped they broke each other's teeth.

————————

In the bright light of the bathroom, Roger inspected the damage done to his face. His jaw and nose throbbed with pain — not to mention his ribs and knuckles — and he cursed silently as he swished the mouthwash slowly around his mouth. It only reignited the pain. His gums and cheeks burned from open cuts, the result of unnatural collision with his teeth.

Spitting out the green liquid, he splashed his face with cold water. But with his eyes closed, all he could see was Erik Stern's smug face.

The gangly, scowling bastard had only grown in the years since he had left Riverside, and Roger was annoyed to note that the time away hadn't done him nearly as much harm as one could hope.

Roger had been working for Wyatt for several years — one of the youngest boys ever recruited — when Erik walked in, age eleven, and convinced Wyatt to let him join.

No one would suspect a kid as young as him, he said; he was the easiest way to move drugs. Wyatt had been intrigued by the offer and let Erik join.

By fifteen, Erik was Wyatt's second-in-command. But Roger had never liked him. Never trusted him.

Serial killer eyes, he said to Dickie once. *You just know one day he's going to snap.*

It was that bravado and boldness and youthfulness, Roger reckoned, which made Erik the only person to ever leave Wyatt's group alive. And Wyatt loved him like a son. He expected Erik to return.

Which he had. Eventually.

At the time, though, it was a strange transition. One day Erik was filling his car with drugs and sealing them expertly beneath the floor and inside the doors, and the next he walked into Wyatt's office, face calm and determined, and quit.

He had seen a girl, Wyatt told Roger later; he had seen a girl and wanted to be good enough to win her. Wyatt found the whole thing childishly adorable, and as Erik had never been doubted in his loyalty — not once in the five years he worked for Wyatt — he was let go.

Everyone assumed the youthful flame of love would die as quickly as it always did and next time, Wyatt would refuse to let him quit and cite the disastrous ending to the first time Erik found himself lovelorn.

Sure enough, a few years later Erik was in Silverlake running guns, and Eliza was single.

Much to Roger's delight.

He had been in love with Eliza since the day he saw her standing outside of a tack shop with her older sister, laughing about something. Her long dark hair and eyes blacker than coal were striking and alluring.

Roger stood, transfixed, forgetting about the cigarette in his hand and ignoring everything Dickie was saying to him.

And he watched as an old car pulled up alongside her.

Moments later Erik was kissing Eliza, a finger resting casually in the back pocket of her jeans. They got into the car, and Roger had lit another cigarette, feeling thoroughly put out with life.

He saw Eliza around the town quite often after that. She was one of those people who wore joy well. It brightened her entire being and was easily infectious to others. A trait neither Roger nor Erik possessed.

She wore tragedy even better.

Whether it was the death of her sister, the loss of Erik, or her father's drinking – likely all three – Eliza's descent was as breath-taking as it was tragic.

The messiness of it fascinated Roger, and he spent many nights watching her dance and drink after Erik left.

And then one wintery Thursday where the only interesting part of his day had been collecting funds from his runners, he opened his door to see Eliza on his porch.

Her long black hair had been unwashed and greasy, her eyes were hooded and swollen, her lips chapped from the cold; her hands were tucked beneath her armpits and she was rocking back and forth on the balls of her feet. Not anxious to leave, he realised, anxious for whatever it was he could offer. A twitch he'd seen a thousand times.

Not sure what to think but intrigued all the same, he'd waved her inside and brought her to the sitting room.

Even fragmented, Eliza was defiant and bold. She walked without fear into his sitting room, ruffling the snow out of her hair.

She tossed her damp coat on the chair beside the fire before holding her hands out over the flames, not even bothering to look at him.

He remembered gazing at her profile, the heat of the fire causing her skin to glow orange. He remembered wanting to know if she burned so lovely on the outside because her insides had long turned to coal and ash.

'Did you know I'm scared?'

Her voice was deeper than most of the women he knew, and there was a lilt to it he thought was the best sound in the world. But her question threw him.

'Is it a gun you want?' He searched her face, trying to determine if she was running, chasing or dying.

'No. I don't need a gun.' She pulled a knife out of her coat and let the firelight glint off it. 'I have this.'

If there was a better sight than that of Eliza Owens, messy and dark in the gloom of his sitting room, holding a knife and looking unconquerable, Roger would have sold his soul to know what it was.

'You don't know what you want?' His intrigue was enough to distract himself from his arousal.

'I don't want to think,' she murmured. 'I don't want to feel.'

He pursed his lips in thought. 'They have therapists for that, you know? Shouldn't go to a drug dealer if you're sad.'

'Therapists help you find the source of your problem, help you solve it. I don't need help solving it. I don't need help identifying it. I don't even need help accepting it. A therapist won't tell me anything I don't already know. And a therapist won't turn off my memories.'

He mulled that over for a few seconds before he walked over to his box on the coffee table and pulled out a bag. Returning to the sofa, he sat down and motioned for her to sit beside him.

'What do I do?' she asked after a beat.

'Are you going home?'

'I ...' She ran a hand through her hair and her face crumpled. Her eyes were glazed and bloodshot, and still somehow the most mesmerising pair he'd ever gazed into. He was so captivated, he almost missed her next words. 'I don't really have a home anymore.'

Without meaning to, Roger found himself reaching out to cradle her face. He brushed his thumb over her skin, enraptured by how soft it was. They were so close he now knew that she smelled like chocolate and cigarettes.

He wondered what she'd taste like.

'Do you want to take it here?' he murmured, grazing his fingers over her cheek and neck. 'You can stay.'

In truth, he didn't want to let her go.

She raised an eyebrow, but she didn't pull away and his heart began to thrum in his chest. 'I'm not going to have sex with you for drugs.'

A low laugh left him, and he moved closer, drawn by her fire. 'I'm a drug dealer, baby. I'm not a pimp.'

'I'll cut your dick off if you try.'

'Good,' he said with a smirk, wanting her more than ever. 'It's not fun if it's not a challenge.'

Roger did love a challenge.

The rest of the night had passed too quickly for his liking. Eliza sat in a daze on his sofa, staring at the ceiling, and he read a book and listened to the steady sounds of her breathing.

In the days that followed, he fell ever more in love with her, only to be driven increasingly frustrated by how little she cared.

Eliza barely acknowledged his existence. Not the way she had ever acknowledged Erik's existence.

So when Wyatt told him that Erik was working for him in Silverlake, Roger hadn't enquired further. He had also never mentioned it to Eliza. Seeing Erik back in Riverside not only disturbed Roger, it angered him. He wanted Erik gone.

More than anything, he wanted to forget the look on Eliza's face when she had seen Erik.

Now furious and in pain, Roger left the bathroom and walked into the sitting room.

He was about to turn on the television when he caught sight of something.

A smirk curved his lips and he walked outside and tapped on the car window.

Eliza opened the door and stepped slowly out of the car. There were deep circles under her eyes and she could have used a good meal, but he found her as intoxicating as ever.

He cocked his head, eyes roving over her. 'Didn't expect to see you so soon, baby.'

'I don't want to talk.'

'Fair enough.'

He stepped closer, one hand moving to the small of her back. His other hand traced slowly down the side of her face.

'Coming in?' he said softly.

Before she could answer, he was kissing her.

Everything hurt. Inside and out.

Erik squeezed the bridge of his nose and winced. Going to town had been a monumentally poor decision.

'I feel like it should be of note that I was handling the situation flawlessly until you arrived,' said Miles, dropping down beside him and lighting a joint. The smoke curling off the end mixed with the smoke from the dozen or so candles that Miles always had lit. An ode to his obsession with good smells. The mixture was heady and pungent, and it made Erik's head spin ever so.

'I would've been inclined to punch him even if he'd been a thousand miles clear of her,' said Erik, taking a sip of his whiskey and grimacing. 'I *loathe* him.'

Miles held up his hands. 'You're not alone in that, brother. But I still think you did yourself no favours by jumping in.'

'It certainly wasn't the reunion I wanted.'

They had been in the shop when Miles told him to grab something from the back and disappeared. Erik returned to find him gone. It took only a minute of looking around to see Miles, Eliza and Roger across the street.

Everything after that was a bit hazy, but the parts which remained clear made him ache.

She hadn't even looked at him. It was that, he knew, which upset him more than anything else. Even if it was irrational, he hoped she would have said hello, smiled, said anything.

Not that he deserved it. He deserved a shotgun to the face.

But still, it stung.

'Ryan was in a bad way,' Miles remarked, lips pursed, voice quiet and sad.

'How long's he been like that?'

'Since the funeral, bro. Never snapped back.' Miles worried the corner of his fingernail before adding, 'I don't know how you two ended up with such useless fathers.'

Erik frowned, guilt flaring inside him. 'I think everything got to him in the end.'

'Not an excuse.'

'Maybe not,' said Erik, still inclined to defend Ryan. 'One more glowing achievement I can add to my record.'

'That's not on you.'

'I killed Sam.'

'It was an accident, EJ. And you didn't put a glass in his hand.'

'I may as well have.'

'How?'

'I put his daughter in the ground.'

'On accident.'

'It doesn't matter.'

'It does.'

They glared at each other until Miles held up his hands and went into the kitchen. He busied himself with making sandwiches, still smoking the joint. It made Erik smile.

Miles always had something in his hands. As if he had to be continually occupied. If he wasn't moving about, he was eating; if he wasn't eating, he was smoking. Well, he was smoking most of the time; he hardly stopped for eating.

The doctors all told Miles that he smoked too much, and each time Miles answered with a promise to quit the day it affected his running or his sex drive. Thus far, neither had suffered a downturn, so Miles kept right on smoking.

'And Eliza?' he prompted, words muffled as he barely moved his lips, trying not to drop the joint as he spread mustard on the bread.

'What about Eliza?'

'Are you going to leave it at that or go and see her? Maybe try and leave her with a somewhat better impression of you?'

Erik rubbed his face roughly. 'Going to see her would put a hole in the plan of avoiding her, don't you think?'

'*EJ* ...'

'Yes, Miles?'

Miles held out a sandwich and glared pointedly at him. 'Go see Eliza or I will beat you to death with a spoon. You owe her that much.'

Erik held his gaze for a second before he stood and walked over to take the sandwich. 'If I see her ... If I see her, I don't think I'll be able to stop myself from begging her to take me back.'

Miles stamped out the joint and spread his palms across the worktop. 'You put yourself in self-imposed exile for five years. The worst that can happen is you both get a bit of closure.'

'That is definitely not the worst that could happen.'

'Don't make me get my spoon.'

Erik rolled his eyes and ate dutifully, mulling over what he should to do. More than anything, he wanted to see her. He wanted to talk to her. It was another stupid idea, but he'd always known he was a fool.

'I'll go,' he said at last.

Miles shot him a thumbs-up. 'Good boy. Swing back by before you leave town. I mean it.'

Erik nodded and left, his heart pounding, his mind going a mile a minute.

He had less than no idea what he was going to say when he finally spoke to Eliza.

CHAPTER FOUR
It Makes No Sense

It was well after sunset when Eliza left Roger's house. The sky was pitch black and the rain was coming down in a half-hearted drizzle. The forecast predicted heavy rainfall for the next several days and the gardens and lawns were already saturated and filling with muck, the roads ankle-deep in runoff.

The end of summer always brought rainy weather to Riverside, but it beat the chill which came with winter. Still, the constant rain this time of year made her think of the night before Sam died and the Paige who never showed, and Eliza felt gloomy by the time she reached the ranch.

The lights in the house were on when she pulled up, and she took a moment to gather her wits about her before stepping out of the car and jogging up the path into the house.

'Mags!' she called. 'Sorry I'm late, something –'

She stopped dead.

It wasn't Maggie who stepped out of the kitchen to greet her.

Hair a messy disarray from the rain, eyes piercing and filled with worry and confusion, hands jammed into his pockets, body tensed, Erik was the most comforting unwanted visitor she'd ever had. And the half of her that didn't want to run to him, wanted to punch him.

If the new habit he had picked up in the five years he was away was popping up at random whenever she least expected it, she was going to be seriously annoyed.

But for a split second she was nineteen years old again, a misunderstanding filling the air between them with tension, and she braced herself to apologise, only to remember that she owed him nothing. They had been nothing to each other for five years. The last time she had trusted him, he left her at her sister's wake, thinking the whole thing must be some sort of nightmare.

The anger returned full force and her hand balled into a fist around her keys.

'Hi,' he said. He looked more uncomfortable than she could ever remember seeing him.

Somehow that just annoyed her more.

'What are you doing here?' she snapped.

'Can we talk?'

'No,' she said flatly. 'Get out.'

'Please.' He seemed to be dredging his soul for the courage to remain there. His nearly-black eyes were even blacker in the darkness. He looked haunted and gaunt and she wanted to make it better. Which, in turn, made her want to scream.

She crossed her arms and glared at him. 'About what? What could you *possibly* have to say to me?'

A long, lingering silence followed her question.

Erik took several deep breaths as if he was having trouble dragging air into his lungs. At last, after clenching his jaw several times, he looked at her and said, 'I love you.'

A snort of disbelief left her. It turned quickly to a laugh.

'I'm serious,' he said.

'No,' she said, voice now strangled. 'You're delusional. You don't love me.'

'*Yes,*' he said emphatically. It was as if such a question was almost offensive to him. 'I do.'

'Bull. Shit.'

Erik dragged his fingers through his hair and gripped at the roots. He looked at her beseechingly. 'Look, can we — can we just sit and talk? No fighting. I don't want to fight. I didn't come here to fight.'

Eliza glared at him for several long seconds. 'Fine,' she muttered, walking past him. 'Make it fast. I'm tired.'

'Were you at your parents'?' he asked.

'I was at Roger's.' She pulled a can out of the fridge, cracking it open with her index finger and leaning back against the sink. 'You?'

Her words caused his expression to darken. 'Don't tell me you're actually friends with him?'

'*Friends* isn't the word I would use,' she said mildly. '*Friends with benefits*, maybe.'

The look on his face gave her a small measure of satisfaction. 'You know what he is,' he said, voice clipped. 'You know what he does to people and how he uses them. How can you be near him?'

'Maybe I like sleeping with him.'

Erik's lips had even lost their colour. 'You're lying.'

'I don't see how it's any business of yours. You lost the right to have any indignation over my life choices a long time ago.'

'I know — fuck, I *know*.' Erik stepped towards her and she held up a hand. He stopped, crestfallen. 'But why Roger?'

'Get off your high horse. You worked for Wyatt, too. It's not like he's so much worse than you.'

Erik opened and closed his mouth several times in disbelief, his hands on his hips. 'I don't — nor have I ever — sold someone laced shit.'

It was the last thing she'd expected to hear, and she stared at him in astonishment. 'Roger doesn't lace his drugs.'

'Oh yes, he does.'

'I buy off him at least twice a week —'

A sudden crashing sound from the adjoining room made them both jump.

Eliza quickly put down her can and stepped into the sitting room; Erik followed.

The window had been blown open and the curtains were billowing. A vase that had been on the nearby table was in pieces on the floor and an icy chill had filled the room in the few seconds the window had been open.

It didn't help that the wind was whistling so wildly outside it almost seemed to be screaming.

Shivers running up and down her spine and arms, Eliza closed the window, stepped carefully around the shards, and headed back into the kitchen, head spinning somewhat.

She picked up the half-drunk can and downed it before glancing back at Erik. But she didn't have to worry about a long awkward silence. Awkward conversation beat it to the punch.

'Miles says you're living here now,' said Erik, gesturing around.

'You want to know about my living arrangements?'

'No,' he said. 'Yes. I just — I just want to know if you're okay. I want you to be happy. That's all. I didn't want to leave it like that. Earlier. That wasn't — that wasn't how I wanted things to go. I'm sorry.'

She crossed her arms and let out a long sigh. 'And how did you want it to go?'

His laugh was rueful. 'I have no idea. A talk. Find out how you've been. I've thought about you — more than I've thought about anything else.'

Her eyes narrowed. 'Is that right?'

'Yes.'

'No.'

'No?'

'Yeah, *no*. You don't want to know. You don't want the truth, Erik. You want to know that you did the right thing. You didn't. Now go home.'

She could see the muscle in his jaw working anxiously, but after a long pause, he nodded. 'All right. If that's what you want.'

The defeated tone tore through her, and her anger, like her self-control, shattered. Before he could move, her next words left her lips without permission. 'I still don't know what happened.'

'Neither do I,' he whispered.

'You couldn't – there's no way you should have been able to do that. It doesn't make any sense.'

She looked at him for answers and saw only the same confusion.

There was something so strange about staring into the face of someone who was both family and stranger and not know what to say. The years had put so much distance between them, so many questions. Grief and bitterness were almost physical entities in the room. Yet the feeling of knowing Erik better than anyone else had not changed. Erik had just always been something she was certain of. Until he left. And sometimes, even now, it was hard to believe he could have let her down.

'I haven't gone back,' she admitted. 'I used to go to those woods all the time. It was our place.'

He nodded. 'I remember.'

'So many times, I've walked to the trailhead, thinking maybe I could go up. I wanted to. I have a thousand happy memories up there to outweigh the last one. But I can't.'

Tears filled his eyes and he looked away, jaw clenching, nostrils flaring, clearly trying desperately to maintain his composure.

She straightened up, mind moving faster than she could process thought. 'You're leaving tonight?'

He cleared his throat before replying. 'Yes.'

'When?'

'After I say goodbye to Gloria and Miles.'

'Go with me,' she said before she could stop herself. 'Go with me to the woods.'

'Eliza —'

'You owe me that much, Erik.'

He sighed and gestured to her. 'You're not even sober, babe.'

'Then it's a good thing I'm not going alone, isn't it?'

They glared at each other for several seconds before Erik nodded. 'All right,' he said heavily. 'I'll go with you.'

It took only a moment for Eliza to change into her hiking boots and grab a thicker coat. Erik was wearing jeans and his heavy leather boots, and she half hoped he'd get blisters on the climb. It was petty, but she didn't care.

The drive passed in deafening silence, neither of them wanting to speak first, neither of them knowing what to say at all. The last time they'd made this drive, Sam and Maya had been with them, jolly folk music blasting from the speakers as they sang along, laughing, high on life and all the possibilities the future would bring. It was the memory of another life, and Eliza hated the people in that memory, envious of their happiness.

Erik parked on the side of the road just at the start of the trailhead, knowing more from instinct where to stop than from actually being able to see anything. The locals all knew of the hidden ditch.

'We should wait until morning,' he said, peering out the window. 'It's not safe to go up this late.'

'We've gone up in the darkness a thousand times,' she retorted. 'Don't tell me you're scared now.'

'Everyone feels invincible at nineteen. We were proven wrong.'

With a scoff, Eliza opened her door. 'I never felt invincible,' she said pointedly. 'I just knew that between the two of us, we could handle anything.'

Erik looked startled. For a minute he said nothing, and they continued to stare at each other. Then he cleared his throat and squeezed the back of his neck in agitation. 'And now?'

'I hate you. But I don't doubt your ability to back me up. Come on.'

It was enough to get him out of the car.

The trail up the mountain was traversed only by locals and the few mountaineers brave enough to go into the untended wilderness. The forest was known to be inhabited by bears, wildcats, wolves, coyotes, moose and other things Eliza had no desire to come across in the dark. Still, she was not afraid of them. She never had been. Most animals wanted about as much to do with people as they did with machinery. It was the rare rabid animal which forced humans to cross paths with them in these woods; most avoided the trails.

And people scared her more.

They wound their way up the trail, boots squelching in the muck, breath coming out in clouds.

'There,' said Erik a few minutes later, pointing ahead.

They were standing in the same place they had been five years ago.

A violent shiver snaked over her skin and a second later she doubled over, vomiting. Her wet hair fell into her eyes and Erik drew it away from her face and rubbed her back as she heaved.

'Are you all right?' he asked when she finally managed to take deep, shuddering breaths.

'Peachy,' she said, spitting and wiping her mouth.

They looked in tandem at the tree a few paces away. It was a gnarled tree, the leaves nearly all fallen away with the autumn. In the night, it was simply a black, twisted shape. Forbidding and eerie.

'You barely touched her,' she mumbled. 'I still don't understand it.'

'Neither do I.' He took a cigarette out and lit it before continuing. 'Doesn't make it better. Doesn't make it less my fault.'

'I've seen you shove people ten times as hard and that didn't happen,' she mused, more to herself than to him.

She sat down on the wet forest ground, water instantly seeping into her trousers and chilling her. But she didn't bother moving. Erik hesitated before sitting down beside her and drawing his legs into his chest.

'Did you ever figure out who the caller was?' she asked. 'The fake Paige?'

He shook his head and blew out a cloud of smoke. 'Believe me, I tried. One of the first places I went – after – was to see her parents. I wanted to know if there was something I was missing. Think I did more harm than good by asking, though.'

Eliza felt wretchedly sorry for them and didn't know what to say. Silence descended again, heavy and unwelcome. Unable to stand it, she stood and walked over to the tree.

'I looked it up,' she said, reaching out and running her fingers over the bark. 'The amount of strength it would take to send someone flying like that. It's not humanly possible.'

'I can't explain it,' he said softly from behind her. 'I wish to God I could.'

Eliza looked back at him. A rush of anticipation spread through her veins as she considered it. 'Could you throw me that far?'

Fearful horror flashed across his face. 'What?'

'Hypothetically.'

'Hypothetically? *No.*'

She fixed him with an even stare. She wanted to understand. More than anything else in her life, she wanted to know what had happened that night. How it could have happened.

She wanted to know who had spoken to her sister, how Erik's small push had sent Sam flying; she wanted to know how one small fight had taken her entire life away from her.

It was clear, however, that her desperation wasn't shared.

'This was a bad idea,' he said. 'We should go.'

'Go if you want to,' she retorted, anger returning. 'I want to know what happened.'

'So do I!'

'Are you afraid of what we'll find?'

'Only an idiot wouldn't be,' he said derisively. 'I don't know what happened that night. I've been trying to figure it out for five years. I have no answers for you, Eliza. All I can say is that I am so beyond sorry. I can never make it right, babe. Never. I will never forgive myself. And I'm so sorry.'

'Yeah,' she croaked. 'I'm sorry, too.'

In the distance, thunder boomed mere seconds before lightning shot across the sky, illuminating the world in the briefest of flashes.

She leaned against the tree and curled her fingers over the bark. It smelled of life despite how dead it appeared. The line between life and death seemed like it could be as wide as the ocean or as thin and frail as thread.

Eliza felt her throat start to close and she breathed rapidly, trying to get air into her lungs. It was becoming harder and harder, like trying to breathe through a plastic bag.

'Hey! Hey!' Erik was suddenly by her side. 'Breathe, babe. Breathe. Calm down. It's all right. Everything's going to be all right.'

It didn't feel like it was going to be all right. They would leave the trail and he would disappear again and she would have to go back and face the ruined, pitiable shells of the parents who had once been her solid ground. Sam was gone, and she was never coming back, and it made no sense.

None of it made any sense.

Erik wrapped his arms around her, and she gripped his coat so tightly her fingers hurt. Stars were exploding in front of her eyes and she was so dizzy the only thing keeping her upright was Erik's hold on her.

'I've got you,' he said, cradling the back of her head with his hand. 'I've got you, babe. You're going to be fine. Just breathe.'

She drew in a ragged breath and said very quickly, 'You don't.'

'I've got you,' he said again. 'I've got you.'

How long they stood there in the pouring rain, next to the tree where her sister had died, clinging to each other, neither of them could have said. Five years of questions and bereavements, of loneliness and longing, of guilt and rage, bound them together in the cold, rainy night.

Another clap of thunder finally broke them apart and Eliza suddenly realised how cold she was, even so close to Erik. She pulled away, crossing her arms protectively over her chest.

'Maybe we should go,' she said, teeth starting to chatter.

Erik nodded. 'The rain's only going to get worse.'

'Are you leaving?' she asked suddenly, searching his face. 'When we get back, are you leaving?'

He held her gaze with a heavy expression of his own. 'I should,' he said. 'I know that I should. Coming back here was a bad idea, I never doubted that. But now ...' He bit his lip and brushed black hair out of his eyes. 'If you ask me to stay, I will. Anything you want, tell me and I'll do it.'

Eliza deliberated. She wanted answers, and she'd run herself in so many circles. Having Erik there to help would be more than she'd had to go on for the past five years. And, although she'd never admit it to him, she was only brave enough to investigate if he was there with her. She didn't want to face the past alone.

'Stay,' she said at length. 'Until we know what happened. We're not together, we're not friends, we're just going to figure this out and then you go. Do that and I'll forgive you.'

Erik was quiet for a long time. The rain continued to lash down upon them, threatening pneumonia. Neither moved.

'All right,' he said, voice barely audible. 'I'll stay.'

CHAPTER FIVE
Contemplations and Conversations

By the time dawn crept into the world, Erik had been sitting in the armchair in the corner of Eliza's room for hours. He was nearly done with the mystery novel he'd plucked off her bookshelf, but he was forcing his way through it.

He'd told Eliza he would go back to the apartment once his clothes were dry, but the buzzer had long since sounded and he had yet to make a move towards the door.

His thoughts kept straying to Paige. A decade old memory of her, hazy and put together mostly from the facts he learned later, kept dancing through his mind. It was hard to recall what she looked like. That beautiful, troubled girl he met at the camp Gloria sent him to one summer.

It had been a little kid's haven; a summer of playing in the creek, building campfires, climbing trees and rocks, learning to erect tents, filter water, fish, forage and hunt.

Three weeks in, Paige arrived.

Erik remembered being endlessly fascinated by her long blonde hair and the vast assortment of freckles on her face that he attempted to count one afternoon. They held hands and kissed awkwardly. And at twelve years old, it felt like the most perfect thing in the world. First love was like that. All or nothing.

Everyone told him it was because they were young. That love wouldn't always feel so immediate, so consuming. He'd wonder, years later, what they would say about him and Eliza.

Near the end of that summer, Erik realised Paige was different.

It fascinated him in the beginning. The highs were exhilarating, and the adventures which ensued seemed one step short of magic; the lows were unexpected and sudden and came crashing down upon them.

Seemingly at random, she would burst into tears, tear at her hair, scream and shout and accuse him of things.

The first time it happened he thought she was playing a strange sort of game and wanted to be let in on the joke. But then it happened again. And then again. Like there were two Paiges, and he had to protect one from the other.

As time went on, Erik felt an increasing sense of responsibility toward her. Unable to save his mother, he'd been desperate to save Paige. He kept her secrets and helped her disinfect her cuts, feeling somehow honoured by being let in on such a secret, on being the only one who could help her.

When Erik confided in Gloria, she told him to be careful, and to mention it to Paige's parents.

'Don't keep secrets like that to yourself, Erik,' she advised. 'Especially when they involve blood.'

Her words echoed in Erik's head for the rest of his relationship with Paige, but for some reason he never felt like it was his secret to share. He never thought he'd really *lose* her.

When Erik found Paige on the bathroom floor a year later, her arms gashed from wrist to forearm, he remembered swearing to God that he would never keep such a secret again so long as she was saved.

She had been saved. That time.

Not the second.

He didn't keep secrets anymore.

Head now pounding, Erik blew out a ring of smoke and closed the book, no longer even pretending to read. His eyes went to Eliza automatically. She looked tired and anxious, even in sleep.

He wanted to crawl in beside her. The urge was nearly overpowering, and he knew if he let himself entertain the idea, leaving would be a hundred times more difficult. Instead, he stubbed out the end of the joint in the ashtray, stood and stretched, and scrawled a quick message for her on the notepad left out on her desk. He then put the book on the bedside table and slipped out of the room.

The old house was creaky, but Erik was light-footed and barely made a sound as he changed into his now-dry clothes, leaving the shirt and pyjama bottoms Eliza had let him borrow in the washer.

He was just tying the laces on his boots when the overhead light snapped on and someone cleared their throat behind him.

Erik looked over his shoulder. 'Good morning, Maggie,' he said in a low voice, standing up and donning his coat.

Maggie was a tall, wiry teenager with slightly terrifying ferocity in her glare. 'What are you doing here, Erik?'

'Just leaving, actually.'

She crossed her arms. 'You shouldn't've come back.'

'I don't disagree.'

'*Are* you leaving?' Dislike dripped from every syllable.

'You asked me that already. I take it you don't mean the house this time?'

'You know what I mean.'

He ran a hand through his hair and shrugged. He didn't know Maggie well – hardly at all – and it wasn't the first time he'd dealt with unmasked contempt, but it still stung.

'I was going to leave,' he said as evenly as possible. 'Eliza asked me to stay.'

Maggie rolled her eyes. 'Eliza doesn't know what's good for her.'

A wave of irritation passed through him, overpowering the sting. 'Eliza doesn't need you as a bodyguard.'

From the look on Maggie's face it was clear she disagreed. 'Yeah, she does. You being here will ruin what little progress she's made.'

'I'm not here to ruin her life or your life or anyone else's life. I was planning on leaving, she asked me to stay. I owe her that.'

'You owe her five years,' said Maggie acidly. 'Since that's not something you can provide unless you're harbouring time-travel abilities unbeknownst to the rest of us, you should do what you've been doing and disappear.'

Erik took his keys out of his pocket and walked towards the door. He paused with his hand on the knob, the cold metal a blessed relief against his sweaty palm. 'I don't need to explain myself to you, Maggie,' he replied, unable to look back and meet her accusatory gaze. 'I appreciate that you care about Eliza, but you're not the only one.'

'You're such a selfish dick.'

Erik closed the door on her hatred. 'I'm not denying that,' he muttered to himself.

The brisk morning sent chills over his clammy skin and he jogged the rest of the way to the car, more than ready to leave.

He supposed a better, more selfless person would have left differently, would have stayed away, or would not have ended up in his position in the first place. But he was keeping his word to Eliza. Even if it wasn't the right thing to do, he'd broken enough promises.

The drive to Miles' apartment went quickly, and to his relief Miles was still sleeping when he jimmied the lock and crept inside. Collapsing on the squishy sofa, Erik dragged a blanket over his body and was pulled instantly into a deep slumber.

He dreamed he was back in the forest, fighting with Sam, only this time instead of throwing her against the tree, he punched his hand into her chest and tore her heart out, crushing it with frightening force as she fell, blood pooling around her.

The screams that filled his ears belonged to Eliza and Paige.

He awoke soaked in sweat and disgusted with himself. Gagging into his fist, his stomach rebelling, it took all his efforts not to vomit on Miles' sofa.

Several minutes passed before he was able to get control of his panic and calm down. Only then did he notice Miles watching him from the kitchen.

'You know you move a lot when you sleep?' Miles noted. He retrieved a bottle of water from the fridge and threw it to Erik, hitting him square in the chest.

'Thanks.'

'You're welcome.'

Rolling his eyes, Erik took a long swig, head pounding. He forced a cough to clear his chest. 'What time is it?'

'Almost twelve,' said Miles, nodding to the clock on the microwave. 'Thought you were leaving town?'

'I was,' said Erik. 'Now I'm staying.'

Miles raised an eyebrow.

Erik shrugged and took another sip of water. His mouth felt furry and his throat was disgustingly raw. When he could talk again, he added, 'I owe it to Eliza to find out how Sam died and what went down that night.'

'You pushed her; she fell and hit her head, no?' Miles leaned down on his elbows and shrugged. 'That's what you both said. Doesn't seem like there's much of a mystery. Unless I'm missing something?'

Erik put the bottle down and lit a cigarette. It tasted foul, but he felt calmer almost instantly. 'She didn't hit her head,' he mumbled after a few drags. 'We were fighting, that much's true. I'd asked Eliza to marry me — '

'Fuck, I didn't know that. What'd she say?'

'She said yes. Sam wasn't happy about it.'

'Wait, why?'

Erik scratched his chin, making a mental note to trim his beard later. He was also in dire need of a shower; his hair was so oily he could have moulded it into another shape when he ran his hand through it.

'You remember Paige?' he asked after stalling for several seconds, heartrate picking up.

'Paige,' said Miles blankly. 'Paige Osbourne? Paige the strange?'

Erik frowned. 'Tactful.'

'Sorry, brother. You know what I mean.'

'Whatever. Yes, her,' he continued. 'Someone spoke to Sam pretending to be Paige. Paige who has been dead for years.'

'Wait, what?'

'Yeah. I felt like I'd been shot.'

After stubbing out his cigarette, Miles prompted, 'So wait, what'd she say to Sam?'

'No idea.' Erik held out a hand. 'That I'd hurt her or something. Some bullshit line I'm sure Logan cooked up just to mess with us.'

Miles rubbed the corner of his eye, face screwed up in thought. 'Hurt her how?'

A question that had been haunting Erik for years. 'I don't know. We didn't find out.'

'Maybe she said you beat her? Or raped her?'

Bile rose in Erik's throat. The unwanted images that suggestion prompted made his whole body feel tight and itchy with disgust. He said, very quietly, 'If someone said that to me ... I wouldn't have thought twice about it. I'd have reacted first. Fucked them up and not waited for answers.'

'Yeah,' said Miles softly. 'Same.'

Erik clenched his jaw, tears stinging his eyes. 'God, why did any of this have to happen?'

'I don't know, brother.' Miles heaved a sigh. 'What happened next?'

It took Erik a minute to force his mind to focus. He'd somehow managed to both relive that night a thousand times and bury it in the back of his mind. Accessing it felt like swimming in sludge. 'When she started in on us for getting engaged, we pried the Paige thing out of her. She and Eliza got physical. I didn't think, you know? I just stepped in. Seeing her grab Eliza like that ...'

Miles walked over and sat beside him. He put a hand on Erik's back and offered him a smile.

Erik had to take several deep breaths before he could find his voice. 'I pushed her backwards. Only I didn't. She went flying.' He shook his head and held out his hands in bewilderment. 'She flew clear across the path and hit the tree.'

Even knowing what had happened, it still sounded so impossible.

Miles stared at him. 'Okay, you've lost me. Were you on a hill and she fell backwards?'

'No. If anything she was uphill from us.'

'And you pushed her.'

'Gentler than I've pushed you.'

Miles stood and beckoned to him. 'Show me.'

'I'm not going to shove you, Miles.' The mere suggestion filled Erik with terror.

'Why not?'

'Because I'm scared that I'll kill you as well, all right?'

Miles took him by the arm and hauled him up. 'You're not going to kill me. We've had more than a few scuffles. C'mon.'

'No.'

'Yes.'

'No.'

'Yes.'

'No.'

'This could go on a while, EJ. Just push me. I'm cool.'

After several long seconds of glaring at each other, Erik pushed him. But fear kicked in and he didn't push hard.

Miles rolled his eyes. 'That's pathetic. Like being kissed by the wind. Try again.'

Erik pushed him half-heartedly.

'Was that how hard you pushed her?'

'Miles –'

'It's okay.'

Belatedly, and with mounting anxiety, Erik shoved him. Hard.

Miles was forced to take two steps back. No more.

They looked at each other with matching expressions of bafflement.

'And she went flying? Like in the movies?'

Erik nodded.

'Yeah, that's weird, bro.'

Neither seemed to know what to say next and the silence dragged on with increasing heaviness. The clock on the chimney mantle ticked, and outside the rain was still hammering away; every once in a while, thunder boomed, and the lights flickered. The gloomy atmosphere did little for their dark thoughts.

Miles tapped his fist on the table with anxious energy and made a face. 'Dunno, man. It could have just been a weird kick of adrenaline. You hear on the news of people lifting up cars, jumping over things that they normally couldn't've jumped over, having hair's width escapes. Not everything's explainable.'

'Yeah, maybe,' said Erik. He didn't think so somehow. But he wasn't sure what he *did* think.

'So,' said Miles, 'are you going to help Eliza figure out what you did or are you going to figure out who was impersonating Paige?'

'How about both?'

'I can do both.' Miles winked at him. 'Town's been a little dull these days. Could use a good adventure.'

'Either way, I told Eliza I would help her figure it out. She needs some closure. I do too. Maybe if there was an answer, I'd stop having nightmares about it.'

'That bad?'

'I keep waking up expecting to actually find my hands soaked in blood.'

Even admitting it felt strange. Like he was admitting he was a murderer. Just like his father.

But the look Miles was giving him wasn't one of fear or revulsion. He looked worried for his best friend. 'Christ, man. That's not good.'

'Tell me about it.'

Not wanting to think about it any longer, Erik cracked his neck and announced he was going to take a shower.

He paused in the doorway and glanced back at Miles, suddenly uncertain. 'It cool if I stay here for a while? If it's not, I can check into the B&B.'

Miles, who had started loading dirty laundry into the washing machine, rolled his eyes and threw a sock at him. 'Don't be an idiot, of course you're staying. I'd be insulted if you preferred a B&B to me.'

Erik flashed him a grateful smile before heading to the bathroom.

It was good to be home.

CHAPTER SIX
Dear Diary

A week later, Eliza agreed to meet Erik and Miles at Joanie's to talk. It was a brief, succinct exchange of texts and Erik's stomach twisted into ever-tightening knots in anticipation of seeing her again.

When they arrived at Joanie's, Eliza nodded stiffly to Erik, but she gave Miles a hug, her entire demeanour shifting at the sight of him and it was impossible not to feel jealous.

He drowned the feeling with coffee and tried to pretend it hadn't bothered him as Eliza and Miles began rehashing everything they knew about the events surrounding Sam and the fake Paige.

'What about Maya?' said Miles. He was stirring a spoon around his cup mindlessly, always filled with excess amounts of energy. 'Would Sam have told her who it was?'

'No,' said Eliza. 'Maya was just as shocked as the rest of us.'

'And Paige's parents know nothing?'

Erik shook his head. The memory of asking wasn't one he relished rehashing, either. 'Although,' he allowed, 'I did secure permission to beat the teeth out of whomever was impersonating their daughter.'

It had been a personal request from Paige's father, Rupert. He'd been as furious and confused as Erik.

Miles nodded ponderously and ran a hand through his hair, sending it every which way. 'Fair enough. All right. And your parents?' he asked, glancing at Eliza. 'They wouldn't know anything?'

Mention of her parents darkened Eliza's expression and she shook her head.

'I'm out,' said Miles. 'Anyone else have any suggestions?'

Erik pulled a packet of sugar from the jar and tore at it agitatedly. 'Sam gave you no indication that anything was wrong in the days before she died? She didn't ask to speak to you or ask how we were getting on? Nothing out of the ordinary?'

Eliza frowned in thought. 'The day before, she asked me how things were going with you. That's the only thing I can think of. It just seemed like sister stuff. She didn't want us moving too fast.'

Miles pursed his lips and held out his hands thoughtfully. 'Could be something there. Then again, I've had similar conversations with my brother and sisters, and I've never heard a bad word against their respective partners.'

'She didn't want to accuse me without proof.' Erik felt his eyes burn as he thought of Sam. 'She was a good person.'

Eliza nodded, picking up a sachet and tearing at the edges, unconsciously mirroring Erik.

'Hang on,' he said. He had been going over every memory he had of Sam and a sudden random one was now replaying vividly in his mind's eye. 'Didn't Sam have a diary?'

Miles' eyebrows went up.

'She did,' he continued, looking at Eliza, who was staring at the pile of sugar with wide eyes. 'I remember her asking us if we'd seen it once. She thought you might've been snooping. Have you found anything in them?'

'I found a few,' she admitted. 'Nothing really recent, though.'

'Doesn't mean there aren't recent ones,' said Miles. 'Where'd you find them?'

'Back of her closet.'

'Do you think your parents might have come across them?'

She shook her head. 'They haven't touched Sam's room since she died.'

The trio exchanged long looks.

'Could be something,' said Erik softly.

Eliza nodded, although she looked thoroughly ill by the thought of going to her parents' home.

'Let's go then, chickees,' said Miles, clapping his hands together. 'No time to waste.'

Erik tossed a few notes on the table and led the way out to his car. The rain had let up somewhat, though the cool, wet air lingered and the clouds lay heavy and thick upon the sky, blotting out the sun.

They climbed into Erik's car, Miles in the passenger seat, Eliza in the back, and Erik drove the familiar route to Maplebrook. The oddest feeling of déjà vu hit him. How often had the three of them been together under better circumstances?

Miles glanced back at Eliza. 'They going to be home? Cos I should tell you I am thoroughly disinclined towards familial awkwardness. One sign of heavy silence and I'm outie.'

Eliza leaned forward and ruffled his hair. 'I'll give you a signal of when to run for it.'

Miles winked at her, and Erik felt another stab of jealousy at their easy banter. Not wanting to acknowledge it, he opened the window and lit a cigarette. Glaring at the road, he tried not to think about how much he'd missed out on. How much he missed them, even now, as they sat beside them. He didn't know their jokes or their private exchanges and each time they smiled at each other, he felt a little more left out.

He almost felt relieved when he parked in front of Maplebrook a few minutes later.

'Are you sure about this?' he asked, glancing back at Eliza.

She ignored him and exited the car.

'All right, then,' he muttered to himself as he unbuckled his seatbelt.

'At least she's letting you in breathing distance,' said Miles. 'Small blessings, brother.'

They exchanged grimaces before stepping out of the car. Externally, Maplebrook had not changed much since last he'd seen it. The flowers still burst forth with intensity, the creek still rushed alongside the garden, the trees still clung to their blossoms and fruits, the statues in the garden still glared and glowered, their eyes seemingly watching at all times. But the moment they stepped inside, it was like time had crept like an infection. Everything smelled strongly of alcohol, cigarettes and moth balls; the fake flowers which had been put out for the wake were still in their vases, dusty and gloomy after five years. The photographs of Sam on the wall had been scrubbed to the point of shining, but the floors were grimy and untended, and tracks of dirt and filth stained them beyond repair. It looked nothing like his memories.

A ghost house for a haunted family.

Erik swallowed hard, his heart pounding, and followed Eliza up the stairs to Sam's old bedroom. Miles trailed behind, taking in the state of the house with a hand over his mouth, the sleeve pulled down to mask the stench.

Sam's room was untouched; even the clothes on the floor had not been put away.

'Christ on a unicycle,' said Miles quietly when he'd closed the door. 'Eliza, my love, we really must talk to your parents about the detrimental side effects of denial and shrines.'

'One's a drunk and one's a mess,' she muttered, jamming her hands into her pockets. 'There's not much to do.'

Miles reached out and squeezed her shoulders, and Erik looked away.

'So where shall we start the creepy search first?' asked Miles. 'Under her bed? On the shelf? In a drawer?'

'Let's start with the closet and then go from there.'

As one, the trio opened up the double doors of the closet and began sorting through the piles of toys, dolls, clothes, art projects and supplies, ribbons and trophies, academic textbooks and journals, novels and biographies, until finally Eliza found the pile of old diaries she'd stumbled across after Sam's wake.

Miles picked one up, only to hesitate before opening it. 'Is it wrong to snoop?'

'It's okay,' Eliza assured him. 'She'd look in my diary for answers.'

He quirked an eyebrow. 'Do you have a diary?'

'No,' she said.

'That's exactly what someone with a diary would say,' he teased before opening the notebook.

Eliza handed another to Erik and then picked up a third one to browse through.

Erik looked down at the tidy scrawl. It was from when she was thirteen. The summer she decided she wanted to be a veterinarian.

When the first pile of diaries proved unhelpful, they fanned out in their search, gingerly moving things about and opening the various notebooks, journals, leather-bound books, sketchbooks and hand-bound collages they found. It felt intrusive and creepy, and Erik silently apologised to Sam. Again.

'I've got a diary from when she was ten,' said Miles five minutes later, tossing it onto the bed.

'Twelve,' said Erik, holding up another.

'This one's from when she was eighteen,' said Eliza, flicking through it.

The pile grew larger and larger as they unearthed more diaries from behind the bookshelf and under the bed. There were dozens more in a floorboard hiding place. It became easier to tell which were from what year after they opened enough of them. She had a flower phase, with at least five diaries adorned in various types of flowers and petals; there were some from when she was a teenager with classic movie stars on the front and inspirational quotes on every other page; there were more adult looking ones starting from when she was seventeen, leather-bound, hand-pressed paper, handwriting almost perfect by then.

'Makes you think she wanted to write a memoir or something,' said Miles, flipping through one with pursed lips.

Erik looked up from rifling through one for dates which corresponded to the months before her death. 'Or she didn't want to forget anything.'

Eliza gave him a small smile before she picked up another journal. 'This one's from that year.'

'Anything relevant?' asked Miles.

'Yeah, maybe ...' She trailed off, prompting them to crowd around her as she held the diary aloft for them all to read.

28 May

The strangest thing happened today. After Maya left for class, my phone rang from an unknown number. I was waiting to hear back about the job, so I answered it.

The girl told me her name was Paige Osbourne and that she's an old friend of Erik. I asked her why she was calling me – I ought to have asked her how she even got my number because I'm still so confused – and she said that Eliza was in trouble. Odd, right?

Trouble. What a weird thing to say.

I asked what she meant, and she said Erik was dangerous to be around and she had proof. And, because I'm me, I agreed to meet her.

Smart Sam. Real smart.

I am such an idiot.

This is the opening to a horror movie, I swear to God ...

But I can't ignore something like this. If Eliza's in danger – or perhaps Erik, for all I know – then I've got to figure out what's going on, don't I? I can't just ignore a warning. And if she's completely insane, at least I know I made the effort. Maybe I can get her some help or something.

But if she's right – if there's something about Erik that we don't know, then I owe it to Eliza to find out. Don't I?

I feel so awful not telling her about this right away. But if she tells Erik and there's something to it ...

None of us ever told her how worried we were for her – getting into a relationship with the son of Logan Stern. I know it's wrong to judge someone by their parents, and I've tried so hard not to, but the stories ...

I sound like a monster.

This is why I'm not telling anyone. Not even Maya.

My fears could be entirely unwarranted, this girl could be completely crazy – maybe she's some lunatic come out of the woodwork, obsessed with Erik for whatever reason. I'm sure there's an explanation. Plenty of people were obsessed with Logan after the murder. Seriously, the world is so gross sometimes. I don't even understand how people can lust after murdering rapists. I actually feel sick just thinking of some of the letters and boxes that were sent to the Stern house while he was in prison.

Christ, poor Erik. If he is messed up, it's undoubtedly because of that.

*And even if Erik's done something
wrong, that's no reason to suspect he'll
do something to Eliza, is it?*

*God, I wish my brain would shut up.
Now that's all I can think of. I count the
seconds until he drops her off and I keep
checking her skin for bruises. Which is
exactly what Miles told Eliza he used to
do for Erik when they were kids.*

I feel sick.

*I'm meeting Paige on Friday. My diner,
so at least I won't be alone. Whoever she
is, I'm just crossing my fingers she's a
harmless loon with no truths to share.*

*I don't know how I could ever tell Eliza
that there was something wrong with
Erik.*

S.A.O.

Erik finished reading a beat before the others and dropped heavily onto
the bed. He put his head in his hands and pressed until stars exploded in
front of his eyes. Panic closed his throat and quickened his heart. He
needed a distraction before he passed out.

To his utter relief, Miles provided him with one just as his hands and
mouth went numb.

'Roadside Diner.'

Erik looked up, blinking hard. 'What?'

Miles held out a small piece of paper that had been tucked into the next
page. A receipt. It was old and had a coffee stain in the centre. 'She met
Stranger Danger at the Roadside Diner. It's more than we had an hour
ago.'

Realisation dawned on Erik and he looked at Eliza. 'That's where Logan
met you.'

'Yeah,' she mumbled, paling considerably. ''Cos that's where Paige told
me to meet her.'

They all exchanged weighted looks.

'This is getting so weird,' said Miles.

'This is so messed up,' said Erik.

'That too.'

Eliza let out a long breath and sat beside Erik on the bed. 'If she'd told me, we could have sorted it out together,' she said, voice laced with anguish and regret. 'We could have found out the truth. None of this would have happened. That stupid fight wouldn't have happened.'

Erik reached out to take her hand, only to realise it was no longer his right, and pulled back. 'None of this should ever have happened,' he said, wishing he had a cigarette just to have something to do with his hands. 'What happened in the forest was entirely my fault — *whatever* happened in the forest. This thing — this weird, random, meaningless prank — at least this we can find an answer to.'

Eliza looked at him with tired eyes. 'And about what happened in the woods?'

Erik shook his head. 'I still have no more clue than either of you.'

'There's another entry,' said Miles, who had continued flicking through the pages of the diary. 'After she met fake-Paige.'

He held the diary out to Erik, who took it with a sigh, and angled it so that Eliza could read it also.

30 May

I can't wait until Maya arrives. This living apart situation is such a joke. When she gets the job and we can finally move in together, it'll be too soon. Living with Mama and Daddy is fine and all, and I'm not trying to complain, but it really is driving me up a wall.
THEY'RE. ALWAYS. HERE.
Whatever. I digress ...

I still can't get what Paige said out of my head. She was such a strange girl.

She was small, and so, so quiet. Almost like a doll. Breakable. I thought she would disappear into the booth.

The other thing I can't get past is how young she looked. She was so baby-faced, it was actually bizarre. For a nineteen-year-old, she looked about fifteen. Maybe.

She wanted to know about Eliza. Straight away. I'm not keen on sharing Eliza's private life with my parents, let alone a complete stranger, and I asked her what business it was of hers.

'Don't you know about Stacey Stern?' she asked.

That shut me up.

I sat with her for a while after that, not really knowing what to say. She asked me if I was going to keep my sister safe. I said I would. What else could I say?

Do I believe it? Why would it be a lie? This stranger ... I want to believe her. It seems cruel not to. But believing her means believing Erik – little Erik Stern who is like my brother – is capable of such things.

My heart hurts. My head hurts a whole lot more.

I think I hear Maya outside. I'm still not sure if I'm going to tell her. Not yet. Not until I know what to do.

S.A.O.

Erik stared at the words long after he'd finished reading. They may as well have been burned permanently into his retinas. His eyes were watery and sore, his throat burned and raw. He felt far from all right, but there wasn't anything anyone could do about that. The disgust and childhood terror were burying themselves where they belonged, and fury was bubbling anew in his veins.

'I want to find this girl,' he said thickly, looking first to Miles and then to Eliza. 'I want to find her. Either she's lying, or someone hurt her.'

Miles squeezed his shoulder. 'I'll go get you some water. You're a really unfortunate colour.'

'Thanks, M.'

Erik waited for Miles to leave before looking at Eliza. He wanted to know what she thought of what they had just read. If she had questions.

Before he could ask, Eliza reached out and took his hand. He started, not sure how to react, and stared at her. His chest hurt from the strain of it.

They gazed at each other for a moment, neither sure what to say next.

The floorboards creaked outside, and Eliza let go of his hand a second before Miles walked in and handed him a glass of water.

'It's getting late and I've got a few deliveries to do,' he announced. 'Do you wanna pick this back up tomorrow? I don't know about you two, but this mess has me exhausted and depressed, and I could use a good distraction.'

Erik glanced at Eliza. He wanted to leave more than anything. From the look on her face, she wanted to be anywhere else, too.

'Ready to go?' he asked.

'Yeah,' she grunted. 'I've to head back and get Maggie. She'll be out of school soon.'

'Sure,' said Erik.

He let the other two walk out ahead of him. Alone in the bedroom he felt like an intruder, but his legs were locked.

'I'm sorry,' he whispered, looking at a picture of Sam on the wall. 'I'm so sorry.'

He stared at the photograph for a second longer before walking over to the bed, picking up the diary and tucking it into his coat pocket.

With a last glance at the far-too empty room, Erik trotted down the stairs.

The drive back to the centre of town passed in tense, strained silence. No one seemed to know what to say and Erik was certain he couldn't string together a coherent sentence even if he'd wanted to.

They turned onto Main Street and Miles tapped on the window. 'This is me,' he said, waving towards the grocery shop where his car was parked.

As Erik turned in, his eyes instantly went to the two men smoking on the bench out front.

'If it isn't Tweedledum and Tweedledee,' he muttered.

'Just don't do anything stupid,' said Miles. 'I don't need to bail you out of jail tonight. I'm too tired.'

Roger was sitting beside his brother Dickie. Ever one for appearances, Roger was dressed in clothes more expensive than Erik's car. It wouldn't have been half so grating if everyone didn't take the façade at face value and assume that good presentation meant good morals.

Roger winked at Erik and blew a ring of smoke in his direction. Erik's grip on the wheel tightened. The knots in his stomach physically hurt and he imagined what it would be like to rearrange Roger's entire face. It was immensely satisfying.

'See you tomorrow,' said Eliza, pulling him from his downward spiral of blood-stained daydreams.

'Eliza?' It left him before he'd thought through what he wanted to say.

'Yeah?'

He sighed. It was, technically, none of his business. 'Never mind,' he said. 'Be careful.'

'You too,' she said, closing the door behind her and donning her coat as she walked towards the footpath.

It took all of Erik's strength not to get out of the car as Roger placed a hand on Eliza's waist, his finger hooking casually, tauntingly in the loop of her belt buckle.

Erik drove off before he committed intentional murder.

CHAPTER SEVEN
The Haunted

The house smelled of cooking chocolate and flour, fresh flowers, and the smoke curling from the joint Roger and Eliza were sharing. It was a home clearly looked after by someone other than Roger, but it made the atmosphere cheery and welcoming.

Roger did all his business from his home. Not many dealers did. But even the local authorities bought from Roger, and most had sat for a drink in his sitting room, asking about the paintings on the wall and what his thoughts were on the local elections. He was known to most, feared by some, and mistrusted by more, but he was needed by many, and they were not afraid to use dirty money when it came so finely wrapped in Roger's nice house with its good smells and false hospitality.

Eliza hadn't said much since he picked her up, and Roger was using all of his self-control to keep from enquiring as to what might have happened between her and Erik. There was something reassuring about the hatred and jealousy in Erik's expression when Eliza left his car, but that did not quell Roger's curiosity, nor his own jealous feelings.

He felt sick thinking of Erik's hands on Eliza, his mouth on hers, the two of them —

Roger dropped the butt of the joint into the ashtray and walked into the kitchen.

Beth, his cleaning lady, chef, and general sounding board for his various complaints, looked up from the pastries she was baking and gave him a smile. 'Long day, boss?'

'And seems to be getting much longer,' he said. His eyes went to the croissants and his stomach grumbled. 'Those smell good.'

'They'll be cool in an hour,' she said, placing another batch in the oven and dusting off her hands. She frowned when she caught sight of the look on his face. 'You all right?'

'I'm fine,' he said. It wasn't convincing. He glanced at the wall, knowing Eliza was somewhere on the other side, and raised an eyebrow at Beth. 'Do you think she'll ever like me?'

'Of course,' said Beth. She was, aside from Dickie, the only one who seemed genuinely fond of him. 'We both know she doesn't have a problem with what you do and aside from that you're a catch.'

Roger smirked at her. 'Aside from that I'm a catch, huh?'

Beth kissed his cheek and stepped around him to put the milk back into the refrigerator. 'I like my men on the calm side of the law, as you well know, boss. And you're not my type.'

He put a hand over his heart. 'Ouch.'

Beth laughed and went back to work.

Still smiling, he filled a glass with orange juice and returned to the sitting room.

He'd only just sat down when Eliza looked up at him and said abruptly, 'Do you remember my sister?'

Her question threw him. 'I do,' he said after a pause. 'She was nice. She loved to dance on tables, if I remember correctly.'

He had never understood how Sam had died — the newspapers said it was an accident and Eliza never spoke of it — but he wondered, often, if there was more to the story. Erik's prompt departure two days later was far from unsuspicious to him.

He leaned back, appraising her thoughtfully. 'You okay?'

'I'm tired, Roger,' she said after a while, her secrets locked away where he would never glimpse them. 'I'm so tired of everything.'

He put his hand over hers. 'You need to find the joy in life more, baby. I've always said that.'

'I have nothing to be happy about.'

'Got all your fingers and toes; that's something.'

Eliza snorted and held up her other hand, examining it absently. 'I suppose.'

'I don't know what I'd do if Dickie died,' he admitted. 'And we're not even that close. He's an ignorant bull most days. But he's still my brother.'

She snorted and dropped her hand. 'Well, as you can see, I'm handling it incredibly well.'

'Grief takes different paths for different people, lovely. Ain't no shame in that.'

Eliza looked at him, her dark eyes piercing even without a change in expression. Desire swelled inside of him and it was impossible to think of anything but her mouth.

'You're the only one who doesn't want me to go back to who I was,' she said. 'Why's that?'

A smile spread across his face as he leaned in and traced her jaw with his fingers.

'One should never go backwards,' he said before kissing her. She tasted like coffee and cigarettes, and she felt like glass in his hands.

Glass he never knew the strength of. Glass he feared already had one too many cracks.

———————————

A loud knocking roused Eliza from her slumber. She blinked heavily and turned over. Roger was passed out beside her, eyeballs rolling around beneath his closed lids.

The knocking continued, jarring the heaviness of her head. With a low groan, she stood and stumbled out of the bedroom, the freezing air biting angrily at her bare skin. When she reached the door, she put her hand on the knob, but didn't open it straight away. Roger knew far too many questionable people.

'Who is it?' she called.

'Your friendly neighbourhood Pitbull.' It was Miles. 'Open up, baby girl.'

Confused, she opened the door. 'What are you doing here?' she hissed. 'Roger's going to lose his shit.'

Miles was clearly unbothered. He looked her up and down and wiggled his eyebrows at her state of undress. 'I always did like your choice of undergarments. Sexy legs.'

'What do you want?' she asked, glancing over her shoulder at the bedroom. Roger was still snoring away soundly. It generally took a mammoth effort to wake him, but he would be far from amused if he found Miles there.

'Just finished my morning shift at work and figured we could head down to that diner,' he explained. 'You know, get this thing sorted out. I don't like seeing my boy all guilt-ridden and I don't like all these memories being brought back up for you. So I figured it was as good a time as any to gather everyone together and whatnot. But if you're busy ...'

Eliza rubbed her eyes. 'Yeah, all right. Let me get dressed.'

'Oh, don't,' he said, wiggling his eyebrows at her bare chest. 'I like this look so much more.'

'Eat me.'

A wolfish smile spread across his face. 'Baby girl, I am more than happy to repeat that glorious experience.'

Eliza shook her head, laughing, and walked to the bedroom.

'You look like a damn skeleton,' said Miles when she returned a few minutes later. He shrugged off his coat and held it out to her. 'I swear, one gust of wind and you'll blow away.'

She glared at him even as she donned his coat. 'I'm not a feather, Miles.'

'No, but you weigh about the same.'

She didn't know what to say to that. She had no excuse. Not that she needed to give one, but it was a constant source of tension between them. For a long time, Miles hadn't felt it was his place to say anything. Now that they were closer, their friendship far more cemented, he made it perfectly clear what he thought of her choices. Though much of what he said hurt, Eliza felt no strong desire to change. She felt no strong desire to do much of anything except figure out what happened with Sam. The lack of answers kept her stumbling on and she needed Miles too much to argue with him.

'Let's go,' she said wearily.

Miles led the way down the steps. 'Do you have some deodorant or anything on you?'

'Why?'

'Because I don't want to be in the car when Erik smells Roger on you,' he said, deadly seriousness. 'In fact, I don't want to be in the same county.'

Eliza pulled a bottle out of her bag and sprayed herself. 'Better?'

Miles sniffed dubiously. 'Yeah. At least now you don't smell like rat. What do you see in dumbfuck Roger, anyhow?'

'I don't see anything in him,' said Eliza, getting into the car. 'That's the whole point.'

'If you were looking for a feelings-free deal, you could've knocked on about fifty other doors in town,' said Miles. He started the engine and pulled slowly onto the main road.

It was a still, grey morning and there was little traffic as most were in school or work, and the queue outside the fast-food joint was empty when he pulled in and ordered them coffees and doughnuts.

'I don't mind Roger,' she said at last. 'I don't like him, but he doesn't ask anything of me. He doesn't care that I don't talk to him or entertain him or take care of him. He's glad he gets laid and I'm glad I don't have to care. It works.'

Miles let out a low whistle.

'What?'

'Erik really ruined you for relationships.'

She shrugged. 'Maybe you only get one shot.'

Miles looked like he was tempted to smack her upside the head; he settled for throwing a piece of doughnut at her. 'You sound like a mopey little teenager – holed up in your bedroom writing angst filled poetry about the one that got away. Shut up. It's obnoxious.'

'Not everyone is looking for a relationship just to have one,' she retorted, bristling at the implication. 'The point of life isn't to be in a relationship. The point of life is to live it however you want, and I don't want anything less than what I had. I can fuck whomever I want and it's none of your business because you're my friend, not my boyfriend.'

'You're right,' he said after a long pause. 'It's six shades of shit. I'm sorry.'

She didn't reply, but the tension slowly dispelled.

A few minutes later, they pulled up in front of Miles' apartment. Erik was sitting on the steps smoking, his headphones in, staring off into space. Eliza didn't fail to notice that he had cleaned up somewhat since last she'd seen him. His beard was less haphazard than before. His thick dark hair was brushed back neatly. The only sign that he hadn't slept were the bags under his eyes and the enormous cup of coffee he was drinking.

It took him a moment to register that they were there; he started, nodded to them, and stood stiffly, stretching. He looked far too good and she scowled out the window, refusing to acknowledge his existence.

'Hey,' he said, climbing into the back of the car.

'Good morrow, brother,' said Miles, handing the bag of doughnuts back to him and pulling out onto the main road. 'Ready to see the infamous diner?'

'I'm dancing on the inside.'

'Can I ask,' Miles continued, taking the exit onto the motorway, 'what exactly it is that we're going to enquire upon arrival? We can't really ask if they remember a quiet, sad girl who looked fifteen from five years ago and if she perhaps left a forwarding address on the receipt she may or may not have signed. Because they might think we're not normal.'

'This was your idea,' said Eliza, glancing over at him, glad of the distraction.

'That doesn't mean it's solid or likely to work. I'm fully aware of how full of shit I am.'

Erik let out a rueful chuckle.

'We have to start somewhere,' said Eliza. She suddenly felt clammy and gross, and in desperate need of a shower. Her clothes smelled of Roger's aftershave and the lingering scent of drugs, sex and smoke. She gagged involuntarily, and her hand went to her mouth.

'Are you all right?' said Erik, leaning forwards.

She nodded, not looking back at him. 'Car sick,' she mumbled.

'Here,' he said, holding out a bottle of water. 'Have as much as you want.'

Eliza shook her head and pressed her face against the cool glass of the window. The motorway out of Riverside was one of the most scenic routes in the county. The only surroundings were the distant mountains, rivers, forests, waterfalls, rolling hills and fields. Everything was so natural, untouched and untamed. Just watching it flash by soothed the ache in her chest.

For most of her life, Eliza had dreamed of disappearing into the hills and never coming back. She loved the idea of solitude, loved the quiet that came from being by herself. A quiet she had rarely been able to find in daily life. Everyone seemed to want something, everyone had an opinion that they felt obliged to share, everyone had a problem that they wanted fixed even when it was futile, everyone wanted something from her.

Only Erik had fit so well into her life that she hadn't had to fit him anywhere. She never needed to make time for him or fill the silence or explain her thoughts. He was just there one morning, as if he had always been there. Her friends, her family, her job, they all required effort; she had to remind herself to act a certain way, be the person they needed or wanted. She was happy to do it, happy to be that for the ones she felt had earned it. But with Erik she had never had to try, she had never had to think. Everything just was. She missed that more than she could say. She hadn't just lost her sister that week. She lost her fiancé, her best friend, her support system. Her family crumbled. In the space of a week, her life became a building of dust on a foundation of water.

And now everything was mud.

It was a relief when Erik, still leaning in, pointed ahead.

'There.'

'Precisely the sort of place where someone would go to get murdered,' said Miles, peering at the diner dubiously. 'I hope you've all had your injections because I'm fairly certain that the seats are going to be filled with needles, bits of glass and chewing gum.'

'One of those things is not like the other,' said Erik, bemused.

'Gum is disgusting, and all open-mouth chewers ought to be shot,' said Miles derisively. He turned off the engine and stepped out, grabbing his long coat from the backseat and donning it in spite of the warm weather.

Eliza giggled and ruffled his hair.

Inside the diner, the air was thick with the smell of coffee, baking pastries and bread, and sizzling meats, giving a comforting air to the otherwise gloomy establishment. They sat down at a booth in the corner and looked around.

'I like it,' said Eliza. More so now that there was no sign of Logan. It was no wonder Sam had frequented it. She'd loved rustic, vintage places. Chewing gum under tables wouldn't have scared her off.

'Me too,' said Erik.

'Heathens,' said Miles. He looked around with an expression of open distaste. 'We're not going to eat here, are we?'

'It looks fine,' said Erik, signalling a waiter. 'Stop being snobbish.'

'Not wanting hepatitis does not make me snobbish, you cretin.'

The waiter came over and Erik ordered a pot of coffee and three cups. When they were left alone again, an uncertain silence descended, each one waiting for someone else to come up with what to do now that they were there.

'Paige told you to come here,' said Miles. 'Yeah?'

'Yeah,' she said.

Miles' brow furrowed. 'I wonder if she thought Sam would come since they'd met here already.'

'She didn't mention Sam,' said Eliza.

'Maybe she felt comfortable here,' said Erik. 'Sam clearly did. And if you were going to have a supposedly important meeting with someone, would you pick a place no one knew you or a place you knew already?'

'I would bring them to my flat,' said Miles, making a face and drumming his fingers on the table. 'I don't have important conversations in public.'

'Some place no one knew me,' said Eliza. 'Or the mountains.'

Erik picked up a packet of sugar and tore at the corners. 'See, I'd go to a place where I was comfortable.'

Miles rolled his eyes. 'Well, we've all established that we can never have private conversations in the same location and thus will never imbue each other with secrets to keep. What a relief. We still don't know if there's anything here to go off of. You don't have a picture of Paige hidden away in the back of your wallet by any chance, do you?'

Erik shot him a look.

'Cranky. Cranky.'

The waiter returned and placed a pot of coffee and three cups down in front of them. 'Anything else?' he enquired, holding the tray against his side. He looked at them knowingly. 'You folks aren't from around here.'

'What gave us away?' asked Miles, and Eliza had a feeling it was only Erik's glare which kept him from adding something like, 'Personal hygiene?'

'Our little hole doesn't exactly entice out-of-towners,' said the waiter. 'We only get the odd one. Aside from that, it's the regulars which keep us in business.'

Miles nodded and nudged Eliza with his foot.

Erik sat back, smiling in an open and friendly manner at the waiter. 'Don't suppose you recall anyone by the name of Sam Owens?'

A shadow passed across the waiter's face and he nodded sadly. 'Old Sammy? Of course. She was a regular here for a while. Terrible shame what happened to her. We even put up a memorial for her after the accident.'

Eliza straightened up. Erik reached over and took her hand, signalling her not to say anything. Her hand opened, their fingers interlacing automatically.

Miles busied himself with pouring them all coffee, his expression a dead giveaway.

'Did you know Sammy?' prompted the waiter.

'We did,' said Erik smoothly. 'It's actually on her behalf we've come. See, her mother was cleaning out her bedroom recently – it took a while, you understand – and she came across Sam's diary. There was an entry in the diary about a woman she met here, just a few days before she died. It was an odd encounter and we told Mrs Owens that we would do our best to track down the woman, just to give her peace of mind. She's convinced drugs were involved.'

The waiter nodded understandingly. 'That was some time ago. She often stopped here because it was halfway between her home and her school. She spent several nights a week doing coursework here, complaining about exams. We were fond of her and her girlfriend. Don't remember the girlfriend's name, though. If you're curious, the memorial's still up in the corner – over there.'

Eliza looked where the man was pointing. There was a corkboard with tacked-up photographs and writing around the side. It was hard to make out what exactly was written or posted on it, and she stood up and made her way over. As she walked, she recognised the pool table by the window. She recognised the jukebox, too. Realisation hit her like a bucket of ice water.

'This was where she did her photography assignment,' she said to no one in particular. 'She had to capture small town life.'

Erik, who had followed her to the board, pointed to a picture of an abandoned building in a back wood somewhere. 'Oh my God.'

'That's our cabin,' said Miles, also having followed them. He sounded equally as dumbfounded.

'What?' she asked.

'I brought Paige there,' said Erik, his voice so soft it was hard to hear.

Eliza's eyebrows shot up.

'You can get there up the side trail,' said the waiter, coming up behind them.

'There's also an entrance from the park,' said Erik quietly. 'Outside of town.'

'Step two,' said Miles, and Eliza nodded.

The waiter wandered over then, clearly intrigued. 'Do you really think whomever she was meeting with might have had something to do with her death?'

'I don't know,' said Eliza, stomach so tight she wanted to double over.

'I'll ask the others if they remember anything,' he said. 'Have some coffee and chill out. I'll see what I can find.'

They thanked him and returned to their table. Eliza sat down heavily. She felt mentally wrung-out and all she wanted was to curl into a ball on her bed and never move again.

'At least he's not totally useless,' said Miles. 'And we'll go up the trail next.'

Eliza scratched absently at a cut on her hand, anxiety mounting. When it began to bleed, she stopped and rubbed her eyes roughly. 'Yeah, sounds good.'

'You tired?' asked Erik, concern clear in his voice. 'You look exhausted.'

'Perpetually.'

'Especially so today?'

'You're observant,' she snapped.

'Fine,' he said, taking a sip of coffee. 'Sorry I asked.'

Eliza leaned back, mouth a thin line. She almost apologised.

'You can crash at mine instead tonight, if you want,' said Miles, the meaning clear in his eyes. 'You can have the bedroom. We'll take the sofas.'

Erik looked between them. 'Am I missing something?'

'No,' said Miles. 'Just thought I'd offer.'

Eliza rolled her eyes. 'I'm fine. I've to pick Maggie up from school.'

'Is Mitch back in town?'

'Tonight.'

Miles nodded, lips pursed. 'What was he doing this time?'

'Buying more livestock. He's looking to expand a bit for next year. If the turnaround is good, we'll be able to fix up the barn next summer. It's in rotten condition – literally.'

Erik failed to mask his curiosity and asked, 'You planning on staying there?'

She shrugged. 'I'm not really planning on much of anything. I live there. I work there. Whatever happens, happens.'

'I like your aimlessness, darling,' said Miles, winking at her. 'But the offer stands.'

'What offer?' asked Erik.

'I asked Eliza to help me deal.'

'Why?'

'Because it's good money.'

Erik shot him a look that Eliza couldn't decipher before looking back at her and offering a tentative smile. 'Do you still ride?' he asked, clearly hoping to steer the conversation in a new direction.

'Not for a long time,' she muttered, crossing her arms over her chest.

'Oh?'

'What is this, twenty questions?'

'I just want to know what's new in your life.'

'Why?'

Erik's jaw clenched and his nostrils flared, but he didn't respond. After a beat, he slid out of the booth. 'I'm going to take a piss. And then let's go up the trail. No one here knows anything.'

Eliza watched him go and tried not to feel bad about being so brusque.

'You could cut the man a break,' said Miles quietly. 'He's trying, baby girl.'

'He shouldn't.'

'If he's going to be sticking around, he might as well be up to date.'

'Miles?'

'Hm?'

She squeezed the bridge of her nose. 'Shut up. Please. Just shut up.'

An apologetic look spread across his face and he let the subject drop.

They sat in silence for only a moment before the waiter returned. Beside him was a woman with her hair in a net and her face slightly sweaty from cooking.

'This is Nina,' he said, motioning to her. 'She and Sam knew each other fairly well.'

Nina bobbed her head. 'Yeah, Sam didn't bring a lot of people here, so I think I remember the girl you're talking about. Short little thing with blonde hair?'

'That sounds about right,' said Eliza, suddenly tense. 'Do you happen to know her name?'

'I don't, sorry,' said Nina. 'I can tell you she was odd. Didn't order anything. Didn't eat. Hardly did anything but stare at Sam each time they met up.'

'I thought she was an ex,' supplied the waiter.

Eliza and Miles exchanged a look before she spoke. 'They met up more than once?'

'About three times,' said Nina. 'Maybe more. I remember finding it odd because the meetings looked really intense, but I can't actually remember hearing the girl speak. She was a frail little thing. I don't even know how she got here. I think she might have lived around here and walked, because there was no car or bike or anything out front, and she certainly didn't come and go with Sam.'

'Well, that's not suspicious,' said Miles drolly. 'Thank you, Nina.'

Erik, who had just returned and was hovering behind them listening, cleared his throat.

Nina looked back at him.

'Do you remember anything we might use to identify her?' he asked. 'Anything odd or unique?'

Nina shook her head after a few seconds. 'I mean, she wasn't the sort of person you'd pick out in a crowd. Very everyday looking.'

Eliza sighed. 'Thank you,' she said, disheartened. 'It's more than we had.'

'Can I get you any food?' asked the waiter.

'No,' said Eliza, motioning to Miles, who began sliding out of the booth. 'I think we're going to go. Thank you, though.'

It was raining lightly when they left the diner, perfectly echoing Eliza's grim mood. She drew up the hood of Miles' hoodie and crossed her arms to ward off the chill.

Miles donned a beanie that crushed his messy blonde hair down around his face before he waved a hand towards the trail. 'Up the creepy dirt road?'

'Onwards and upwards,' said Erik, sticking a cigarette between his lips and lighting it as they walked.

Queasy with anticipation, Eliza led the way up the trail. It was largely overgrown, and the wet grass dampened her legs with every step. The path hadn't been traversed in years, that much was clear. The muck was deep and caked quickly to her shoes. But if the town park was on the other side, that made little sense.

She reached the top of the hill and glanced back at the other two. 'Left or right?'

Miles opened his mouth, closed it, and then shrugged.

Erik's brow furrowed as he looked first left and then right. 'Left,' he said slowly. 'I think.'

The path curled around a wooded bend and let out in a large field. On the other side of the field, half hidden by tall grasses, was a tumbledown shack. It looked entirely unwelcoming and a flutter of unease went through her chest.

They reached the cabin and fanned out, scrutinising the scene for anything that might give a clue.

There were none.

'Okay,' said Miles, stepping away and glaring at the top of the shack. 'So, we know that we were here, and Paige was here, and Sam came here to take photographs. Think it's important?'

'I have no idea,' said Erik, walking around from the side of the cabin. 'Probably.'

'God, I haven't been here since …' Miles shrugged and didn't elaborate.

Eliza bent down and examined a garden that was so overgrown it was simply an explosion of grasses and petals. 'How many times did you two meet here?'

'I don't even know,' he mused aloud. 'I never thought to keep track.'

There was a stone with grass and dirt coating it, and Eliza brushed it clean until the engraved words were clear.

'*Blackwater*,' she read.

Miles bent down beside her. 'We just called it Shithole.'

She cracked a smile and he nudged her with his shoulder.

There was a smashing sound and they looked up to see Erik kicking in the door. He disappeared a second later.

'Come on,' said Miles. 'He's going to fall in a hole or something.'

With a last glance around the overgrown field, Eliza followed Miles into the house; almost immediately the stench of mould, damp and rot reached her nose.

'Lovely,' said Miles. 'Should have hired a housekeeper.'

They moved carefully through the house, mindful of debris and nests and broken furniture. All pieces from different eras, likely brought in at random times over the years by squatters.

In the doorway of what may have been a sitting room at one point, there was a strange symbol on the ground. It had mostly faded. She cocked her head to the side, trying to remember if she'd ever seen it before.

'We did that,' said Miles. 'Just after EJ's mother died. We thought doing a spell might bring her back to life. Obviously, it didn't work.'

'I didn't know that.'

'Yeah,' he muttered. 'I think that was the day Erik lost faith in just about everything.'

Eliza wanted to cry at the thought of them trying something so innocent, so desperate, and walked quickly past the symbol and into the adjacent room.

Erik was there already, but he was standing stiff-backed and his eyes were fixed on something in the corner.

'What is it?' asked Miles.

Without a word, Erik walked over to the corner. He bent down and picked up a book.

Eliza glanced at the cover with a small frown of confusion. It was one of a series of horror novels for teenagers; she had read a few in school. Mindless scares that wouldn't make her blink now.

She looked at Erik. 'What's wrong?'

'This belonged to Paige,' he murmured, turning it over in his hands. The book was ruined from the weather and most of the pages were stuck together, the paper warped and close to disintegrating. 'Why is this here?'

'Perhaps she left it sometime,' said Miles. 'When you two met up.'

'She didn't,' said Erik. 'This was her favourite. She brought it everywhere.'

He stood, the book still in his hands. He didn't say a word as they combed the rest of the house for any other clues. But all they found was the book.

When they returned to the car an hour later, they stood in the drizzle, no one sure what to do next.

'We can check the surrounding towns,' suggested Miles.

'And what?' said Eliza, crossing her arms to ward against the autumn chill. 'Ask if they know of a small blonde girl?'

'What else can we do?'

'I don't know,' she admitted.

Erik held up his hands. He'd been smoking nonstop since they left the cabin and his skin was off-colour with shock. 'Perhaps we should change gears.'

'To what?' asked Miles.

Despite knowing how it would sound, she took a deep breath and said, 'I think it's something supernatural. Magic.'

Erik inhaled sharply on the cigarette and began to splutter and cough. 'Excuse me?' he choked out.

Miles smirked. 'That so hard to believe, brother? I always thought you believed in the strange and unusual. We did freaking spells as kids.'

Eliza's brows shot up. She'd thought his words in the cabin had been a one-off event to make Erik feel better. 'Like more than one?'

'Hell yeah,' said Miles. 'I considered myself a wizard until I was eleven.'

She grinned. 'What happened when you were eleven?'

'My letter from Hogwarts never came.'

But Erik didn't look half as ready to buy magic as an answer. 'I'd be more inclined to believe you conversed with ghosts than believe I've got magic.'

'Why?'

Erik looked away and put the cigarette back between his lips. 'Then again,' he added, words muffled around the cigarette, 'the ability to kill people isn't really a gift, is it? Perhaps this is just one more thing to thank my father for.'

No one knew what to say to that. They stood in the rain, each wondering what to do and where to go next. All wanted answers; none knew where to start.

Miles was just reaching into his pocket for the car keys when the door to the diner opened and Nina stepped out.

'You're still here,' she called, jogging over. 'Good.'

Eliza's heart instantly began to gallop in her chest. 'What's up?'

'I remembered something,' she said. 'About the girl. You wanted to know if she had any unique features that you might identify her with? I only just thought of it – her neck. She was wearing a scarf most of the time – which I thought was odd considering it wasn't cold or anything – and I thought it was two tone wool because I didn't really look at it closely. But it wasn't. I only realised as she was leaving, and I remember thinking then that she had a good reason for being so quiet and reserved. Her neck – it was badly bruised. Blackish-blue, you know? Like someone strangled her. Or tried to. Maybe Sammy was trying to get her to come forwards and whoever did it attacked Sammy. Like drug dealers or something. Maybe her mother's right.'

They gaped at her.

Nina gestured over her shoulder. 'I've got to head back in, but I thought you should know.'

'Thank you,' said Miles, the only one of them capable of forming a sentence.

When Nina disappeared back into the diner, Eliza glanced at Erik. His eyes were wide, and his hands were shaking, and he looked close to passing out.

'The only drug dealers in town are Roger and the rest of Wyatt's boys,' said Miles quietly. With a grimace of resolve, he put an arm around Erik's shoulders and steered him into the car.

Eliza climbed into the front seat, her mind swirling with confusing thoughts.

'Bruises don't last five years,' said Miles when he'd closed his door.

'She's dead,' said Erik, voice thick and hoarse. 'She's dead. I saw her body in the casket.'

'She might be dead,' said Miles, looking back at him. 'It seems like she's still hanging around. And maybe she's got something to say.' He scratched his stubble thoughtfully. 'You did say you'd be inclined to believe in ghosts.'

'I was being sardonic, Miles.'

'Well, I think you were right on the money, man.'

They stared at each other until Miles shrugged and started the engine.

When Miles pulled up back into the town centre, it was a little over an hour left before the school let out for the day.

'Do you want to meet up tomorrow?' said Miles as he turned off the engine. 'See if we can't figure this whole mess out?'

'Tomorrow,' she said as she got out of the car. 'I'll meet you both at Joanie's.'

'See ya then,' he called.

Without looking at Erik, she walked up the street and turned left, taking a roundabout route to Roger's house.

He answered almost as soon as she knocked. His short brown hair was wet from the shower and he was only wearing trouser bottoms, the array of tattoos on his torso on display.

'Back so soon, baby?' he said, winking at her. 'Couldn't stay away?'

Eliza stepped past him into the warm house and hung her sodden coat on the heavy metal coatrack. Tying her hair back from her face, she walked without asking into the sitting room and dropped down on the sofa. Roger was a lowlife, but she knew he was no girl killer. He wasn't evil or stupid enough to stoop so low. She wasn't sure she could say the same about Wyatt, though.

Roger sat down beside her. 'How long you got?' he asked.

'I have to pick up Maggie at four,' she said.

He nodded and held out a tightly rolled joint.

As she smoked, Roger typed away on his laptop and she stared at the ceiling and thought of Paige Osbourne's short life.

She felt a great swell of compassion for those whose pain had no source but their own minds. It was wretchedly unfair.

'Penny for your thoughts?'

Eliza glanced over at Roger.

'You looked miles away,' he observed. 'Long day?'

She shrugged. 'Day's only halfway through.'

He chuckled and closed his laptop. 'Get up to much?'

'Went to a diner with Miles and Erik. And then a hike.'

'Oh?' There was a sharp, familiar edge to Roger's voice. One laced with jealousy and contempt. When she didn't elaborate, he prompted, 'Why is Erik staying in town?'

'Why don't you ask him?'

'I'm asking you.'

'You think I know Erik's mind.'

'Don't you?'

'Not anymore, no.'

'Are you two getting back together?'

'No.'

Roger made a noise of disbelief.

'You're ruining my mood,' she said irritably. Roger's jealousy was as exhausting as it was exasperating. 'I'm bouncing. Maggie's expecting me.'

'Look, I don't care if you're sleeping with someone else,' he snapped. 'But do me the courtesy of telling me.'

Eliza rolled her eyes before forcing herself to stand. 'Why does everyone want to know what I'm doing on my own time? I owe none of you a thing.'

His eyes narrowed. 'So there is something going on.'

'Christ on a bike. Goodbye, Roger.'

Before she was even halfway across the room, Roger was in front of her. He grabbed her by the arm and spun her around, his mouth colliding with hers.

She shoved him away. 'What the fuck, Roger?'

'Don't forget that I'm the only one you can stand to be around, baby,' he said acidly. 'You can't be by yourself with your own thoughts for more than a minute. That's why you come to me. That's why you need me.'

Eliza donned her coat and opened the door. She paused to glare back at him. 'I never denied that. But if you want me to keep coming around, get yourself together. I don't have the patience to deal with jealousy from my drug dealer. I can get drugs off Adrian Kane. At least he won't care who I speak to.'

She was halfway out the door when Roger caught her hand, gentler this time. 'I'm sorry,' he said, not insincerely. 'I just — I don't like him. Erik. I've never trusted him. You know what they say about him. He's dangerous.'

She was starting to get the impression that Roger had the emotional consistency of a faulty wire. She opened her mouth to contest it and he held up a hand.

'Don't defend him,' he growled. 'I've never asked you about your relationship with him because I half don't care and I'm half afraid to find out. You may not care about me, baby, but I care about you and I don't want to see you get hurt.'

Eliza didn't care enough about Roger to be properly angry, or properly understanding, or anything really. 'Don't take out your shit on me,' she said after a drawn-out pause. 'If you can calm down, I'll come back, but don't lose your head around me. I'll knock your teeth in next time.'

Roger nodded, clearly relieved. 'That's fair enough.'

She thumbed at the road. 'I've got to go get Maggie.'

'All right,' he said. Leaning in, he kissed her cheek and stepped back. 'I'm sorry I kissed you like that. I was jealous. I know I don't have the right to be, but I am. I've never made it a secret.'

'I know.' Though she found it hard to care. 'See you later.'

Outside in the cool air of the early evening, Eliza walked down the main road towards the school, her thoughts frayed and disjointed. More than anything, she wanted to be nineteen again, happy and certain and carefree.

More than anything, she wished Sam was there to tell her how stupid she was being.

After picking up Maggie, they went for pizza and shopped before heading back to the ranch. Chores kept them busy most of the evening and Eliza was more than ready for bed when at last she bade Maggie goodnight and headed into the bathroom.

As she walked past the mirror in the hallway, something moved in the corner of her eye and Eliza stopped dead.

There, in the mirror, was Sam.

Eliza spun around.

Sam wasn't there.

She glanced back at the mirror.

Nothing.

Heart hammering, Eliza pulled out her phone and dialled Miles' number. Her hand went to her forehead as she tried not to panic. It was hard to draw breath.

She wanted to cry. She wanted Sam to come back.

'Baby girl,' he answered. 'You miss me already?'

'I just saw Sam,' she croaked, almost hyperventilating.

Miles was silent for a very long, sickening pause. And then, 'We'll be there in ten minutes.'

Eliza slid the phone back into her pocket and stared at the mirror. Her sister's reflection felt burned into her eyes. It took almost five minutes to move from the hallway, down the stairs, and outside.

Eliza was sitting on the front step, staring into the night, unable to relax, when they appeared a few minutes later.

Erik was out of the car before Miles even stopped. He darted to her side and kneeled before her. He took her hands. She let him.

'Are you okay?'

'No.'

Miles sat down beside her and put an arm around her shoulders. 'What happened?'

'I was just walking through the hallway when I saw her in the mirror.'

He squeezed her arm. 'Anything else happen?'

She shook her head.

'Do you want to stay with us tonight?'

'I can't leave Maggie here,' she said. 'She might ...'

What? Would Sam hurt someone? Eliza felt wretched for even considering it.

It was Erik who said, 'I don't think it's the house that's being haunted.'

Both Eliza and Miles looked up at him.

'What do you mean?' she asked.

'I think it's us,' he murmured. 'I think it's you and it's me. I'm being haunted by Paige; you by Sam.'

Now that he said it, she wondered why they hadn't considered that. Perhaps ghosts didn't haunt places. Perhaps ghosts haunted people.

'Why?'

'If I knew that, I'd be able to stop it.' Erik sat down on her other side. 'Do you want us to stay here tonight?'

The thought of having Erik around for the night made her chest quake, but the thought of him leaving was even worse.

She sighed heavily and nodded. 'Fine. But keep quiet. I don't want Maggie to feel weird.'

She led the way up the stairs to her room and they tiptoed in behind her.

Miles dropped into the desk chair and Erik sat on the windowsill and opened it before lighting a cigarette.

Eliza sat cross-legged on her bed and stared at the mirror, silently praying Sam would return.

CHAPTER EIGHT
The Weight of History

In the days that followed, Eliza found herself staring at every mirror she passed, increasingly desperate to see Sam again. She went days without sleeping or eating; she was in a kind of daze.

The desire to see her sister, to ask if she was okay, to find answers, became an all-consuming, gnawing ache. The problem was that neither Erik nor Miles had been able to provide more answers or suggestions and none of them knew where to go next. The diaries and the cabin had only conjured more questions and as the days passed, she felt even more adrift than ever before.

A few hours into a mindless walk she didn't remember starting in the first place, Roger's car pulled up beside her and the window slid down.

'You okay, baby?'

She blinked back at him, unable to find the energy to answer.

'Get in,' he said. 'You're going to freeze to death.'

Eliza sighed heavily before acquiescing. He drove back to his house and led her inside. It was warm and smelled of Beth's cooking.

Instead of taking her to the sitting room, he took her to the bedroom and held out two tablets. 'Take these. You look like crap and you need to sleep.'

Eliza swallowed them unquestioningly and let Roger take off her coat and shoes.

'Lie down,' he said.

She dropped onto her back as he slowly pulled off her jeans. She was asleep seconds later. This time it was a black sleep, deep and undisturbed.

When she awoke, Roger was fast asleep beside her, his arms around her stomach. Her movement jolted him awake and he pressed against her, his arousal obvious.

'You feeling better?' he murmured.

'Sure,' she said, not feeling much of anything but empty.

'Good.'

It was silent and distracting, but far from satisfying, and afterwards she sat up and checked her phone. She had slept almost fifteen hours. Hungry and stiff, she dressed and texted Miles to meet her at Joanie's.

Below his name, a text from her mother made guilt well in the pit of her stomach. She stared at it for almost five minutes, uncertain and racked with more guilt because of it.

'What's up?' asked Roger, pulling on a pair of trousers. 'You look like you're going to throw your phone.'

'My mother wants me to come for dinner this week,' she said.

He zipped his jeans and walked over to her. 'How's your dad?'

'Drunk.'

'If you want company,' he offered, 'I can go with you. People are disinclined to be awkward when there's company.'

She nodded slowly. 'You may have a point.'

Clearly not expecting her to agree, he hesitated a moment before asking, 'Do you want me to come?'

She pursed her lips and tried to imagine how that would go. Her parents knew Roger in passing, but not well. She wasn't worried what they would think of him; she was worried about what state he'd see her parents in.

'It doesn't mean anything,' he said quickly, misinterpreting her silence. 'I want to help. No strings, Pinocchio.'

'Yeah,' she said at length. Bringing Roger would at least prevent her mother from asking her to stay the night. 'Okay.'

A look of surprise flashed across his face. But instead of saying anything, he nodded and led the way out of the bedroom. Relieved, she followed him after sending a reply to her mother that they would be there.

'Let me know?' he called when she reached the door.

Eliza nodded and left.

The mid-October air blew the leaves along the ground and sent chills up and down her spine, but she was shivering for more reasons than one.

Miles was there already when she arrived at Joanie's. He pushed a cup of coffee towards her pointedly. 'You look terrible, baby girl.'

'That's because I feel terrible,' she said, dropping down into the other chair.

'Drink.'

She gulped down half the cup before taking the cigarette he proffered.

'You at Roger's?'

'You know I was.'

Miles put his hand over hers and raised both eyebrows. 'Sam's not the only thing haunting you.'

'No,' she whispered. 'She's just the only one that's real.'

He raised her hand to his lips and kissed it, but he didn't seem to know what to say to that.

She looked at her coffee, wanting to cry. 'I wish none of this had happened. I wish everything was different.'

'I know.'

'But if Sam is haunting me, I don't think I want her to stop.'

The admission made her throat tighten, and Miles moved his chair closer and wrapped an arm around her.

He kissed her temple. 'There is another way to think about it,' he said softly.

'What's that?'

'Maybe Sammy's not haunting you,' he said. 'Maybe she's watching over you.'

Eliza looked at him, choked up with a hope she never wanted to let grow, but which blossomed inside her at his words regardless.

'Miles?'

'Yeah?'

'I really love you sometimes.'

He leaned in to catch her eye. 'I do it for the smiles. And you've got one of the best smiles I've ever seen.'

It was impossible not to smile at that, and she buried her face in the crook of his neck.

Bottled sunshine, that was Miles.

———————————

The drive to Turner Cross took two hours on a clear day. In bad weather, it took almost three.

Rain lashed against the windshield for most of the way, but it lessened to a slow drizzle when Erik stopped outside of the Osbournes' home.

He knocked twice on the door and bit his fingernail in agitation as he waited for it to open. He'd come by often enough over the years, but he always felt like he was intruding.

Sun answered and a surprised smile lit up her face. 'Erik!'

'Hi,' he said, scratching the back of his head as his discomfort skyrocketed. 'May I come in?'

'Of course.'

She kissed his cheek as she always did when he dropped by and waved him inside.

He followed her through the house and into the sitting room. Rupert was at the table, typing away on his laptop, but he closed the lid when he caught sight of Erik. He stood and gave Erik a hug.

'I'm so sorry to bother you both again.'

'Don't apologise,' said Sun. 'You know you're always welcome.'

When they'd sat down at the table, Erik took a moment to steady himself. Then, forcing a smile he didn't feel, he said, 'Did Paige ... Did Paige ever mention anything odd in the weeks before she died?'

The colour drained from their faces and he felt instantly horrible. All he ever brought them was bad news and more questions.

'Is this about the impersonator?' asked Rupert.

Erik nodded. 'We may have an idea, but I want to run over everything before I accuse anyone.'

'Good idea,' said Sun softly.

'Did she say anything to you? All I remember was coming up for the weekend, going hiking, and then she phoned me later that week to come down.'

Sun tucked her hair behind her ears and leaned forward on her elbows. 'She didn't say anything when she went down to see you?'

Erik frowned in confusion and shook his head. 'She never came down to see me.'

'Yes, she did,' said Sun. 'I remember because it was raining. I didn't want her to cycle.'

He stared at Sun, heartrate picking up. 'I never saw her.'

'Perhaps she was meeting someone else,' said Rupert. 'Lied to us. She had a habit of doing that.'

Erik leaned back in his chair and thought about that for a moment. In the weeks leading up to Paige's death, he'd seen her constantly. He'd fretted about her depression and didn't like to leave her alone. They'd meet at the cabin and pass the hours together. Him avoiding Logan — who, at the time, was fighting Gloria for custody — and Paige avoiding her fears and an unconquerable sense of loneliness and desolation not even he could fully fix. But Paige didn't have a huge circle of friends. Outside of a girl named Karen, she'd spent all her time with Erik. Rupert's suggestion left him with even more questions.

'Do you mind if I look in her room?' he asked.

Rupert nodded. 'I've looked through her room hundreds of times. There's nothing there. But if it will put your mind at ease, go ahead.'

Erik thanked them and walked down the hall to Paige's old bedroom.

When he was alone, the door closed, he pushed the bed aside and took out his pocketknife. Paring up the carpet, he pulled it back; there, hidden from the world, were several diaries beneath a loose floorboard.

He remembered Paige telling him once how proud she was of her hiding place. He'd never wanted to pry into her private demons before. But now he doubted everything and had to know.

Erik stuffed them into his bag. Placing the carpet back carefully, he moved the bed to its former place and spent the next few minutes simply browsing around the room and turning things over in his hands.

Everything still felt like it belonged to Paige. A girl who loved life and had a mind that turned it grey and frightening. She deserved so much better.

'I'm sorry, Po,' he said, placing his hand on the desk still covered with her belongings. 'I'll figure out what happened.'

He wondered if the chill that ran down his spine was from his own anxiety, or some other presence.

He wondered if he was losing his mind.

———————

When Eliza and Roger arrived at her parents' house the following night, she still couldn't believe she'd actually brought him. And she wasn't alone in that thought.

The look of shock on her mother's face when she opened the door was proof enough. But the house had been tidied somewhat and the windows were open, letting in fresh air and for half a second Eliza relaxed.

And then she realised.

'Where's Dad?'

Mira let out a tremulous sigh. 'The pub.'

Eliza wanted to scream.

'I'll get him,' said Roger quickly, departing before they could protest.

Eliza looked at her mother. Only when she heard Roger's car start did she speak. 'He needs help.'

'Your father isn't that heavy,' said Mira.

'*Dad* needs help.'

Mira's face fell. 'I know. I've tried.'

'He's going to get himself – or someone else – killed. Just like last time.'

'I hide the keys. He walks or takes a taxi.'

Eliza shook her head. 'Sam would be so disappointed. The last time he was like this, she was the one who got hurt. Who's next? You?'

For a long time, Mira said nothing. But then, 'I know. You're right.'

Eliza didn't want to be right.

It was almost an hour later when Roger returned with Ryan. Eliza helped him lug her father upstairs to her parents' bedroom. After depositing him face down on the bed, they closed the door.

'I'm sorry,' she muttered, leaning back against the wall, legs anything but steady. 'Jesus.'

Roger waved off her apology and brushed hair out of his eyes. There was no judgement in his gaze and she felt a rush of gratitude. 'It's fine,' he said. 'It's not on you. His daughter died.'

'We all lost Sam.'

'I know.' Roger drew her close and wrapped his arms around her. 'Want to go?'

'All I do to them is leave.'

And she hated Erik for doing just that.

Dinner was a subdued affair, but it was clear her mother was grateful for the company. Still, Eliza was utterly relieved to get into the car and head back to the ranch an hour later.

Roger said nothing on the way home and when they arrived at the ranch, he only kissed her cheek before she got out.

'He'll be okay,' he called after her. 'It just takes time. He snapped out of it before, didn't he?'

'But what if he doesn't?'

'He will.'

She nodded, feeling numb. ''Night.'

''Night, baby.'

Roger's car was barely down the drive when movement to her right caught her eye and Eliza turned to see Erik walking over. She hadn't even noticed his car, which was obscured by the night.

He was so lanky that he always seemed to be strolling. There was nothing reticent about his demeanour, however. Anger seemed to spill from every pore. He stopped a few paces away from her, hands jammed into his coat pockets.

She stared back at him defiantly, daring him to say something and too tired to start.

He took the bait. 'You two have a good time?'

Eliza leaned against the paddock railing and crossed her arms. 'Are you bothered that I'm carelessly fucking or that I'm carelessly fucking him?'

He looked close to imploding at her words. 'Let's start with him since I'll grant you that the former is none of my business, although I won't deny that hearing it makes me want to set myself on fire.'

Those words gave her a rush of satisfaction and she smirked with cold contempt. 'I don't have feelings for him,' she said bluntly. 'I don't have feelings for him, or for AJ or Derek or Martin or Miles –' She stopped short. She hadn't meant to mention Miles.

Erik looked ready to be sick. 'Miles? *My* Miles?'

'Does that surprise you?' she snapped back.

He looked like he was having trouble standing and he opened and closed his mouth several times. 'Why in the name of *God* did you go near Miles?'

She shrugged.

'That's it? That's what you're giving me?' Erik's voice had taken on a wheezing quality. 'He's the closest thing I have to a *brother!*

'You left me! At my sister's wake!'

'Because I hated myself for what I'd done! I was terrified I would hurt you!'

She let out a strangled noise and slammed her hand against the wall of the barn. 'You did! If you loved me, you wouldn't have left!'

'I never stopped loving you.'

'Bullshit.'

'It's true.'

Thoroughly fed up, Eliza turned and stormed into the house. Her heart was racing, and her lips were trembling, her cheek twitching from nervous energy.

She made for the press beside the sink and pulled out a bottle of bourbon. She took a long swallow and leaned against the sink, knowing without looking that Erik was behind her.

He'd followed.

She was both furious and relieved.

Why was he staying now? Why couldn't he have stayed when it mattered?

'I didn't leave because I stopped loving you,' he said softly. 'You can't honestly think that.'

'Maybe. Maybe not.' Eliza turned around. She clenched her eyes shut. Her head had started to ache. 'Doesn't change the fact that I hate you for what you did. I hate that you left me. I've tried to rise above it and see your side of things and I do – I really do – but you chose your own guilt over me – and don't say you didn't, I can see you opening your mouth.'

Erik closed his mouth, but it was clear he wanted to protest.

'You killed Sam. It was an accident. I know that. I've never doubted it. You didn't mean to kill her. But the fact remains that you did. You killed her and instead of sticking around to help – to make up for it – you disappeared. You left me with my grief and my mother's depression and my father's drinking. So, I tried not to care. It didn't work. I went months without sleeping. But the nightmares wouldn't stop so I tried to drink until I blacked out. That worked for a while, but then it didn't, and the nightmares came anyway. I tried to kill myself. Twice. Almost succeeded the second time. Miles is remarkably persistent when it comes to forcing someone to vomit up a bottle of pills – and him coming by was sheer happenstance, by the way. He wanted to know if I was up for the movies.'

Erik stepped closer, tears in his eyes.

'Don't.' She held up a hand and backed away. 'You don't get to give me belated comfort. I don't need it. I learned how to function and on days that really bite, I go to Roger. Why not? Roger wants sex and I don't care enough to object. What does it matter to me? Sex lost all meaning a long time ago.'

Erik's face was devoid of all colour by this point. When he spoke, his voice was so thick with emotion the words were hard to make out. 'And you think it's any different for me? You think I just moved on and forgot about you? That I could do that?'

'How should I know? I don't know you anymore. Sometimes I wonder if I ever knew you at all.'

He walked over and took the bottle from her hands, drinking a considerable amount before wiping his mouth and putting it down. Erik had once sworn to her he would never touch the stuff. How very long ago that was.

'I've slept with people too if you want start taking count,' he said bitterly. 'Trust me, babe, we'll both be in the double digits as something tells me there's a lot of people you're leaving off your list. It's easier not to be heartbroken if there's distraction around. But that doesn't mean that every second I was inside of them I wasn't wishing it was you. I *hated* them for not being you.'

His breath caught, and he took a ragged, rattling breath. He sounded close to tears when he continued. 'I've loved you since we were sixteen years old and thought life would never be more complicated than finding jobs and figuring out the tax system. That hasn't changed.'

Despite herself, Eliza snorted. 'I still haven't figured that out,' she admitted. Taxes would forever baffle her. Just one more thing she wanted to run to her father about. Just one more thing she couldn't go to him for.

Erik's lips twitched. 'I don't think anyone has. One of the greatest conspiracies of life is the how and why of the tax system. Right up there with cauliflower and the purpose of wisdom teeth.'

'Cauliflower really is useless.'

'Broccoli's poor, rejected cousin.'

They looked at each other, anger no longer emanating from either of them. Erik was staring at her in a strange way, his dark eyes somehow darker. If that was even possible.

He gave her a small half-smile and stepped back with a resolute nod. 'I should go. I keep trying and failing to leave you alone. Seeing Roger didn't help. I'm sorry. I only came by to see how you were.'

She found she was actually surprised. 'All this and you're not even staying for a cup of coffee?'

'I don't think that's a good idea.'

Eliza's eyebrows knit together in confusion. 'Because *now* things are awkward between us?'

'No,' he murmured. 'Because I can't stop staring at your mouth or thinking about how good you used to taste and all the things I'd very much like to do with you, and it's taking all of my self-control to walk away from you right now.'

'Gentlemanly.'

'My thoughts are anything but,' he said huskily, eyes flicking to her lips again. The look on his face was so heated and full of desire that Eliza nodded and let him leave.

She leaned back against the wall and took several deep breaths. Her legs felt jellied and her lips pulsed.

'Crap,' she muttered under her breath.

CHAPTER NINE
Collide, Combust

For a few days, the search for answers was put on hold. Miles was given more shifts at the shop to cover for two of his co-workers who were out with a horrible virus; and Eliza was working all hours at the ranch after a storm tore the roof off the barn and four of the animals were injured.

Left to his own devices, his thoughts intrusive and overwhelming, Erik found himself aimless and pensive. So when he spotted Roger leaving The Weaver, several days after his confrontation with Eliza, black ledger in hand, Erik's tenuous grasp on coexistence vanished.

Within an hour, he was outside Roger's door with no plan; Erik was simply bursting with an unquenchable need to punch him in the teeth.

'Well, well, well if it isn't Riverside's black sheep,' said Roger upon opening the door. He was wearing an ironed shirt and expensive shoes and smelled strongly of expensive cologne.

'If it isn't Riverside's resident scum-bucket,' he retorted.

Roger's lip curled in open contempt. 'What can I do for you, Stern?'

Erik gestured to the street behind him. 'I've been told not to discuss personal business in view of others, Kray, but if you're so inclined we can hash it out right here.'

Roger stepped back. 'Come in then,' he said disdainfully, waving a hand. 'It's not like I have better things to do.'

'I'm sure.' Erik followed him inside and closed the door.

Roger's house was unexpected. Black leather furniture, a clean and recently vacuumed rug on polished wood floors, and a kitchen devoid of dirty dishes and sparklingly clean was not what he would have guessed.

He looked at Roger, eyebrow raised. 'You clean?'

'I have a housekeeper,' said Roger. 'And she cooks. You should think about hiring someone. Damn handy.'

'Selling opiates and stimulates as lucrative as ever, I imagine,' said Erik. 'I assume you're still trading in other areas as well?'

Roger dropped onto his sofa. 'Is that why you're here, Stern? Come to scold me? I seem to remember you handing out a few white bags in your day.' He cocked his head mockingly. 'Get off your high horse and go pester someone else, you fruit fly. You're less welcome than a pile of shit.'

'I can't imagine scolding you would do much good.' Erik glanced about the room, eyes landing on a large wooden chest with a lock on the front. He had seen the inside of that chest too many times and his eyes narrowed. 'And I gather you don't have much to fear from the authorities since at least a third of them are customers. But I will say this: keep selling in Riverside and we're going to have a problem.'

Roger chuckled, entirely unintimidated. 'Is that a fact? You've certainly found moxie on the road. I admire that. Coffee?'

'I'm all right,' said Erik. 'Thank you.'

Roger sat up and poured himself a large cup of coffee and lit a cigarette, before leaning back on the sofa to appraise him. 'You didn't seem to have a problem running guns and stolen goods for Wyatt.'

'I haven't sold anything in years.'

'No,' said Roger, smile widening, wolfish and knowing. 'You just bloody whatever poor shmuck he sits in front of you.'

A sick shiver went over Erik's skin. 'At least I've not sold laced shit.'

'You keep hurling that accusation, Stern, but you've never proved anything. Even Wyatt believes you made that up.'

'Is that right?' Erik regarded him, wrath building steadily. 'And Sam?'

Roger's face went white. 'What?'

'It was Dickie who drugged her,' said Erik coldly. The memory of that night came back to him like a bullet as the sound of Sam crying echoed in his ears.

'Dickie wouldn't —'

'You sure about that?'

They glared hatefully at each other.

'You should stop, Roger,' said Erik quietly. 'Riverside has enough problems without your help.'

'This isn't about guns or drugs. We both know the only reason you're making this your business is because of Eliza. I wonder what she'd think of you coming over here to scold me. Can't imagine she'd be delighted about it. She hates busybodies.'

Erik tried to ignore how the mere mention of Eliza made his blood thrum and his chest shake. 'I'm not discussing Eliza with you.'

'Oh? Isn't that why you're here?'

'One word about her from you, Kray, and I'll break your teeth. Don't push me.'

Roger's expression darkened with unmasked hatred. 'You should go back to Silverlake. Wyatt misses his dog.'

The clear desire Roger had for him to leave gave Erik an edge he hadn't known for certain he possessed. He grinned with affected mockery. 'Do I frighten you, Kray?'

'Frighten me? No.' Roger put the coffee cup down and stood. He walked towards Erik slowly, expression quietly menacing. 'Piece of advice: you should know when you're on the losing side of a fight.'

'Is that right?'

Roger stopped within swinging distance. 'What is it you think you can threaten me with? I have more money, more friends with more guns; more influence, more power. I'm kindly giving you this one chance to leave before I become truly annoyed and make it happen. Who will side with you against me? You're the son of a murdering rapist. I run this town now that Wyatt and your dearly departed dad are gone.'

'Eliza will side with me.' Erik cocked his head to the side. Taunting. Daring him to contest it. 'That must burn you up inside.'

It was enough. A flicker of doubt passed over Roger's face a second before he raised his fist. Erik ducked and caught him around the middle, sending them both crashing to the ground.

Erik's hand closed around his throat at the same time Roger lashed out, his fist connecting with Erik's ribs.

Pain shot through his torso and Erik had to force himself not to curl into a ball from the force of it.

He let go of Roger's throat and punched him hard, twice, before Roger rocked forwards, smashing his head into Erik's face and dislodging him.

They both scrambled to their feet. Erik's nose was bleeding profusely, the taste of iron strong on his tongue. Roger's eyebrow was ripped open, his eye bloodshot, his teeth stained red.

Roger wiped blood from his mouth. 'It never ceases to amaze me that she stooped to your level,' he spat. 'How much did you have to manipulate her for that to happen?'

'At least she was with me for more than my drugs,' said Erik, flexing his fingers and wondering just how many times he could beat them into Roger's face before he lost feeling. 'Does it bother you? Knowing that she's only with you to get a fast fix?'

Roger smiled viciously. 'Does it bother you knowing that she spends her nights with me and will hardly look in your direction?'

Erik lunged at him. They collided with the wall, the force knocking the wind out of them both. Roger buckled, and Erik rammed his knee up, forcing Roger to fold in half.

Erik slammed Roger's head against his knee and shoved him away.

Dazed and bloody, Roger still managed to right himself and dived, catching Erik around the middle. They fell backwards onto the coffee table and pain exploded through Erik's body.

He slammed his hands against Roger's chest –

And Roger went *flying*.

He collided with the opposite wall and crumpled, plaster and dust covering him, books and trinkets cascading everywhere.

Erik looked down at his swollen hands and unclenched them, his heart pounding with fear.

Again. It had happened again.

'Stay away from her,' he said, barely finding his voice. 'And stop dealing in Riverside. I find out you haven't, I'll be back.'

He was halfway out the door when he heard Roger's grunting reply.

'I'll be waiting.'

The cool air felt like a kiss of reprieve as Erik stumbled down the street, wiping blood off his face. The grocery shop was only around the corner, but he wasn't sure he wanted to see Miles. He wanted to see Eliza, which was a monumentally awful idea before even taking into account the fact that he had just beaten Roger to a pulp. And yet he wanted to see her more than anyone else. She was the only one who'd ever been able to make the demons in his mind shut up.

His feet seemed to make the decision before his brain could raise any objections, and he climbed into his car and made his way to Calico.

The ranch was abuzz with activity when he arrived. The small area in front of the house was filled with workers' cars.

Erik parked behind a farmer's truck and got out. The barn was an absolute disaster from the autumn rains, but it was clear they were making progress. More than twenty people were hard at work moving debris and picking up boards with long, rusted nails sticking out.

He spotted Mitch and walked over. Covered in muck and dust, sandy hair sweaty and matted, Mitch was a comforting, familiar sight.

He laughed when he caught sight of Erik. 'Who messed you up?'

'Got into a fight with my toaster,' said Erik, wiping blood out of his eye. 'How's the clean up going?'

'All right,' said Mitch. He brushed dirt off his hands absently. 'Could be worse. The Callaghans and Rosenbergs came over to help us, which is taking a load off.'

'Want an extra pair of hands?'

Now that he was there, Erik wanted something to occupy himself with. He also wasn't sure tracking Eliza down and then dodging answers was the best course of action; hard labour seemed a good middle ground. At least he could take his anger out on a building site with relatively no fallout.

Mitch nodded. 'If you're up for it?'

'Got a spare set of gloves?'

And so, for the next few hours, Erik found himself picking up pieces of the ruined roof and lugging them to the flatbed for transport, and lifting beams with several of the others to put them back into place, and securing tarp onto the rooftop to keep out wind and rain until the new roof was put on. It was hard, repetitive work which required all his concentration and little by little his anger dissipated.

He was so focused on what he was doing that he didn't notice Eliza's arrival until he stepped off the ladder and turned around, almost colliding with her.

'Hey,' he said, wiping sweat from his face with the back of his arm.

She took in the state of him with raised eyebrows. 'Nice face.'

'I made it myself.'

154

Her lips twitched. 'What happened?'

'I had a disagreement with Roger over the distribution of drugs within town limits,' he said as he led the way over to the hose. He turned it on and took a long drink before turning around to face her.

'You had a disagreement over drugs,' she echoed, tone disbelieving. 'Drugs wouldn't happen to be spelled T-E-S-T-O-S-T-E-R-O-N-E, would it?'

Erik turned the hose off and cracked his back. 'Can't say for certain, babe. He's a bit childish.'

She crossed her arms, thoroughly unimpressed. 'Was there something to warrant this lovely display of machismo or did you just go over and beat the tar out of each other because you were pissed off?'

'Both?'

'*Erik.*'

He shrugged, although he silently hoped she wasn't actually angry. 'Look, we were going to have it out eventually. Roger's never liked me, and I've never liked him. It's been in the cards for years. I just hastened up the date.'

'Because of me.'

'That might have had something to do with it,' he allowed.

'Maturity is widespread in Riverside.'

'We try.'

The look of irritation on her face made him deflate somewhat and he ran a hand through his hair. He took a deep breath before saying, 'Look, I saw him selling —'

'You did, too.'

'Not to people like your dad.'

'Roger would never sell to my dad.'

'So the other alcoholics and drug addicts don't matter?'

Eliza rolled her eyes. 'Don't pretend to be fighting for those who can't help themselves. This isn't about him selling; it's about me buying.'

It was a few seconds before he answered. 'I talked to Miles about the drugs. He said you've been doing them for a while.'

Eliza scowled. 'What I do in my own time is my business. I work, I pay my bills and I do what I want because despite what you and Miles might be inclined to think, my life is my own and I only have to answer to myself.'

'I'm not debating that,' he retorted, although it would have been false to say that he did not *want* to debate it. 'Doesn't change the fact that I'm worried. Doesn't change the fact that he's dealing to people who don't have the strength or self-awareness to say no to that shit. He's scum, Eliza. I'd hate the guy even if you weren't with him. Hell, I hated him when we worked together. I've thought of beating the brains back into his skull for years.'

She said nothing, and the silence dragged on. He rocked back and forth on the balls of his feet, not knowing what to say next. Not knowing how to approach her anymore.

A cool breeze picked up and he walked over to the fence where his coat was hanging. Donning it, he pulled a cigarette out of the battered box and inhaled several times before turning back to face her.

Eliza had remained where she was, watching him with an inscrutable expression. He used to know what she was thinking better than he knew his own mind. Now he couldn't read her at all.

That realisation, amongst a multitude of others, broke his heart.

He walked slowly back over, desperate for some kind of reaction.

'Babe?' he prompted when he couldn't stand it anymore.

Something in her dark eyes changed and she held up her hands. 'I can't do this anymore, Erik. I can't. Not with you. You need to go. I thought I could handle you being here long enough to sort out what happened with

Sam, but I can't. You're sticking your nose where it doesn't belong, acting as if you still have a say in my life and I'm tired of it. Just go.'

Her words hit him like a punch, but he did not fight them.

'All right,' he said softly. 'I'll go.'

To his surprise, Eliza shook her head in disgust. 'Figures.'

He did a doubletake. 'You want an argument?'

'I didn't think you'd agree so quickly.'

'It's what you want.'

'Is it what you want?'

Erik felt slightly dizzy. A few of the workers were watching them, each at least peripherally aware of who they were and what they might be fighting about.

He glared venomously at them before looking back to Eliza. 'Babe, if you want me to leave, I'll go.'

She scoffed and turned away. 'You never could fight for anything.'

The words felt like a slap. 'Come again?'

'You heard me,' she said, walking off.

Erik watched her for about three seconds before he strode after her.

They went around the corner of the barn to the paddock fence where the cows were milling about, mooing for food and restless with the threat of more bad weather.

'I never fight for anything? Really?' he snapped, catching up with her. 'Screw you, Eliza.'

'Why did you even come back?' she cried. Her voice was far too loud in the quiet, wooded area, but he was too angry to cringe at the thought of the workers overhearing. 'Why now after all this time? Gloria didn't need your help. You could have sent her the money. She's had other tragedies in her life before this and you never returned for any of them. Certainly not for a death you were both relieved by. Why now? You did enough damage leaving! You didn't need to come back and pour salt into wounds that have festered for years! You're an infection, Erik!'

He looked away, eyes burning. He had tried very hard not to give the matter much thought. If he admitted to himself that he used his father's death as an excuse to return, it would lead him down a road he wasn't prepared to deal with.

'Silence? That's all I get?'

He had to force his throat to open. 'What do you want me to say, Eliza? You know me. You know me better than anyone. You know why I left. You know why I'm back. Just tell me what to do to. Tell me what you want. I'll do anything.'

'Make it better.'

'How?'

'Come here.'

Erik moved towards her without hesitation. She fit against him perfectly, every contour of her body a complement to his own. She wrapped her arms around his waist and tucked her head against his chest.

It had been so much easier to have boundaries when the distance had been physical. Holding her, feeling her against his body, Erik felt nineteen and irrational, and knew that his last reserves of standoffishness were fast evaporating.

Eliza's hands curled into his jacket, lifting it slightly and sending a chill down his spine and he was suddenly very aware of her proximity, of her smell. It was overwhelming.

An old, familiar ache filled his body and he drew back, his mouth dangerously close to hers.

'Eliza ...'

He couldn't move away from her. Every fibre of his being was on fire. His heart was pounding so hard that his hands would be shaking if they hadn't been holding her.

She met his gaze, eyes heavy and hooded, dark with want, and nodded. Erik was kissing her before his brain could even register what was happening, his hands sliding down her back and drawing her in closer.

It wasn't close enough.

Five years of horrible need burned through him and he wanted to consume her.

That thought made him draw back, gasping, even as everything inside him screamed not to.

Her lips were swollen, her hair hanging in front of her face, framing her tantalisingly, and it took all his power not to pull her close once more.

He was far too aware of his skin and the lower half of his body definitely disagreed with his brain. He had to clench his fists to steady himself.

Eliza bit her fingernail, clearly not knowing what to do either.

'I love you,' he said plainly. 'I love you and I will find out what happened. I swear.'

'And then?'

'I haven't the slightest idea,' he admitted. 'But maybe — maybe we can start over.'

Eliza didn't look wholly convinced, but she didn't pull away, and Erik was grateful for small victories.

He held out his hand and when she took it, the relief almost knocked him over. They walked back through the field and parted ways at the barn.

The rest of the day passed in a flurry of activity and Erik was glad of the distraction. He vented all of his frustration into the work and by the time the sun was setting, his muscles ached and his hands were blistered, but the barn looked infinitely better and he felt less frayed.

He was just climbing off the ladder, stomach growling with hunger, when Eliza approached him again. She was covered in dust and muck and her hair was matted with sweat. A shot went through him and he smiled sheepishly at her, his mind instantly replaying the kiss — and all he wished had followed.

'Dirt looks good on you,' she teased.

'I was just thinking that,' he said, winking at her.

She thumbed over her shoulder. 'Maggie's making dinner and there's always extra. You can stay if you want. A thank you for lending a hand and all that.'

'Cos we don't pay around here,' said Mitch cheekily, appearing behind her. He was half soaked — from sweat or a hose, it wasn't clear — and had a noticeable amount of shavings in his sandy hair. 'We'd love it if you stayed.'

'Sure,' said Erik. He couldn't stifle the smile which spread across his lips as he held Eliza's gaze. 'I'd love to stay.'

He followed them up to the farmhouse, picking idly at his blisters.

The heavenly smells of sizzling steaks, roasting potatoes, steaming vegetables, baking bread, and some sort of cake that smelled chocolatey, greeted them upon entry.

Maggie glanced up as they entered the kitchen. She smiled at her brother and Eliza, but her smile vanished at the sight of Erik.

'Erik's staying for dinner,' said Mitch, kissing his sister's cheek before going to the sink and washing his hands. 'A thank you for helping out today.'

'I see,' said Maggie. It was quite impressive how much dislike she could pack into two short words.

'Simmer down, sassy,' said Mitch. 'You always liked Erik.'

'I liked cheese until it gave me food poisoning.'

Erik walked over to the sink, rolling up his sleeves. 'I promise not to poison you, Maggie. Sound fair?'

'I can't promise the same thing,' she rejoined, turning back to cooking; behind her, Mitch was making faces and gesturing humorously.

Erik smirked and sat down at the table, taking the proffered beer from Eliza and winking his thanks.

'When was the last time you worked on a farm?' asked Mitch.

'It's been a while,' said Erik. 'Most of my work is indoors of late. It's nice to change things up.'

'Where've you been working?'

'Silverlake, but I miss home.'

'You sticking around for a while, then?'

Erik looked at Eliza. 'I suppose we'll see.'

She gave him a small smile before glancing down at her phone and staring with obvious determination.

The rest of dinner passed uneventfully, with Mitch gallantly maintaining the bulk of the conversation, and far too soon Erik was taking his leave. But Eliza walked him out to his car and it was hard not to love even so small a gesture.

He opened the car door but didn't get out straight away. 'About earlier ...'

She raised an eyebrow.

'I don't regret it,' he said. 'Not for a second.'

'Okay,' she said. 'Drive safe.'

It was clear that was all he was going to get. With a small smile, he got into his car and left. The roads were mostly empty, and he got back to Miles' faster than he otherwise would have. Certainly not enough time to gather his thoughts.

The lights were on in the apartment when he stepped inside. Miles was on the sofa in the sitting room, smoking a joint and watching old sitcoms.

Erik dropped down beside him, propped his feet up on the coffee table, and took the joint when Miles held it out.

'You smell like cow,' said Miles, kicking him with a socked foot that smelled no better. 'Go shower.'

'I was at the ranch.'

Miles whistled in surprise. 'How was that?'

'Eventful.'

When he didn't elaborate, Miles nudged him again. 'Man, why don't you talk to me?'

Finger slowly tapping the ash off the tip of the joint, Erik looked at him. 'We talk all the time.'

'We talk shit. We talk about Eliza, we talk about this ghost, we talk about the past and the present. We don't ever talk about you. When I'm upset, I tell you exactly how I'm feeling and why. I give you the details because that's what friends do.'

'We're more than friends, Miles. I didn't think I'd have to explain myself to you.'

'Just because we're family doesn't mean I can read your mind.'

'What do you want me to say? You want me to tell you what's on my mind right this minute?'

Miles sat back and held up his hands. 'It's a start.'

'Fine,' said Erik quietly. 'I'm angry.'

'I already knew that.'

'Then why'd you ask?'

'Details!' Miles ran a hand through his hair and widened his eyes. 'Dear God, you are the most frustrating man I have ever met in my life. Which, to be quite honest, is fitting, seeing as how Eliza's the most frustrating woman I have ever met in my life. I don't know why I had to pick the pair of you — I really don't.'

Erik narrowed his eyes as jealousy burned through him once more. 'You wanna talk about Eliza? Fine, let's talk about Eliza. She told me you two were together. Let's talk about *that* because I've wanted to drink bleach ever since I found out.'

The coloured drained from Miles' face and he sat up. 'Oh,' he mumbled, eye twitching. 'That's why you're angry.'

A heavy silence fell.

Erik hated it. Things with Miles couldn't be heavy. Miles was the only light thing in his life.

He hadn't wanted to say anything about it. Some things were best left alone. He had hoped to just forget about the whole thing. But scattered around intrusive thoughts of his father that he could never be rid of, the memory of killing Sam which would haunt him until his last breath, the constant, horrible, unwavering ache of missing Eliza with every fibre of his being, wanting her there more than anything, he now had not only with the image of Eliza with Roger, but, to twist the knife further, the image of Eliza with Miles.

But he couldn't lose Miles. Not ever.

So he sat. He smoked. He stewed.

After an awful stretch of quiet, Miles gestured cautiously between them. 'Do you wanna know what happened?'

Erik held out the joint and shook his head. 'I'd rather take a cheese grater to my dick.'

'For what it's worth, I was going to tell you,' said Miles. His unhappiness with the situation was audible. 'I just didn't know how. It's so nice having you home that I didn't want to ruin it.'

A wave of nauseated relief swept through Erik. 'I know,' he grunted. 'I'm not upset with you. You didn't do anything wrong.'

Miles leaned back and ran a hand through his hair. 'Man, you must have a golden dick or something. I've never seen anyone so hung up like she is with you.'

'She's not the only one,' said Erik. He rested his head against the cushions. 'I miss her.'

'No other woman compares, no?'

'Sure,' he allowed. 'Plenty compare. But it's not about checking off boxes.' His mouth turned down bitterly. 'And now she's with Roger.'

Miles grimaced in sympathetic agreement. After a moment's hesitation, he clapped Erik on the knee. 'We good, brother?' He didn't sound sure.

Erik nodded. 'Always.'

'Good. Cos I missed your ugly-ass face. Don't want you leaving quite yet.'

'I love you, too, dick-weed.'

Miles grinned around the joint.

They smoked until they could finally sleep; Erik slipped into blackness which ebbed into nightmares, and awoke sometime around midnight, sweating profusely and shaking with guilt, staring at his hands to reassure himself that they were not covered in Sam's blood.

For five years he'd stared at them and wondered how he'd killed Sam. For five years he'd stared at them and thought only of the damage they could do to Eliza. And for five years, he'd been a mess of confusion and fear.

He put his head in hands, his fingers twisting painfully in his hair, and cried until he was too tired to do more than stare blankly into space, torturing himself by replaying everything over and over and over again.

Around midday, Gloria called and invited him over for dinner. Glad of the excuse to do *anything* but think, Erik arrived early. The difference between the home Gloria had raised him in and his childhood home with his parents was still startling. A quiet, cosy house that smelled clean and felt beloved, it was the only place that came to mind when he thought of home.

She greeted him warmly on the doorstep, a spatula in hand, and ushered him inside. Everything smelled like cayenne pepper, chili powder and sizzling meats; his mouth watered at the same time his stomach rumbled.

'I may just become attached to having you around,' she told him as she went back to cooking and he began setting the table.

'How's work?' he asked.

'Same ol', same ol'. You know how it is.'

Erik nodded in understanding. 'Yeah, but you can vent to me.'

With a motherly smile of relief, Gloria launched into a rant about the dentistry and Erik listened, mostly glad just to be around her again.

The fajitas she'd made were so heavenly, he had third helpings and dessert.

'It's nice to have you home,' she told him for the fifth time when they were on the porch swing an hour later, drinking wine and rocking slowly back and forth. 'It's too quiet around here without you.'

'Think I'll be around for a while yet.'

'Good,' she said.

He lit a cigarette and glared out into the night. His mind went automatically back in time.

'What're you thinking about, sweetheart?' she asked, nudging him with her foot.

'How did they meet?' he asked quietly. 'Logan and Ma?'

Gloria's expression instantly saddened. 'He just showed up with her one day,' she said. 'They went from nothing to something overnight. I think she thought he was mysterious and wanted to fix him. But some people can't be fixed.'

Erik silently wished people who cared so deeply didn't trust so freely. 'What was Logan like as a boy?' he wondered aloud. 'I never thought to ask.'

'He was terrifying.' Gloria made a face. 'Like a kid in a horror movie.'

A chill went over Erik's skin. 'What do you mean?'

'He always liked to hurt things. Animals, people.'

Erik looked over at her, heartrate picking up. 'Did he ever hurt you?'

She nodded once and tucked a strand of black hair behind her ear.

'I'm sorry,' he whispered. He reached out and squeezed her hand.

'None of his shit is on you,' she assured him. 'And whatever his sins, I loved your mother, and I love you.'

Erik drained his glass of wine before resting his head on her shoulder. 'Thank you,' he murmured. 'For everything.'

Gloria kissed the top of his head and wrapped her arm around him. 'You're very welcome, sweetheart.'

He stayed for a little while longer before bidding her goodnight and driving back to the apartment.

Miles was already asleep – and snoring *loudly* – when he stepped inside. Erik dropped onto the sofa, in no mood to dream. He turned the light on and pulled Sam's diary out of his coat pocket. Instead of going to the entries towards the back, the ones just before she died that were filled with confusion regarding Paige Osbourne, Erik opened the first page.

It was dated seven months before her death.

17 November

I'm absolutely exhausted. My week's been an unending marathon of essays, exams, presentations and studying. It's so good to be home again. Mama promised a huge dinner and she didn't disappoint. Macaroni, fresh bread, fried chicken, mashed potatoes, tomato soup, salad with homemade dressing, margaritas, and chocolate fudge cake for dessert. Dear God, I am so full. BEST MOTHER EVER.

The best part about the whole night – aside from being back home – was seeing Eliza. She looks amazing! Stupid Eliza and her ability to stay in shape without even trying. I swear she's secretly a man. Everything she eats just falls off her body. She got a haircut and I'm so jealous. I never could pull off blunt ends, but somehow she manages it.

Erik couldn't take his eyes off her the whole night. Those two are ridiculous. They've been together for ages and still act like they're only now falling in love. It's cute. It makes me miss Maya. She's in Greenvalley until the end of the month and I've got to say, I am no fan of long-distance. This is so shit. Phone calls and letters don't compare to the real thing. And I miss sex.

GOD, I MISS SEX.

How is it possible to be horny all the time? I feel like I'm going mad. I even talked to Eliza about it after Erik left. (Where did he even go? It's not like he goes home. Mama always says he can stay, but he never does more than a night or two. Which is weird, because he's here for breakfast every day.) Anyway, she was absolutely no help. Apparently, a lack of sex isn't a problem for her. I asked her what Erik was like. (And now I'm wondering if all sisters discuss this sort of thing or if we're just weird. I mean, I know we're weird, but I like it.) She told me they were together almost a year before they had sex. Erik's idea, apparently. I was shocked (and, okay, I didn't believe her at first), but she told me he's beyond messed up thanks to his dad. Sex scares him. Which I suppose makes sense. And it explains why Eliza worries so much about him and always goes the extra mile to make sure he's okay. But ... sometimes I worry she loves him too much.

I'm happy for them. I really am. But more than I miss having my sister all to myself, I worry that she's quickly becoming Erik's entire world. Then again, maybe I need to get better about telling Maya everything. Maybe that's how it should be. She pours so much information into our conversations, spilling every detail of her life with such vivid description. I can't do that. I think things over too much, and then I write about them. Aside from here, where I know even my mother won't look – holy lord am I glad we respect privacy in our house – I have few enough places to dissect my thoughts.

Maya ought to be first for me the way Erik is first for Eliza. Perhaps it will come in time. I mean, it's not like Eliza and Erik have a perfect relationship. I know they have their issues. If half the things she suspects about his past and his job and his family are true, maybe their giddy relationship is the way it is to offset things. And she worries about him all the time. I almost wonder if I should tell him about how bad her anxiety is. But surely, he must know? I can't be the only one she calls at four in the morning during a panic attack. But you wouldn't guess she had a care in the world if you watched them smile at each other.

It worries me. I think she's so happy to throw people off how scared she really is. Ever since Daddy almost died. After I almost died. Now she gets attacks about Erik dying. His old connections make her worry. There's no way Erik doesn't know, but I don't know how to bring it up without looking nosy. I just want to ask how he helps her. Sometimes I feel like I'm failing her because I never know the right thing to say.

But I'm overthinking things again. Too many margaritas. I need to get some sleep and then get some.

S.A.O.

Erik stared at Sam's words about Eliza with shock. He knew Eliza had anxiety, but four am phone calls were news to him. He was also curious about what Eliza had said to Sam about his past and his job. He had been truthful about the illegality of it — if not exactly forthcoming. From the moment he and Eliza met, life seemed to start over and everything that happened between them was easy and clear and honest.

But the past was a shadow that lingered like depression, and over the months Erik had strung bits and pieces of it together for Eliza, slowly revealing just how sordid his life prior to her had been. She had never flinched, never showed any pity for him, never asked him questions he did not want to answer, or questions with answers not even he could give. She listened, she kissed him, and she left it alone.

With Eliza, Erik had felt safe for the first time in his life. But he'd always just assumed she'd share her problems. Worse, perhaps, had been his assumption that she had fewer problems than him.

Leaving Sam's diary aside, he began leafing through Paige's once more. Nothing in the diaries was dated, so he had to read the first few pages of each to put them into sequential order. In addition to not dating anything, there were no breaks in paragraphs, and entries were broken up only by a small star on one line between chunks of text.

He'd read three already, but it wasn't until he was halfway through the fifth one that he found his name.

Very quickly, the sentences began to crawl under his skin, into his heart, and rot.

> *I don't know what's wrong with me. I can't stop crying. Nothing makes sense. All the time.*
>
> *I want to die. I'm sick of everything.*
>
> *I called Erik's house. I need to see him. He didn't answer. Second time, his father answered and told me Erik was on his way. I asked if he meant the cabin by the diner. He said yes.*

FUCK!

It was all but carved into the page. The next few pages were so torn Paige had skipped them.

His hands trembled as he reached the next entry.

> *I can't get clean. Six showers and still nothing.*
>
> *I can't look at Erik. Everything about him makes my skin crawl now.*
>
> *Does he know?*

And then, below those —

I'm done.

Erik read and reread everything, tears of anger and heartbreak filling his eyes.

'Oh God,' he whispered, his hand going to his mouth as bile burned his throat. 'Not you, too.'

As if his words were a summoning spell, the air crackled and to his shock, Paige was suddenly standing before him. She looked the same as she had when last he'd seen her. Blonde hair, green eyes that knew too much, pale and freckled face.

'Paige,' he said. 'What happened?'

She stared at him for a second before her eyes went to the diaries. 'I went to meet you,' she whispered. Her voice sounded odd and distorted, and yet so familiar it *hurt*.

'I didn't know,' he promised. 'Jesus Christ, Po. I'm so sorry.'

She flickered, but she didn't attack him.

Another few seconds passed and then she disappeared with a flash of light, the image of her ghost tattooing itself on his retinas.

Shaking like a leaf, he sat back down and rolled a joint.

It was another couple of hours before Miles woke up.

Erik hadn't moved and there was a pile of ash on the ground beside him.

His hair mussed in fifty different directions, Miles took in Erik's appearance and raised an eyebrow. 'Something on your mind, brother?'

Erik held out Paige's diary, his finger saving the page. He stared at the top of Miles' head as he read.

After less than a minute, Miles looked up at him with horrified eyes. 'You think Logan attacked her and she killed herself after?'

'Yes.'

'Jesus. Christ.' Eyes wide, Miles disappeared into the kitchen. When he returned, he held out one of two glasses of whiskey.

Not caring that it was seven in the morning, Erik took the glass and downed it. He grimaced and squeezed the bridge of his nose. 'I hate him so much, Miles.'

'You and me both, brother.'

The silence fell, heavy and choking, but neither knew what to say next.

CHAPTER TEN
One Step Forward, Two Steps Back

The air around Eliza's childhood home was always heavily scented with flowers and pine, but inside all smelled stale and wretched.

Her father was passed out in the sitting room, an empty bottle of bourbon on the floor.

She stopped in the doorway and regarded him with a feeling of deep, desolate sadness. She only had one bad memory of him before Sam's death: the car wreck where his drinking nearly killed Sam.

After that day, Ryan hadn't touched a drop.

The rest of her memories were so good that it somehow made the shell he'd become even more heartbreaking. The memories she clung to were of him being there to give her soup when she was sick, or glare at her when she came home late, or ground her when she got drunk.

One occasion in particular was the night she, Erik and Sam had all come home hammered. Ryan sent each — even Erik — to separate rooms and grounded them all. Eliza had found this immensely funny at the time, but in the morning, Ryan proved as good as his threat. Gloria was downstairs at eight o'clock, ready to drive Erik home, with zero sympathy for his hangover, and grounded him double the time Ryan had.

When Erik was allowed over two weeks later, Ryan cuffed him affectionately, told him he hoped the hangover taught him a lesson, and went right on back to treating Erik like the son he'd never had.

That was what dads were supposed to do. They were supposed to protect their daughters and dance with their partners in the kitchen and have smiles to spare. They weren't supposed to drink themselves to death and keep their families wide awake with an overwhelming, unconquerable fear.

With a heavy sigh, she walked over and sat on the table across from him. She nudged him with her foot until he opened his eyes. His hooded, glazed, bloodshot eyes.

'Elle?' he mumbled. 'What are you doing here?'

'You're killing yourself,' she said matter-of-factly. 'You're killing yourself and you're killing Ma and you're killing me. We've already lost Sam. Unless you want this family to lose you too, get your act together.'

'Elle —'

'I don't care,' she interrupted, hands together. She was trembling from the entire exchange. From having plucked up the courage at last to say something.

She needed her dad to be okay, so she could fall to pieces. She couldn't do it first.

'I don't,' she affirmed. She said it more to herself than to him, but he didn't need to know that. 'We all have our problems and none of us are doing well. Get it together or I'll help Ma move out. I'm serious. She needs her husband and I need my father.'

She raised her eyebrows at him pointedly before standing and walking away. She stumbled to her car and drove slowly, entirely on autopilot. She pulled up in front of Roger's without even processing what direction she was driving in.

He let her inside and she collapsed on the sofa, shaking badly and wanting to hurl. He didn't ask. He draped a blanket around her shoulders and handed her a joint.

It was moments like this where Eliza remembered why she came to Roger at all.

The first hour passed in a haze of silence and smoke; there was a twisted serenity to avoidance.

The serenity was broken, however, by the ringing of her phone.

She looked at the name on the screen for almost a minute before answering. 'Hi, Ma.'

'Your father said you came by earlier,' her mother said softly.

Eliza stared at the ceiling. Unlike her childhood home, unlike the ranch, Roger's ceiling had no cracks, no cobwebs, no age. Everything was scrubbed clean, pristinely painted, unblemished and unaged.

'I'm surprised he even noticed me,' she muttered.

'Elle ...'

Ignoring the flare of guilt in her stomach, she shrugged to herself. 'It's true.'

'I'm going to talk to him tonight.'

Eliza pursed her lips and said nothing. It wasn't the first time since Sam died that her mother had promised she'd talk to Ryan. Her father had even promised them both that he would try harder.

'I want him to get better, too, Elle.'

'I know you do.' Eliza heaved a sigh. 'Let me know if you need anything, okay?'

'I will,' said Mira. 'I love you, sweetheart. Just try and remember that.'

A lump formed in her throat and it took a minute to force it down enough to reply. 'I know,' she croaked. 'Just wish Dad said the same thing to us every now and then.'

'I know.'

'I love you, too.'

'Call me tomorrow?'

'Sure.'

Eliza hung up the phone. Sinking into the cushions, she put the joint back between her lips and tried in vain not to get her hopes up.

When she left Roger's later that night, she drove to the one place she ever found peace and stumbled up the steps of the crumbling cabin. Even after the haunting visit to the cabin by the diner, this one still comforted her more than any other place in the world.

It had belonged to a number of people over the years and had gone through twenty or thirty different names, none of which ever seemed to stick. She and Erik had named it Willow Lane after a day of exploring the surrounding area and finding numerous willow trees by the brook which ran through the back of the property.

Abandoned for over a decade, the cabin was a shell of its former glory, but there was still something old and stately and wise about the place. There was a reason she had always loved Erik's plan to rebuild it and make it their home. When he left, it became her sanctuary. She'd never even brought Miles.

After two or three hard shoves, she got the door to unlock and stepped inside. The rustling of feathers and scurrying of tiny feet alerted her to the fact that she was hardly the only one inside the dwelling, but wild things had never bothered her, and she walked on through to the old sitting room. She felt safer here than even the farmhouse.

She spread the blanket she'd left there out across the cushions of the tatty sofa she'd bought in a charity shop and dropped down.

The lantern Mitch kept in the truck filled the room with a warm glow of light and she opened her bag and pulled out a book, a large bottle of whiskey, and a bag of cookies.

She curled up and read until the whiskey made her eyelids droop and black sleep pulled her down.

She dreamed she was running through a field with Sam. Up ahead, Erik and Paige waved frantically to them. As if they needed to hurry.

Eliza glanced back and saw Logan —

And woke with a start.

Heart racing and eyes heavy, it took a moment to realise her phone was beeping. She rubbed her forehead, a migraine making itself known.

After several long moments of forced, painful blinking, she raised the phone and looked at the screen.

It was from Erik: *How are you?*

Eliza failed to fight the smile that spread across her face. *I'm at our house*, she wrote back.

Her phone lit up with his name less than ten seconds later and she put it to her ear.

'Why are you there?' His deep voice sent a calming wave through her strung-out body.

'I come here when I can't sleep,' she mumbled, drawing the blanket up to her chin.

'Do you want some company?'

She smiled up at the ceiling. 'Only if you bring coffee and doughnuts.'

'I think I can arrange that. See you in a few, babe.'

Eliza sat up and stared at the wall as she waited for Erik to arrive. It was hard not to get swept up in everything. Hard not to hope.

She groaned loudly at herself and put her head in her hands.

It was only the sound of Erik's car several minutes later which prompted her to move. He stepped out of the car and winked at her as if no time at all had passed. He was wearing denims, leather boots, a long black coat and a beanie pulled low over his ears.

She swallowed hard. He really had grown up *well*.

He raised the coffee and a box of doughnuts. 'I come with deep-fried sustenance and shots of caffeinated blackness.'

She grinned. 'What a gentleman.'

When he was at the top of the steps, Eliza took the coffee and gestured for him to follow her inside. She led the way to the sitting room and over to the corner with the most sunshine.

They sat down opposite each other and Eliza opened the box of doughnuts. He'd brought one of everything and two cups of coffee each.

Something in her chest betrayed her by fluttering and she picked up a cup of coffee to give herself something to concentrate on.

'I've dreamed about you in this house for years,' he said quietly.

His words made her smile stupidly and she looked up. 'I know the feeling.'

Suddenly the air felt heavy. He set his cup aside, and then hers, before taking her hands. 'Eliza?'

'Yeah?' It came out a whisper.

His smile was crooked and uncertain. 'Can I kiss you?'

After a beat of deliberation, she leaned in and brushed her lips over his. He gasped against her mouth and his hands came up to cradle her face and twist in her hair. Everything inside her shivered and she knew she wasn't alone in feeling overwhelmed.

When at last they broke apart, his eyes were heavy-lidded with desire.

'Do you want to go somewhere?' he asked, voice low and husky.

'Okay.'

They left the cabin hand in hand and got into his car. He pulled onto the dirt road and reached out, taking her hand and interlacing their fingers.

Yet the silence in the car was stifling; like a full bus on a hot day when the windows won't open and everyone's breathing and smelling and existing in each other's sticky warmth. She rolled down the window and took several deep breaths before looking over at Erik.

'What are you thinking about?' she wondered aloud.

Erik glanced at her, his near-black eyes unreadable. 'Everything. All of it.'

'So simple, easily analysed topics.'

'Undoubtedly.'

Eliza half-smiled and glanced back out the window. 'What's your plan after this?'

'I don't really have one.'

'What do you want to do?'

'No clue.'

'Aimless.'

'Open,' he countered. 'Free.'

She pondered that as he turned the car down a side road. The trees grew slightly thicker as they drove, only gapping where the water and the bridges popped up like impromptu signals to slow down and pay attention.

The locals called it Windy Hill, although it had a longer, more complicated name that no one bothered to remember. It was a small, beautiful lookout over the mountains and the view was the best around. But the wind was fierce. There was a feeble wooden railing which hugged the edge of the trail in a likely futile attempt to keep people from being blown off if the wind ever became too strong.

As they got out of the car, Eliza looked over at Erik, a rising swell of fondness in her chest. 'If I didn't know any better I'd say we're nineteen and you've come to pick me up from a lesson,' she said. 'Feels like yesterday.'

He smiled sadly at her. 'And another lifetime.'

'True.'

Before she could think of what else to say, Erik drew her into another kiss, his arms encircling her. Instantly, not even aware she was doing it, she fell into him, kissing back with increasing desperation. Her entire body felt like a bow pulled taut and she was ready to snap.

How they ended up against the car, her legs around his waist as he deftly unbuttoned her shirt, kissing every inch of her his mouth could find as if drunk on the taste of her, she didn't know.

When they broke apart, he pressed his forehead against hers, his hands cradling her face. 'Take me back, Eliza. Please. Let me prove to you how much I've changed.'

She was running out of reasons to say no when being with him was the only thing she wanted. But even still, she'd had a very long list of reasons not a couple of weeks ago.

She leaned back, needing to think more clearly, and his hands fell from her face. 'I really want to say yes.'

'But?'

'You left me, Erik.'

A stricken expression crossed his face even as he nodded. 'I know. I know. I'm sorry. I was a dick. I was selfish.'

'What's changed?'

He brushed her hair out of her eyes and his own darted over her face, seemingly memorising her features. 'Maybe now I'm a different kind of selfish.'

She arched an eyebrow. 'How's that?'

'Maybe now I realise that I love you and want to be around you, even when you deserve so much better than my bullshit.'

Wry laughter escaped her lips, and he grinned.

'Please,' he continued. 'Just give me one more chance, babe. Let me show you how good of a boyfriend I can be. I won't let you down again. I swear.'

'You staying?'

'I'm staying.'

'You done with Wyatt?'

He nodded vehemently. 'I told him I wanted out before I came home.'

She tried to find the lie in his dark eyes, but she couldn't. Trepidation and fear mixed with hope and longing in her chest, leaving her somewhat dizzy.

The silence stretched on and on, and she could see the doubt beginning to take seed inside him when at last she nodded. 'Okay.'

Erik stared at her, not seeming to believe her. 'Okay?'

'Okay.'

His face broke into a wide smile and he kissed her again, laughter upon his lips.

'Come on,' she said when they finally managed to stop kissing. 'Let's get out of here. It's freezing.'

'Do you want to head back to the apartment?' he asked.

'Not really,' she said.

'You hungry?'

'We left the doughnuts.'

'Crap.'

After exchanging matching looks of bemused exasperation, they got back into the car and headed into town for pizza.

They were in the midst of eating when Miles appeared.

His blonde hair was a messy disarray and his clothes were rumpled and mismatched, but somehow he made it work. He dropped down into the seat beside them and took off his sunglasses. He opened his mouth to speak, did a doubletake, and then narrowed his eyes. 'You guys had sex, didn't you?'

'No,' said Erik with a cheeky grin.

A smile played on his lips. 'My. Hole.'

'We didn't have sex.'

'You did something.'

Eliza and Erik exchanged smirks and Miles clapped his hands together. 'Thank God. I was getting sick of listening to your angst.'

He launched into the many tales of woe that came from working in customer service. His stories made them all laugh and Eliza found, to her surprise, that she was enjoying herself. For the first time in a long time. And that feeling held for the rest of the day. None of them mentioned Sam or Paige or Roger, none of them dragged in darkness.

When Erik drove her back to the farmhouse that night, he walked her inside. Maggie, as usual, glared at him when he sat down at the kitchen table. Unlike his sister, Mitch seemed delighted and told Erik they could use an extra set of hands on the ranch if he was bored.

The dinner passed in easy company and it was closer to midnight than twilight when Eliza and Erik headed up to her room.

But long after Erik drifted off, his arms locked around her, Eliza stared at the wall, unable to sleep. Having hope and laughing only reminded her of how easy life had once been – and how easy it had been to lose everything.

Very quickly, her mind was in overdrive. Her thoughts wouldn't stop.

Everything was going and going and going and going.

Her fear skyrocketed and all she could think about was death. Losing her mother. Her father. Erik. Again.

She felt like she couldn't breathe.

Careful not to rouse Erik, she slipped out of bed, dressed, and was out of the house and in her car in under two minutes.

Before she knew it, she found herself outside Roger's door. She knocked twice and crossed her arms; her heart was almost flying with how fast it was beating.

The door opened and Roger appeared. His hair was wet from a shower and he smelled like mint and tobacco. 'Where's your boyfriend?'

She glared at him and said, 'I can't sleep.'

Roger smirked and stepped aside, letting her in. When she dropped down on his sofa, he held out a baggie.

'Same as always, baby?'

She took it without a word.

CHAPTER ELEVEN
Surprises

A loud ringing tore her from sleep and she yanked her phone out of her pocket, adrenaline surging through her even as she winced at the pounding of her head.

'Babe.' Erik sounded frantic. 'Where are you? I woke up and you were gone.'

She sat up, clutching her head. 'I'm in town,' she said, coughing to clear her throat. 'Meet you at Joanie's?'

'Yeah, all right.' But there was an edge of concern to his voice.

She ended the call and put the phone back in her pocket. She squeezed the bridge of her nose and tried to force her mind into order. It was an immense struggle.

'Leaving so soon?'

Roger was reading a newspaper on the chair adjacent to the sofa, a cup of coffee half-drunk on the table in front of him. He would have looked entirely at ease had he not been scowling at her.

'Shit to do,' she replied.

'Come here,' he said, holding up a bag between two fingers.

She walked over and held her hand out. He grabbed her by the arm and pulled her onto his lap.

'Roger!' She shoved him back and scrambled to her feet. 'Stop. We're done.'

'Because Erik's back? Are you that easy?'

Snorting in disgust, she turned and walked away from him.

He followed her into the hall and grabbed her hand. 'Just like that? Really?'

'Yes, really.'

Roger's lip curled into a sneer of outrage. 'Then you owe me.'

Not remotely surprised, Eliza rolled her eyes and pulled money out of her pocket. 'There,' she said. 'Now we're done.'

He put a hand out, blocking her path. 'We're not done.'

Without pausing, she ducked under his arm and carried on.

It was hard not to glance back, but she wasn't in the mood to feel bad about Roger's jealousy. She'd never lied to him. He knew what he was getting into and it wasn't her fault he couldn't handle it.

A few minutes later she was at the café. It was mostly empty, and she dropped into one of the chairs outside and tried to source some measure of calm.

To her relief, Ciaran asked her no questions as he brought her coffee.

She'd finished half the cup and two cigarettes by the time Erik appeared.

He kissed her in greeting. 'Good morning, beautiful.'

She smiled automatically. ''Morning.'

'You look exhausted,' he said as he sat down. 'Why were you in town so early?'

Eliza held his gaze long enough for a look of fury to twist his smile into a grimace.

'Roger?' he growled, leaning in. 'You were with Roger?'

'I didn't sleep with him,' she said in her defence. 'I wouldn't do that to you.'

Her words served only to make him flinch. 'Don't – don't say things like that.'

'You'd prefer the opposite statement?'

'I don't want to think about you sleeping with anyone!' he said through gritted teeth. 'What were you doing at Roger's? More drugs?'

She shrugged and picked up a sachet of sugar, tearing at the corners and getting sugar on her hands. It wasn't as if she had a defence. Shit was shit. She knew that.

Erik snatched a cigarette out of her pack and stuck it between his lips. He flicked the lighter open and shut with trembling hands.

'I'm sorry I snapped,' he said at length. She looked up. 'God, babe. I'm just scared for you. I can't – I don't trust him. I don't trust him for one second. Not with you. I don't trust *anyone* with you. Not even me. *Especially* not me. But he's a dick.'

'It's fine,' she mumbled, letting the sugar fall and crossing her arms. 'I shouldn't have gone.'

'Why did you?'

'I panicked.'

Erik put the cigarette between his lips and reached across the table, taking her hand gently. His thumb traced over her skin. 'Why did you never tell me you got panic attacks?'

She stilled. 'Who told you that?'

'Sam's diary.'

'Oh.'

'Yeah.'

'I didn't want you to worry. It makes me seem like a freak.'

'No,' he said. 'It doesn't. Everyone panics. The worst thing to do is bottle it up. That's when it becomes unmanageable.'

'Sometimes I'm not afraid of anything. Just ... *everything.*'

'Me too.'

She got out of her chair and sat on his lap. She leaned into him, fingers curling into the fabric of his shirt, her body complementing the contours of his. His arms tightened around her and for a long time neither moved.

'Will you do something for me?' he asked, kissing her shoulder.

'What?'

'Please don't go to Roger again.'

Eliza leaned back to catch his eye. 'Is this because of the drugs or because you don't trust me?'

'I trust you,' he said. 'I don't trust him. He's a prick, babe. I don't feel comfortable with you near him. Please.'

'The drugs make it stop.'

'Your thoughts?'

'Everything.'

He fixed her with a very serious expression. 'When your head won't stop spinning, come to me. Not him. If — if you really need something, I'll see what I — what I can do. Okay? Don't go to him.'

'Okay,' she said, leaning against him.

She would go to Adrian Kane if need be. Despite Erik's offer, she couldn't bring herself to go to him about it. She didn't want him thinking less of her. She didn't want him to feel like he had to leave again.

Eliza was waiting in the park for Maggie to get out of school a few days later when she heard the car pull up behind her. She glanced around to see Roger's truck. He got out, gaze fixed on her, and gestured for her to wait for him. She sighed heavily but didn't bother leaving.

When he reached her, she raised both eyebrows, waiting for him to speak first.

He cleared his throat after a few seconds of notable tension. 'Are you avoiding me?'

'Yes,' she said bluntly.

Roger's eyes narrowed. The hazel in them looked bright with outrage. 'Do you do everything he tells you?'

Eliza glared at him. 'You're not my boyfriend. You're not my ex. You're my ex-drug dealer.'

'Maybe so, baby,' he said, stabbing his key into his palm. 'But I'd like to think that even if you're not in love with me, you'd at least have the decency to give me an explanation before ghosting me.'

His wording sent a shiver down her spine, but she felt bad all the same. People couldn't help who they liked. Even people like Roger. And was she so much better? Erik seemed to think so, but Erik was hardly a shining example himself. Perhaps they were all as bad as each other. And she'd hated Erik for leaving with no explanation.

The wind blew her hair into her eyes and she brushed the strands away irritably before responding. 'You were a prick.'

He nodded and jammed his hands into his pockets. 'I'm jealous. Sue me.'

'That's no excuse.'

'I'm not excusing it. I'm apologising.'

'You haven't, actually.'

He fixed her with a hard look and said pointedly, 'I'm *sorry*.'

'There you go.'

But it was hard to maintain anger with Roger for long. She had to care about someone to hate them, and with Roger she mostly just felt indifferent.

'Will you go for a walk with me?' he queried, pulling her from her thoughts. 'Please? I want to talk.'

Eliza bit her lip and glanced at her watch. She still had a little while before the school let out. And Maggie was always late. It was more to do with the fact that it would infuriate Erik. But she did feel bad for how things ended between them.

With a nod, she followed Roger down the path.

The air was chillier in the shade of the trees and she crossed her arms over her chest to ward off the cold as they walked slowly up the side trail. Everything smelled of freshly cut grass and damp. Flowers were clinging to the last of summer despite the constant rain, cool days and cooler nights.

'Why do you love him?' he asked as they rounded the bend, a deep frown on his face.

The question surprised her.

'Why ask?'

'Curiosity.'

'I've heard it's detrimental.'

'Humour me.'

'Because he's my best friend,' she said, kicking a rock out of her way. 'Haven't you ever felt that before?'

'Not from a psychopath.' He kicked the same rock she had, only his kick sent it flying into the trees where it landed somewhere out of sight with a *thump*.

'Says the man who sells drugs and uses people.'

'You use people and drugs, baby,' he retorted. 'We're as bad as each other. That's why it's so good.'

'Did you want to talk or just make innuendos?'

'I can do both.'

She sighed and stopped. The wind was picking up and the shaded path felt like it was being enveloped by the encroaching winter's wrath.

'This is pointless,' she said. 'I'm heading back.'

'No, wait,' he protested. 'I want to talk to you.'

'Roger –'

He grabbed her wrist. 'Eliza –'

'Let go of me.'

'Not until you talk to me.'

Blood suddenly appeared in the centre of his chest.

It spread across his shirt, staining his coat and dripping down, soaking his torso. He looked down with disconnected horror; blood began to dribble out of his mouth and down his chin.

Eliza made to grab him as he fell only to be blasted back by an invisible force. She landed on the other side of the path and the wind was knocked out of her. Gasping for breath, she looked up in time to see Roger's body thrown against a tree with vicious force.

Sam's ghost flickered malevolently between them.

Even as panic threatened to set in, the gravity of the situation kept Eliza's head clear. 'Sam, stop!' she bellowed.

But her sister was advancing on Roger, bleeding the life out of him with a furious expression.

'You should know better,' said Sam, voice cold and jarring and distorted. 'We don't like men who don't take no for an answer.'

Eliza ran over and put herself between them. 'Sam!'

This time, Sam vanished, taking the cold air with her. The silence of the forest was deafening in her absence.

'Sam!' she yelled, louder this time, suddenly desperate and close to hysterics. 'Sam!'

But her sister didn't reappear.

Tears burning her eyes, blood pounding in her ears, Eliza bent down and turned Roger over. Blood was beading in the corner of his mouth and every struggling wheeze made the blood bubble.

She put his arm around her neck and heaved him up. The blood soaked into her clothes and warmed her skin. All she could smell was iron and salt.

When they were finally in the car, she sent Maggie a text before driving toward the hospital.

She couldn't stop herself from glancing over at him every few seconds. The pained sounds leaving him were horrible, but each one was a reassurance that he was still alive. That there wasn't yet another body to add to the appalling number they were already at.

Twenty minutes later, he was being seen to in the hospital.

He would be fine.

Eliza wasn't sure she could say the same.

———————————

The day at the ranch had passed rather uneventfully. A new load of shavings came in just after breakfast, and Erik and Mitch spent the better part of four hours shovelling the pile into the shelter of the barn before securing a tarp across the top to keep the rain off. It was the kind of work Erik liked losing himself in. He found the laborious tasks far more rewarding than what he'd done for so long. It helped reaffirm that his decision to stay was the right one.

By dusk, as the setting sun cast the world in shadow, Erik and Mitch headed back towards the house, covered in sweat and dust, their stomachs rumbling. Halfway up the path, the sharp trilling of Mitch's phone cut through the air and caused them both to still in unison.

'Hey, sis,' Mitch answered. Then, 'She's where?'

Erik's gaze snapped to him, anxiety spiking in his chest.

When Mitch ended the call a few seconds later, he looked at Erik, brow furrowed. 'Maggie says Eliza's stuck at the hospital with a friend.'

Erik yanked his phone out of his pocket. He dialled Eliza's number, trying, and failing, to stem his worry.

She answered after several rings. 'Hello?'

'Babe,' he cried, relieved. 'What's going on? Who's hurt?'

'Roger.'

An ill, itchy feeling began to crawl under his skin. 'Roger?'

'It's bad,' she mumbled.

Mitch looked over at him, eyebrow arched in curiosity. Not bothering to ask the specifics — not sure he wanted to know until he could physically do something to help — Erik motioned to Mitch that he was going and jogged outside to his car.

'I'll be there in a few minutes,' he told Eliza. 'Are you okay?'

'I'm fine,' she said unconvincingly.

When Erik reached the hospital a short while later, he found her in one of the plastic chairs in the waiting room speaking with an officer. He recognised the stooped figure as Jared Roberts. A short, balding fellow with a beer gut and hairy ears, Roberts was an unwelcome sight for more reasons than one.

For years, Roberts had harassed Erik over his father. That said, Roberts was hardly the only one who had. Few authority figures in Erik's life had ever contemplated the notion that he wasn't his father's son in every way.

Trying his best to ignore Roberts, Erik went straight to Eliza's side and took her hands. 'What happened?'

'Stern,' said Roberts, glaring suspiciously at him. 'I should have known.'

Erik glared back at him. 'Known what, Roberts?'

'Roger and I were alone,' Eliza cut in, voice sharp and edged. 'I told you that. Something attacked him.'

Although it was clear Roberts didn't believe her, after a dozen more questions, he departed, but not before shooting Erik a look filled with promise.

Erik scowled at his retreating back until he disappeared from view. 'What happened?' he asked when they were alone. He took the seat beside her and put a hand on her back. She was shaking so badly he could feel her vibrating under his touch.

Eliza looked beyond exhausted, and she was wide-eyed and disconnected with shock. 'Roger wanted to talk. Wanted to know why I was with you. When he grabbed me, Sam just showed up and attacked him.'

Fury poisoned Erik's insides. 'He grabbed you?'

'I'm fine,' she said, scratching the back of her head. 'God, Sam ...'

Too angry and worried to speak, Erik pulled Eliza to her feet and they left the hospital.

The sun had already set, and the cold night was not relaxing. Halloween decorations were everywhere, and Erik was far from in the mood to be festive. Especially where it concerned ghosts.

It now felt like ghosts lurked in every shadow. Yet at the same time, he was starting to feel like the ghosts were looking after Eliza. It sure seemed that way. First Paige, and now Sam.

He drove back to the apartment deep in thought. Since he'd been there more than a month, he and Miles had cleared out the study and moved a bed in.

After Eliza had showered and changed, she crawled beneath the blankets and he slipped in behind her.

'Do you want to talk about it?'

'Not really.'

'You okay?'

'No,' she said, voice catching.

He kissed the nape of her neck. 'I love you.'

She wrapped his arms tighter around her waist and said nothing.

He listened to her breathing slowly even out as the exhaustion overwhelmed her and she finally drifted off to sleep. Soon enough, Erik found himself lulled by the steady sounds.

He dreamed of blood and screams and woke with a start after only a few hours.

Not wanting to rouse Eliza, who desperately looked like she needed the sleep, he disentangled himself carefully and climbed out of bed.

In the bathroom, he turned on the sink and stared at the water. All he could see was Roger attacking Eliza. The longer he stared, the worse the images became until all he could see was his father attacking his mother.

Only they weren't imaginings. They were memories.

With a shaking breath, Erik looked up and froze.

In the mirror, staring back at him, was his father.

He whipped around.

There was nothing there.

'No,' he choked out. 'No. No. No.'

Perhaps they should have expected it.

But not him.

Not Logan.

'Erik?'

He looked up. The sight of Eliza sent a wave of complete terror through him.

'I saw Logan.'

Her hands went to her mouth.

Miles appeared in the hall, shirtless and clearly having just rolled out of bed. 'What now?'

Erik couldn't move. His fingers pulled his hair tight enough to be painful, eyes widening. 'What the fuck is going on?'

They stayed awake on the sofa and watched cartoons until the sun rose and the light gave them all a false sense of stability and safety.

But when fear wasn't confined to the shadows, it was so much harder to conquer.

And none of them felt safe.

———————

The day remained grey, and everything smelled like an oncoming rainstorm. Miles branched off near one of the apartment complexes to drop off an ounce, agreeing to meet them later, and Eliza and Erik headed toward Main Street.

He drew her in close and wrapped an arm around her shoulders as they made their way down the footpath.

'You smell good,' he murmured, kissing her cheek.

She grinned at him. 'Yeah?'

'Amazing,' he affirmed. After kissing her again, he cast his eyes around. 'Want to get coffee while we wait for Miles?'

Before she could reply, a shout made them both start.

'Eliza!'

Eliza went stiff at the sight of her mother. 'Hey, Mama.'

Clearly having just finished her shopping, Mira looked from Eliza to Erik with hope in her eyes. 'It's so nice to see you two together again.'

'Tell me about it,' he said with a tight smile.

Mira didn't appear to notice. 'Are you staying in town, then?'

'Moving back,' he affirmed.

'You should join us for dinner tonight,' said Mira. 'It'll be like old times.'

Eliza's stomach tightened at the mere suggestion. 'Old times' sounded like a truly painful idea for an evening.

Erik glanced at her, unsure what to say. Before Eliza could come up with an excuse, her mother ploughed on.

'Ryan would love it!'

Mention of her father made Eliza grimace. Her mother had texted to say that she'd had a long conversation with Ryan, but Eliza couldn't get excited about it. 'I'm sure Erik has better things to do,' she said tightly.

Mira's face fell. 'Oh ...'

'I mean ...' Eliza looked at him, desperate for help.

'I'll be there,' he said succinctly. 'I've missed your cooking.'

Mira beamed at them. The relief in her eyes made Eliza feel wretched for hesitating and she smiled at her mother.

'Excellent!' said Mira. 'Seven?'

'Sure,' said Eliza. She nodded to her mother and watched her leave before looking over at him. 'Sorry.'

He shook his head and raised their interlaced hands. He kissed the back of her hand before meeting her gaze. 'I love your parents, babe,' he said firmly. 'You know that. I don't mind. I just don't want you to feel uncomfortable.'

'Being anywhere near them is uncomfortable.'

'Is he that bad?'

It took a minute to formulate a reply. 'Yeah. He's worse than he was.'

Erik drew her into his arms and kissed the top of her head. 'I'll be there.'

'You promise?'

'I'm not going anywhere.'

They wandered through the town, neither sure what to do. In want of a distraction, and to feel like they were doing something of use, they walked the two blocks to the local library and began combing through the town archives for any other mention of ghosts or hauntings. As they didn't know where to start, they simply started with the present day and began working their way backwards, searching for any unusual occurrences.

'You ever hear of any local ghost stories?' he asked her after a while.

'Dead guy in the inn,' she said after some thought. 'And the haunted lake in the mountain.'

'Any super strong people?'

'Just you. Do you think there might be more?' She pursed her lips in thought. 'In the town, I mean.'

Erik raised a thick eyebrow and looked away from his computer screen. 'Strong jawed and dashing fellows?'

She giggled and rolled her eyes. 'No, Chuckles. Strong. Like, stupid strong.'

'I should have a cool moniker,' he said sardonically, sticking a pen in his mouth before glancing back at his screen. 'I don't even know where to start with something like this.'

'Start picking search words and go from there.'

'I dropped out of school for a reason,' he muttered even as he looked back at the database screen and began to type.

Hours went by without any leads, however, and before Eliza knew it the library was closing, and they were on their way to Maplebrook.

The drive went too quickly and before she could process anything, they were parked outside.

Neither made to leave the car.

'We've seen Sam's ghost and even still I feel like there's more of her in that house than anywhere else,' she said, drumming her fingers on her legs.

Erik took her hand. 'Do you think we should tell them?'

'Tell them that their daughter's lurking around as an angry poltergeist? No. Sam would kill me.'

They both laughed humourlessly.

'I still don't know how to face them after what I did,' he admitted, lips turning down as he rubbed the side of his face in agitation.

'You're not facing them alone.'

With matching sighs, they stepped out of the car and into the cold, damp night. Eliza took Erik's hand and they walked up the path.

But what she found upon entry made her stop dead with shock.

The first thing she noticed was the cleanliness. Everything smelled of soap and leather oil, rather than the beer smell which had hung heavy in the air for years now. They exchanged glances before heading into the kitchen. Her heart was thrumming, and she felt sick with hope.

To her astonishment, Ryan was at the table. He had aged heavily in the last couple of years and the veins had burst in his cheeks and nose. For the first time in a long time, however, he was clean and groomed and upright. There was a cup of black coffee in front of him, and a copy of the newspaper was open to the crossword. It was half-finished.

It was like going back in time.

'Hi, Daddy,' she croaked.

He looked up at her with tired eyes. Tired, sober eyes. 'Hey, Elle.'

She glanced at her mother, too stunned to formulate a question.

Mira smiled at her. 'Hi, sweetheart.'

'I'm sorry about the other night,' her father said, voice raspy, drawing her attention back to him. 'I'll apologise to Roger.'

Beside Eliza, Erik went stiff.

'It's fine,' said Eliza quickly. 'Are you okay?'

Ryan bowed his head and gave her a tight — but not faked — smile of assurance. 'Your mother and I were talking about me maybe taking a few weeks to get my head together.'

Eliza swallowed hard. She was afraid her hope would choke her. 'Good. That's good.'

Ryan turned his gaze to Erik. 'How are you getting on, EJ?'

'Good, sir,' said Erik awkwardly. 'Really good.'

'It's nice to have you around again.'

Ryan held out his hand and Erik shook it with only a minor amount of awkwardness.

Eliza was so thrown by it all that she stayed immobile until Erik drew out a chair for her.

He held her hand under the table all throughout dinner and when they left an hour later, Eliza was sure the only reason she was even standing was because he was there.

Her parents both hugged her goodnight. Soberly. Together. And she was so shocked — and far too afraid of jinxing the joy of it — that she said nothing at all until they were back at the farmhouse.

Erik walked her to the door and she leaned against it, unable to stop smiling.

'That's the first conversation I've had with him in years,' she said at last. 'First time he's even eaten a meal with us since Sam died.'

'It'll be the first of a thousand,' he said bracingly. 'Shit like this just takes time. He's strong, though. If anyone can pull themselves out of it a second time, it's Ryan.'

She leaned in and kissed his cheek. 'Thank you for coming.'

'Always.' With a cheeky smile, he nodded to the door. 'Want company?'

A grin spread across her face. 'If you think you can handle me.'

'I think I'm up to it.'

With matching smiles, they stepped inside, both trying to remind themselves that sometimes it was okay to hope.

Sometimes good things did happen.

CHAPTER TWELVE
Shadows and Stories

A horrible feeling, like she was being watched, tore Eliza from sleep and she sat bolt upright. Her breath came out in an icy cloud. It took a few seconds for her to realise what was happening.

Logan Stern was standing at the end of the bed. Alive or dead, he was one of the most evil-looking men Eliza had ever seen.

'Erik,' she said loudly, not looking away from Logan.

He woke with a start and followed her gaze. The colour drained from his face. He ushered her out of the bed, positioning himself between her and Logan's ghost.

'What do you want?' he asked his father.

Logan cocked his head to the side and then suddenly he was in front of them. He put his palms on Erik's chest —

And Erik was blasted out of the window.

Glass went everywhere; several shards cut Eliza's cheek and neck. She clenched her eyes shut, terrified glass would get into her eyes.

Something then wrenched her backward, slamming her against the wall. Stars exploded in front of her eyes as pain ricochet through her body. When she managed to focus her vision, Logan was leering down at her.

'Pretty little girl,' he hissed, voice crackling and distorted.

Eliza tried to lift her arms, but they were pinned by an invisible force. As if she were a ragdoll, she was then flung onto the bed.

Logan appeared above her. His hands wrapped around her throat. Squeezing tighter and tighter.

And then, as suddenly as he'd seized her, something dragged him away.

Eliza scrambled up, gasping and wheezing.

It was Sam.

Her sister let out a piercing scream and both ghosts vanished with a crackle of energy. The cold left and Eliza was suddenly hot and sticky with sweat.

Gasping, her throat burning, Eliza sprinted out of the room.

Mitch and Maggie had both appeared in their doorways; she ignored their enquiries and all but leapt down the steps.

The world outside seemed far too calm after what had just happened inside. The animals were unbothered by the disturbances and looked up with mild interest as she ran past.

She found Erik on the ground a good distance from the house. He was starting to stir and was able to stand with her help. Blood covered half his face and there were pebbles and bits of dirt caked into his skin. He stumbled a few times, legs unsteady.

'What happened?' he asked, clutching his head. 'Are you okay?'

'Sam is a really good sister for a ghost,' she said, brushing dirt and dust from his hair. She let her eyes rove over him, assessing the damage. He seemed remarkably unharmed for having been thrown so far.

He reached out and traced the fast forming bruises. 'Eliza —'

'I'm fine,' she said quickly. 'I'm fine.'

A throat cleared behind them and they turned to see Maggie and Mitch looking at them in utter bewilderment.

It was Mitch who spoke first. He held out both hands. 'What. The. Hell.'

'Long story,' said Erik.

'Then I'll get the bourbon,' said Mitch.

Maggie looked at Erik. 'You okay?'

He nodded, still clearly dazed. Maggie walked over to them and helped Eliza support him into the house and onto the sofa.

It took several hours of explaining the story before the siblings were satisfied enough with the information they were receiving that they let the matter lie. Mitch took it all in stride, but Maggie didn't seem remotely comfortable with the idea of a haunted house and went to school far earlier than necessary.

Alone and antsy, Eliza and Erik fed the animals and cleaned the stalls, but by midday they were on their way into town. Neither of them really knew what to say.

Logan was not someone they knew how to deal with. Especially now that he was dead.

They were across the street from Joanie's when, whiter than a sheet, Erik stopped short.

Half afraid Logan had reappeared, Eliza followed his gaze.

There, on the other side of Main Street, deep in conversation with Roger, was Wyatt Irons.

Roger was clearly just out of the hospital and looked somehow worse than when she'd seen him last. His brown hair was unwashed and matted, his bruises yellow and purple, his skin sallow.

'I don't believe this,' said Erik under his breath.

'Let's go,' she murmured, tugging on his hand.

It was too late.

'Erik!' Wyatt had caught sight of them and was waving Erik over. 'Come here, son!'

Eliza suddenly wished Miles was there. Miles was a good buffer between her and the parts of Riverside she didn't want to think about. The parts of Riverside that had belonged to Erik before and after her. The parts of Riverside that didn't seem keen to let him go, apparently.

Wyatt pulled Erik into an aggressive embrace when they reached the other side of the road. When they parted, Wyatt turned his attention to Eliza.

'My, my, if it isn't little Eliza!' He kissed her cheek and she fought the urge to cringe. 'Finally caved and took our boy back, I see.'

She had to force a smile.

'How's business?' said Erik loudly, shooting a glare Roger's way.

'Good, good. I had a proposition for you, actually.' Wyatt smiled, cunning and worrying. 'Up for a drink?'

Erik shook his head and wrapped his arm around Eliza. 'No. I'm out, Wyatt. I told you.'

Undeterred, Wyatt chuckled and squeezed Erik's shoulder. 'Come on, son. One drink. I can't do this one without you.'

It was clear from the look on Erik's face that he was having trouble saying no. Eliza disentangled herself from his grip and thumbed over her shoulder.

'I'm going to find Miles.'

Erik's face fell, and he turned to her instantly, putting himself between her and the other two. 'No, you don't –'

'It's fine,' she said sharply. 'I'll see you around. Nice to see you again, Wyatt. Roger.'

She nodded to them, feeling sick with dread, and left without another word. As she crossed the street, she took her phone out of her pocket.

'Miles?' she said when he answered. 'Wyatt's in town.'

'Oh, crap. Where's EJ?'

'I think they're going for drinks.'

'Okay, I'm on my way. You good, babe?'

'I'm good,' she lied as she got into the car.

Not sure where to go, and mind on fast-forward, she drove without thought. Before she knew it, she was outside of Adrian Kane's.

She knocked on the door, so filled with anxiety she wanted to vomit.

The door opened a moment later and Adrian appeared. He didn't look like a drug dealer. If anything, he looked like a banker. As with Roger's charade, it worked in his favour.

His expression turned quizzical when he recognised her. 'Aren't you Roger's girl?'

She held up the money. 'Do you care?'

Without a word, Adrian stepped aside to let her in. She could hear the sounds of his family in the other room, but they went through the hall.

It was a normal home with photographs on the wall and discarded shoes lining the hallway to the study.

Within two minutes, Eliza was back in the car.

She drove to Willow Lane and curled up on the sofa. Only when she was safe in her sanctuary did she finally let herself think.

Since the day she'd met Erik, all she'd imagined was losing him. And every time the ground felt solid beneath them, something came along and threatened to take it all away.

It had happened already. It could happen again. For longer this time. For good.

She sat on the sofa, letting the drugs clear her mind and cloud her anxiety, and at last she was able to breathe.

———————

Erik had been in The Weaver for almost an hour when Miles appeared. For a mild-mannered man, Miles could look tough when need be. Relief and concern vied for control as Erik tried to read his expression. But he wasn't going to ask about Eliza around company, certainly not Roger and Wyatt.

'Miles Hennessey, as I live and breathe,' drawled Wyatt, holding out his hand.

Miles shook it and nodded. There was an unusually cold glint in his eyes. 'Good to see you, Wyatt.'

'Likewise. What you doing here?'

'Keepin' an eye on my boy.' Miles sat down without being asked and waved to several regulars before looking back at Wyatt and Roger, unflustered by their existence.

It was hard not to be jealous of the ease he exuded.

Despite not having spoken to Wyatt in weeks, Erik wasn't surprised by his arrival. It was simply that he'd had nothing to do with it. From the look on Roger's face, he wasn't quite as confused.

'What have I missed?' Miles prompted, looking between the three of them.

'We were just discussing Erik's severance package,' said Wyatt, interlacing his fingers where his hands rested on the table top. His words were polite, but the warning behind them was missed by nobody.

Miles looked at Erik, eyebrow raised. 'Oh yeah?'

'One last job,' said Wyatt. 'Isn't that so?'

Roger smirked around the rim of his beer. Erik clenched his jaw and lit a cigarette instead of replying.

'What sort of job?' asked Miles.

'Now, son,' said Wyatt pointedly. 'That's hardly any of your concern.'

'Erik concerns me.'

'He concerns me, too,' said Roger.

Wyatt chuckled as Erik and Miles shot him looks of loathing.

'Unfortunately,' said Miles, turning back to Wyatt, 'Erik's working for me now.'

Wyatt and Roger couldn't conceal their surprise. Erik kept his face blank and inhaled about half the cigarette.

'Is that right?' said Wyatt, steely gaze going to Erik. 'You never said.'

Erik held out a hand with forced nonchalance, but he struggled to hold Wyatt's gaze. He hated the feeling of disloyalty curling in his gut. 'I did tell you I was out, Wyatt. Miles and I are aiming to be business partners.'

'So, you see,' Miles supplied, 'I have a say in any shit he gets involved in. All Erik's affairs are my business now.'

'He owes me a final favour,' said Wyatt acidly.

Miles' eyes narrowed. 'How much?'

A derisive snort left Wyatt. 'He doesn't owe me money.'

'Then he doesn't owe you a damn thing.' Miles stood and nodded to Erik. 'We have our appointment. Let's go.'

Wyatt straightened up. 'Now, Erik —'

Miles leaned down on one arm and glared at Wyatt. 'Don't forget which town you're in. This isn't Silverlake.'

'You don't have the power to make threats, Miles.'

'Easy,' said Roger, leaning in. 'Don't threaten my cousin, Wyatt. Miles is a pest, but he's family.'

'I wasn't,' said Wyatt. 'I was just reminding him who has the power in this town.'

The look Miles gave him was one of unmasked contempt. 'Remind yourself that it's not you.' He then glanced at Erik and cocked his head. 'Let's go. We're late.'

With a stiff nod to Wyatt, Erik followed Miles out of the pub. 'That wasn't smart,' he said when they were on the other side of the road.

'Getting mixed up with him in the first place was fucking stupid,' said Miles. He pulled out a cigarette and lit it before inhaling sharply. He then pointed a finger at Erik that brokered no room for argument. 'You're not doing guns again. And Elle's not amused, either.'

Erik's stomach dropped. 'Where is she?'

'Hell if I know, but she's the one who told me.' Miles thumbed over his shoulder. 'I actually do have an appointment. You good?'

'I'm good. Go.'

He wasn't, really. Fear of losing Eliza again engulfed his guilty feelings over Wyatt, and he drew out his phone as Miles walked away. But no matter how many times he dialled her number, Eliza didn't answer.

Thoroughly distracted, Erik was halfway down the street when he realised he'd passed by his mother's old church.

It was a small church, built long before Riverside cropped up around it. Old and ivy-covered, there was a wisdom to the building few places could emulate. Surrounded by green grass and trees with leaves clinging to branches as the encroaching winter coaxed them to the ground, and flowers that bloomed a myriad of colours throughout spring and summer, Erik found it a welcome sight even now. Even after all the ghosts.

Perhaps some part of him had always hoped there was an after. His mother had always told him there was. With ghosts coming out of the woodwork, he believed now more than ever, and the wanting left him with questions he wasn't sure he would ever get the answers to, but they were answers he ached for.

If Paige had come back, could she move on? If Sam was around, did that mean he could apologise? If they were there, what did that mean for his mother?

The possibility of those questions having answers propelled him towards the church.

In the front garden, Henry Olyphant, the priest, was bent over, weeding the leaves coating the garden into large compostable bags.

Erik stepped through the gates and walked over to him, hands jammed into his pockets.

'It's been a long time since I've been here,' he said to Henry, voice quiet with his mounting nerves.

Henry looked up, a smile spreading across his aged face. 'Welcome home, Erik.'

'Thanks.'

'Haven't seen you in a while.'

Erik's lips twitched. 'Never was one for religion.'

'And yet I still remember the day your friend Miles asked me if there was a way to talk to the dead.'

A pang went through his chest. So many of his early memories were blurred, or so bloody he forced them from his mind, but that day with Miles stood out more clearly than most.

He frowned in thought. 'That book you gave him, where'd you get it?'

'I didn't give anything to him,' said Henry ruefully. He leaned against his rake and wiped sweat from his brow. 'He stole it from my bookshelf when I left to deal with another parishioner.'

A wry laugh left Erik. 'Yeah, that sounds like Miles.'

'He never did give it back. Expensive book, too. Bought it at an auction years ago. You might see if he'll be so good as to return it to me.'

'Of course.'

Henry smiled at that. It was a genuine smile, grandfatherly and kind, his eyes sparkling with innate compassion. 'Thank you, Erik.'

Erik nodded slowly, wondering how to be casual about his next question. 'Miles was looking for ghost stories we could tell at Halloween.'

'Ah,' said Henry, bemused. 'Don't think there were any stories in that one.'

'No. Not one.' Bracing himself, he added, 'Do you believe in ghosts?'

It was Henry's turn to laugh. 'Even priests have questions, Erik. I don't *not* believe in them. But I doubt they look like Halloween sheets.'

'You ever hear about anything weird in this town?'

Henry scratched the white stubble on his cheek and shrugged. 'Weird how?'

'Just ... weird.' Erik shrugged in what he hoped was convincing nonchalance. 'Might be fun to scare the pants off Miles later.'

Henry smirked. 'Well, all towns have stories,' he allowed. 'Our town's got more than most, that's for sure.'

'Like what?'

'Oh, you know. Legends and the like.'

Erik crossed his arms and leaned against the gate post. 'It's been a while since I've heard a ghost story.'

'You think I got nothing better to do than tell stories, son?' But there was a twinkle in Henry's eye that showed how much he was enjoying the exchange.

'Humour me, Father. Come on. I gotta scare Miles good this year.'

With an amused shake of his head, Henry dusted off his hands and set his rake aside. He moved to sit on the church steps and gestured for Erik to join him.

'Riverside's always had rumours of witchcraft, curses and ghosts. History says sometimes people just disappeared. Sometimes people just went bad.'

'Bad how?'

'Our bed and breakfast made headlines a decade before when a body was discovered under the floorboards in one of the upstairs rooms. A drifter checked in for a few weeks and suddenly disappeared. Whether it was the drifter they discovered under the bed, or someone who met a dreary end by his hand, no one was entirely sure – the body was too badly decomposed to properly identify.'

Erik made a face. 'Anything else?'

'There's the forest near Lake Lally. Some of the more vivid descriptions involve cannibalistic monstrosities, horrible riverbed dwellers, angry spirits of travellers' past, savage scavengers comprised of missing children, and various other colourful stories that the tellers swear up and down to be truth.'

'But you've never seen anything?'

'Not myself, no,' said Henry. 'Your mother actually told me a good few. You probably know them better than I do, though.'

Erik went still. He was sure he hadn't heard correctly. 'My mother?'

Henry nodded. 'She was a good storyteller, your mother.'

'Yeah ...'

Most of Erik's memories of his mother were obscured by the last one. The bloodstained one. He remembered listening to her for hours, finding such comfort in the sounds of her voice. But for the life of him, he couldn't remember what the stories had been about.

'The one about Death,' Henry continued, clueless to Erik's shock. 'I liked that one the most.'

Erik went completely still. The words stirred something in the back of his mind. A tale he should know but couldn't quite recall.

'The one about Death?' he echoed. It felt like his skeleton was shaking inside his skin.

Henry bobbed his head thoughtfully, the wrinkles on his face even deeper as his mind wandered back through the years. Erik wished he had that many years with his mother to comb through. It made something constrict inside his chest to remember that he didn't. He wouldn't.

'Oh,' said Henry airily, 'some story she had about Death in a human form and how he could only come up from the afterlife three nights a year.'

Erik pulled his pack of cigarettes out of his pocket and lit one before replying. 'Like a werewolf?'

'That's three nights a month.'

'Oh, sure.'

'No,' said Henry. 'No, she said Death could only come up on All Hallowtide.'

'What is that?'

'The triduum that encompasses All Hallows' Eve, All Saints' Day and All Souls' Day.' At Erik's blank expression, Henry added, 'The night of Halloween and the two nights after.'

'Now I'm with you,' said Erik, and Henry chuckled. 'Anyway, back to Death.'

'She said she met him.'

'She ... *met* Death?'

Henry heaved a sigh and ran a hand through his snow coloured hair. 'You have to understand, son, your mother was dealing with a lot. Every time she came to me, I asked her to leave your father.'

'I asked her, too.'

They smiled sadly at each other before Erik gestured for Henry to continue.

'She told me that she fell in love with him. With Death.' Henry's eyes were suddenly sad and weary. 'I think she meant she wanted to die.'

Erik nodded, hardly able to draw breath. 'Did she ever say where she saw Death?'

'Out in the forest,' said Henry. 'Best place to start a ghost story, isn't it? I think she went there because she felt safe. Your father hated the forest.'

'Yeah,' said Erik hollowly. He looked at the trees. 'The perfect start to a ghost story.'

After a few seconds of silence, Erik thanked him and carried on through the headstones.

The more he learned, the less he felt he knew.

CHAPTER THIRTEEN
Dark Spaces

Eliza woke up with a dry mouth and an aching head. She was cold to the bone and felt painfully aware of every part of her body. Like she'd been wrung out and beaten with a stick. She licked her lips, but even her tongue felt fuzzy.

On the floor beside her, her phone beeped with notifications. She ignored it and sat up. Her stomach instantly rebelled and she heaved for several seconds, a cold sweat breaking out all over her body. She pressed the heels of her palms into her eyes and took slow breaths.

Adrian's drugs were definitely nowhere near as pure as Roger's. But the thought made her mind drift to Erik's accusation about Roger lacing his drugs. It was hard to know what to believe. In her experience, Roger's drugs were the best in town.

Her phone began to ring. The shrill, jarring sound cut through her skull in painful waves.

With narrowed, heavy-lidded eyes, she squinted down at the name. It was Erik. She was tempted not to answer, but her worry over what might have happened made that impossible. Wyatt wasn't someone she trusted no matter how much loyalty Erik had to him.

After another moment's deliberation, she answered it, face screwing up as her head throbbed. She rubbed one of her aching temples. 'Hello?'

'Babe!' Erik sounded completely panicked. 'Where are you? Mitch says you never came home. Are you okay?'

She squeezed the bridge of her nose as her vision and head spun in tandem. She had to breathe forcefully to keep from getting sick.

She half considered telling him she was at Roger's just to cement how irritated she was about Wyatt's entire proximity to Erik's life, but she didn't. She'd never lied to him before.

'I'm fine,' was all she said.

'Where are you?'

'Willow Lane.'

'Oh,' he said, audibly relaxing. 'Can I come by? I want to talk about yesterday.'

'What does Wyatt want?'

'For me to do a last job.'

Eliza picked agitatedly at a spot on her face. 'Are you?'

'Can we talk in person?' he said instead of answering. 'I don't want to do this over the phone, babe.'

She let out a small noise of disgust. 'That's a yes.'

'Babe, please.' The tone of his voice went straight through her chest. 'It's complicated. Please just let me explain.'

'Fine,' she muttered, rubbing her forehead roughly. It would have been so much simpler if she didn't care. 'I'll meet you at Joanic's.'

'Okay? Okay. Good. Thank you, babe. Now?'

'Fine,' she said again. 'See you in a bit.'

'I love you.'

Not in the mood to acknowledge that she loved him as much as ever, she ended the call and tossed her phone onto the moth-eaten cushion beside her.

Screaming and vomiting both seemed like possibilities.

It took another few minutes to source the ability to stand. Grimacing and breathing with forced slowness, Eliza left the house and made her way back into town. The roads were mostly empty, and the morning felt oddly quiet when compared with the days that had preceded it.

She parked by the library and headed toward the café. While food was an altogether unappealing thought, eating would probably make her legs feel less like string cheese.

Erik was waiting at the front door when she reached Joanie's. He took in the sight of her with unguarded concern and curiosity, but instead of saying anything, he simply kissed her and wrapped his arms around her.

He smelled perfect and her body began to relax for the first time since they'd parted ways.

'What does Wyatt want?' she asked.

He leaned back and smiled sheepishly. 'Do you want some coffee?'

'No, I want to know what he wants.'

'Help.' Erik stepped back, rubbing his jaw. It was clear he hadn't slept either and his eyes were bloodshot and hooded.

'Are you going to?'

He held out his hands. With complete seriousness, he said, 'Not if you tell me not to.'

She almost ordered him right then and there not to do it, but she didn't. Not only wasn't it her place to tell him to do anything, rumours and whisperings over the years lent credence to the assumption that doing so wouldn't be nearly as easy as she might hope. 'How would Wyatt take that?'

'Not well.' He looked at her pointedly, his dark eyes imploring her to believe him. 'But Wyatt's a thug, not a psycho.'

She raised an eyebrow. 'Would he let you walk away, though?'

Erik was quiet for a time before he nodded. 'I think so. On some level, to him, I think I'll always be the beaten-up kid he took pity on. I think I'm the only one he'll ever let walk away for the sole reason that I'm the only one who ever thought of him as something like a father.'

Eliza reached out and put her hand over his. She didn't believe him, and she could tell he didn't much believe himself.

'Do what you want,' she said. 'It's not up to me.'

He covered her hand with his own and looked at her with the same raw urgency he'd always displayed. 'I'll do whatever you want.'

She grimaced and shrugged. That was the problem, wasn't it? She wanted him to walk away and never look back. She didn't want him to ask her if it was the right thing to do.

Neither of them seemed to know what to say then, so they headed into the café.

No matter how hard she tried, Eliza couldn't quite forget Sam's words to her the day before she died.

It's not like we don't know what Wyatt Irons does ... People lie. Guys lie ... Don't be that idiot ...

She wondered what Sam would say about all that had followed that night.

———

Henry's story about his mother had been haunting Erik since he'd heard it, but broaching the subject with Eliza proved more difficult than he'd expected.

He spent the rest of that day watching her, heart in his throat, terrified she would decide she'd had enough of him and walk away for good.

It was only when Eliza and Miles had fallen asleep that Erik slipped out of the apartment.

The forest near Lake Lally was gnarled and dark, not the sort of locale where campers went for a good night's sleep, or hikers went for peace. It was a place for stories, for scares, for disappearances. Not for those who knew what came of shadows and spooks.

Leaving his car on the side of the road, Erik stepped into the darkening wood, unable to quell the feeling that something was about to happen.

He walked for what felt like hours, losing himself in the depths of the forest. There were no creatures, no insects. A quietude that felt deliberate. Erik stopped when at last he reached the lake his mother used to tell him about.

He'd only been standing there a few seconds when he felt someone watching him.

He whirled around and found himself face to face with a man he didn't recognise.

At least, Erik *thought* he was a man. For some reason he wasn't entirely convinced. There was something eerie and ethereal about the stranger. As if he wasn't all there.

Erik took a step back and wished he'd had the forethought to bring a gun. 'Who are you?' he enquired.

The stranger's eyes went black. 'My name is Sael.'

A chill went down Erik's spine and he swallowed hard. 'That doesn't answer my question.'

'I wanted to speak with you.'

'Why?'

There was something familiar about him. But before Erik could figure out where he knew the stranger from, Sael said, 'Because I'm your father.'

For a few seconds, Erik had no reaction at all. He thought perhaps he might have misheard. And then he thought maybe Sael was joking.

When it became increasingly clear from the look on Sael's face that he, at least, believed the words that had just come out of his mouth, a scoff of absolute derision left Erik's lips.

'The fuck you are,' he grunted.

Sael bowed his head, black hair falling in front of his black eyes. 'I am.'

Erik didn't know whether he was more confused or irritated. It was the strangest conversation he'd ever had. And he'd spent the last few weeks chasing ghosts.

'Prove it,' he said.

'To prove such a thing, you would have to come with me.'

'Yeah, that's really not going to happen. I make a habit of not going with weirdos in the forest to strange places. Especially when they tell me they're related to me. I don't have a long list of things I won't do, but that's definitely on there.'

Sael tilted his head to the side, as if confused by Erik's assumption. 'I won't harm you.'

'Somehow I don't believe you.'

'Are you afraid of me?'

'Afraid of some psycho in the forest telling me I'm his son? Yeah.'

'Then I shall return,' said Sael with an almost unsettling air of calm. 'Should you change your mind and desire answers, I have two nights left.'

'Two nights until what?'

'Until I return to the After for another year.'

Despite his derision, Erik's curiosity was mounting. 'The After of what?'

'Life.'

Erik mulled Sael's words over, dissecting each one carefully before replying. 'Why?'

It was Sael's turn to be stumped. 'Why?'

'You said you only have two nights left.'

Sael nodded slowly. 'Death may only come in physical form on All Hallowtide, Erik.'

'That's what Henry said, too.'

'Your mother's priest? Yes, she spoke to him often.'

Erik went stalk still. 'Have you seen my mother?'

'Of course,' said Sael simply. 'She's my wife.'

Erik choked. 'How —'

'The dead do not give their secrets to the living, Erik. If you want answers, you must come with me.'

'I'm not going anywhere.'

But his conviction was gone. The prospect of seeing his mother had made all arguments half-hearted.

Sael bowed his head once more and then disappeared like a shadow into the night.

Erik did a double take. 'Hey!' he yelled at the empty clearing.

But Sael did not reappear.

———————

Eliza woke up to find a note from Erik on the pillow telling her that he would be back soon. It also told her not to worry, which of course made her fear spike instantly.

She quickly got dressed and stumbled into the sitting room. Miles was there already, folding laundry and watching cartoons. He looked like he hadn't slept well and there was an empty mug of coffee beside him.

She held the note out to him. 'Do you think he's with Wyatt?' she prompted after a few seconds.

He looked up from the note. 'I hope not.'

A curl of fear spread through the pit of her stomach and twisted her insides into painful knots. 'Great.'

Miles stood and went to put on his shoes. 'I have some runs to do, but I'll see if I can find him.' He donned his coat and paused to give her a reassuring smile. 'I'm sure it's nothing, baby girl.'

'You're a bad liar.'

'I'm not going to let Wyatt touch him.' He said it with such authority that she found herself nodding.

'I'll tell him to call you the second I see him.'

'Maybe just punch him instead.'

'Oh, I'll do that too. Don't you worry.' He winked at her before darting out the door.

Relaxing proved impossible. She paced around the room until she was dizzy; she sat on the sofa and jiggled her foot until she was too antsy not to move; she made coffee and then didn't drink it.

Less than an hour after Miles had headed out, Eliza got her coat and left the apartment.

The drive to Maya's house took hours, and Eliza arrived late in the day. She parked out front and jogged up the steps.

With a hammering heart, she knocked twice, bouncing on the balls of her feet.

Maya opened a second later. She looked the same as ever, although her eyes were sad and her face gaunt. Maya had agreed to keep Erik's involvement in Sam's death from the police, but she had never forgiven him. The wake had broken them all. Maya drank herself under the table, Erik drove off without a word and never came back, and Eliza only made it home thanks to Miles.

A look of total shock changed Maya's grim expression. 'Hi, Elle,' she said, stunned. 'What are you doing here?'

Eliza crossed her arms as discomfort spread like poison through her chest. 'Do you have a minute?'

'Sure ...' Maya stepped aside and waved her in. 'What's up?'

Eliza took a deep breath, nodded resolutely to herself several times, and said, 'I spoke to Sam. And before you tell me I'm crazy, before you tell me you don't believe it, you need to hear me out. She's dead, I'm not saying she's not. But I saw her ghost and I thought you should know.'

Maya stared at her. 'You saw her ghost.'

'Yes.'

'Eliza —'

'I'm not crazy,' said Eliza. She looked at Maya beseechingly. 'You know I'm not crazy. And there were two other ghosts, too.'

That made Maya do a doubletake. 'What?'

'Paige Osbourne and Logan Stern.'

Her eyebrows shot up. 'Wait. Paige? As in —'

'As in the girl who talked to Sam before she died,' said Eliza, nodding several times, glad that Maya was at least giving her the chance to be heard. 'Logan attacked Paige. That's why she was warning Sam.'

Maya stared at her, clearly dubious. But Maya had known her long enough to know that Eliza didn't make things up. Nor would she ever have lied about Sam.

'Is ...'

Eliza held out a hand and smiled even as her throat tightened and breathing became tricky. 'She's still Sam, you know? Kicked Roger's ass when he was being a dick, too.'

Maya's eyebrows shot up. 'Kicked his ass how?'

'Ghost justice,' said Eliza with a wink. 'I think he needed stitches.'

'Ouch.'

'Seriously.'

They stared at each other for a long time, but dubious as she was, it was clear Maya *wanted* it to be true. The laugh left her abruptly, and then the sobs.

Eliza moved quickly to embrace her. Even now, so many years without a word between them, she thought of Maya as a second sister. One she had so badly wanted.

'Eliza?'

'Yeah?'

'Think I'll see her when I die?'

Eliza pulled back to catch her eye and nodded. 'Yeah,' she said softly. 'She'll be waiting. But she wants you to be happy, okay? Whatever happens, you have to try. You have to make sure that you have a whole life to tell her about when you see her.'

Maya wiped her eyes and nose and cleared her throat. 'I still can't believe that night was real.'

'Neither can I.'

Maya took her hand and Eliza laced their fingers together. 'Thank you.'

'Anything you want me to say to Sam if I see her again?'

For a minute, Maya stared out the window, lips pursed in thought. Then, with a tremulous breath, she said, 'Tell her that I love her. Tell her that she's still the only one I've been able to tolerate long enough to consider marrying.'

They both cracked a strained laugh at that.

'Tell her that I'll be wishing she was there on all the adventures we should have gone on together.'

Tears stung Eliza's eyes. 'I will.'

'Make sure she knows.' Maya smiled brokenly. 'Make sure she knows I still love her.'

'I will.'

For a moment, Maya said nothing, and then, with a smile that only she and Sam could have deciphered the meaning of, said, 'And tell her it rained. Just like I said it would.'

Not sure what that meant, Eliza promised to deliver the message, hugged Maya, and then left. She hoped it was the right thing to have done. Maya deserved more than unanswered questions. And she deserved to know Sam was sticking around.

It was nearly midnight when Eliza got back to Riverside and her phone was beeping with messages she wasn't in the mood to answer.

She had only just stepped onto the path to the grocer's when someone appeared in front of her, stopping her short.

It was Wyatt.

'Hello,' he greeted. 'How are you, Eliza?'

'Fine,' she said warily. 'How's Erik?'

Wyatt's eyes narrowed. 'Didn't he tell you?'

Something about the way he said that made her tighten her grip on her keys. 'I haven't seen him since he left to meet you.'

'Oh sweetheart, he didn't come to work for me. He up and quit without so much as batting an eyelash.'

The tone of his voice sent a chill over her skin. There was something very off-putting about Wyatt. Innately so. Like he knew all the places to apply pressure and enjoyed the potential fallout he could rue. Perhaps that was why he liked Erik so much. Perhaps he wanted to see how much fallout Erik could wreak.

Eliza stepped around him, desperate to put space between them. 'I'm meeting Miles, Wyatt,' she said. 'See you later.'

'Erik's been in this business long enough to know what happens to those who cross me. He's doled out more than enough repercussions to know that.'

Eliza was fairly certain her legs were no longer functional. 'He's what?'

A smirk played on his lips. 'There's a lot you don't know about your boy, Eliza.'

'What does that mean?'

Instead of replying, his eyes went to something behind her. The sudden cold press of metal against the base of her spine made her go very, very still.

'Okay,' she said, holding up her hands. 'Okay, I'm listening.'

'Excellent,' said Wyatt. He nodded to the man behind her, who then shoved her toward the truck.

Wyatt clambered in beside her. 'What's say you and I have a talk?'

She looked from him to the gun in his lackey's hand and, not for the first time, prayed one of the ghosts would reappear.

CHAPTER FOURTEEN
Answers Raise Questions

Erik spent the better part of the morning smoking himself into a frenzy of worry. He'd left Eliza two dozen messages and she hadn't responded to one. He knew she was angry about Wyatt, but the silence didn't feel like a cold shoulder. The fact that Miles couldn't reach her only lent credence to his assumption that something was wrong.

'We should try Roger,' he said after another minute of drumming his fingers on the table. 'See if she's over there.'

'Already did, brother.' Miles shook his head. 'He's not at home or answering.'

'We should go back out.'

'It's pissing rain.'

'If Eliza's hurt —'

The knock at the door made them both jump. Erik shot to his feet immediately, but his hope that it was Eliza turned to confusion at the sight of Roger. Or rather, at the state Roger was in. He was a mess; there was blood, grime and muck all over him.

He looked at them through swollen, purpled eyes. 'Got any whiskey?'

Not sure if he felt like gloating or offering concern, Erik didn't step aside. 'What happened to you?'

'I was trying to help Eliza,' said Roger. He reached up to a cut on his eyebrow and winced as blood dribbled down the side of his face. 'Are you going to let me in or should we do this in the hall?'

Too in shock to refuse, Erik let him pass and shut the door. 'What happened?'

'You really pissed off Wyatt this time.' Roger dropped down into a chair with a grimace. His clothes were soaked as well as dirtied, and water began to pool on the ground at his feet. 'He took Eliza to the cabin.'

A horrible, marrow-deep chill went through Erik. 'When?' he choked out.

'I don't know,' said Roger, visibly shaken by his own knowledge of what that meant for Eliza. 'I found out and voiced my displeasure. He didn't take kindly to it.'

Miles, who had disappeared into the kitchen, returned with an ice pack. He tossed it to Roger before donning his coat. 'We going?'

'Let's go,' said Erik, already halfway out the door, keys in hand.

'What's the cabin?' asked Miles as they jogged down the stairwell to his car. 'Not your cabin?'

'No. It's where Wyatt takes people who piss him off,' said Erik, trying not to remember the last time he'd been there. It was a few weeks before his father died, and he remembered wondering how he was any better than Logan.

The cabin was where Wyatt had him take runners who were caught stealing, buyers who couldn't pay, or snitches. A common location for his nightmares, it wasn't a place anyone went without being bloodied.

Miles eyed him. 'Not for a slumber party, I'm guessing?'

Erik didn't bother to reply as he got into his car and revved the engine. Miles got into the front seat and Roger slipped in the back.

'You're coming?' It was a somewhat rhetorical question as Erik revved the engine the second the words left his mouth.

Roger scoffed. He was still holding the icepack to his head. 'I didn't get beaten up because I *don't* care, shit-brain.'

'Whatever.'

The rain began to hammer down as they headed east on the motorway and very quickly the sides of the road turned from shops, to forests and ranches, and then only forests. It was difficult to see much of anything and Erik was almost vibrating with fear and outrage. He kept dialling Wyatt's number, but there was no answer.

Miles looked over at him. 'Did Wyatt ever —'

'Wyatt's never touched me or anyone he knew I cared about,' said Erik angrily.

'Until you quit,' said Roger.

Miles looked over his shoulder. 'Hey, cuz?'

'Yeah?'

'Shut up.'

It was over an hour before the exit came into view and Erik turned off the motorway and headed up the forested drive. It brought them through a small village and then on into the mountains. The road became bumpy and the trees swallowed them whole.

The gate appeared at last and Erik parked in front of a locked gate. Exchanging wary glances, all three clambered out. The rain had only worsened and in seconds they were drenched.

No one bothered to make conversation as they walked through the cold, wet night.

When the cabin finally came into view, Erik found it hard to even breathe. He took his gun out and checked the clip, glad to find that his hands remained steady.

'EJ ...'

He looked up at Miles. 'What?'

Miles eyed the weapon nervously. 'Gun, EJ?'

'Yeah.'

Erik didn't say anything else as he moved past Miles and headed into the cabin. Miles had always hated guns; Erik had, too, but likes and dislikes were a luxury he'd rarely been afforded.

A few seconds of searching revealed something that was both a relief and deeply alarming.

There was no sign of Eliza.

'Would he have brought her to Silverlake?' asked Roger when they were all back on the porch. 'To the cabin there?'

Erik shook his head, thinking quickly. 'He'd keep her close. He wants me to do what he wants, not turn against him.'

'Charming,' said Miles, lighting a cigarette. His eyes flicked to Roger. 'Good work bringing him here, ass-wipe.'

'I didn't know this would happen,' said Roger. He'd gone the colour of sour milk and was worrying at a cut on his lower lip.

Erik rounded on Roger, rage spiking violently. 'What did you *think* was going to happen when you brought Wyatt here?'

'I was trying to get rid of you, not hurt Eliza!'

Something moved out of the corner of Erik's eye and he turned to see Sael step out of the trees. The rain seemed to slow, the air turned a little colder, and all sounds of the forest disappeared.

All three men stepped off the porch, but where Miles looked wary, Roger's gun was immediately aimed at Sael.

'Who're you?' he demanded.

Sael rolled his eyes and with a wave of his hand, Roger dropped to the floor. 'Tiresome boy,' he said with an air of deep exasperation.

Had he not been filled with terror for Eliza, Erik would have found the exchange immensely funny.

'What are you doing here?' he asked, still holding his own gun.

'No,' said Miles loudly. 'Better question is: *who* are you?'

'Your lady's been taken,' said Sael, ignoring Miles entirely and looking only at Erik. 'I thought you'd like to know.'

Miles, however, wasn't about to be ignored. 'How do *you* know?'

'I know everything that happens in my woods,' said Sael, still looking at Erik. 'I am not meant to interfere in the business of the living, but in this I shall make an exception. After all, you are my son.'

A slightly high-pitched sound of disbelief left Miles. He looked between them in bewilderment. 'You're what now?'

Erik didn't bother enlightening him. He just looked at Sael. Perhaps it was true. Perhaps Sael was his father. Not being related to Logan would be an enormous relief. But Erik didn't care who his father was; if he was Death or simply dead. He cared whether Eliza was safe or not.

'Where is she?' he prompted.

'Not here,' said Sael.

'Do you know where?'

'Yes.'

When Sael didn't elaborate, Erik threw out his free hand. 'Are you going to tell me?'

Sael nodded ponderously. 'Before I do, I should tell you that if you go near her, once again her life is in danger.'

The sensation inside Erik which those words conjured was not unlike being in a plane as it descends. 'What?'

'The only way to return the spirits you have brought to Earth is to come with me.'

'What?' he said again. At the same time Miles said, 'Wait, hold up. The fuck?'

'They're tied to your power,' said Sael. 'Until you can control it, they will be in your vicinity.'

'Dude,' said Miles. 'Seriously?'

Erik shook his head at Miles to be quiet before responding. 'So I'll learn to control it.'

Sael shook his head. 'It will take years.'

Erik stiffened. 'I'm not —'

'You must.' Sael moved closer. 'Logan will never be anything but a danger until you do.'

Erik scowled at him even as the remark made his blood run cold. 'Will you just tell me where Eliza is?'

'Do you wish me to bring her to you?' Sael tilted his head to the side with an insufferable calm. 'It's up to you.'

'Oh, bro,' said Miles irritably. 'Just get her.'

'Please,' implored Erik.

'Will you agree to listen to what I have said?'

He nodded tightly, jaw clenched so hard his head was beginning to ache.

As Sael disappeared, Roger sat up, and Miles rounded on Erik. He held up both hands. 'EJ, what is going on?'

Erik shook his head, utterly lost himself.

'Where'd that freak go?' asked Roger, looking around wildly.

Before either of them could be bothered to enlighten him, the world around them grew unnaturally cold once more, and Sam and Paige appeared.

At this point, their arrival was far from disconcerting for Erik and Miles. Roger, on the other hand, scrambled back in shock.

'Jesus Christ!' he cried. 'What the Hell!'

'Newbie,' said Miles with a scoff. He put a cigarette between his lips and nodded to the ghosts. 'Hi, ladies.'

There was something different about Sam and Paige this time. Something more solid. Their calm, steady voices only confirmed that, and Erik tried not to fret about Logan suddenly appearing.

'Hi, Miles,' said Sam, rolling her eyes at him. 'Looking as greasy as ever.'

Miles winked at her before looking back at Erik, unperturbed by their undead audience. 'What now? I don't think Death Man is going to take no for an answer.'

Paige grinned. 'I'll be sure to call him that from now on.'

'You know what's going on?' asked Erik. 'How?'

'Even the dead gossip,' said Miles, as if he could possibly know such a thing.

Roger waved a hand; he looked very close to passing out for real this time. 'What's going on?'

Ignoring him, Erik looked over at Paige and Sam. 'Is he full of crap? Sael?'

'No,' said Paige. 'Sael tried to bring us to After when we first died.'

'But he couldn't,' said Sam. 'We're tied to you. We can't leave with you here.'

Erik stared at them. 'How is that possible?'

'Cast any good spells lately?' Paige's question was rhetorical. Erik had told her about what he and Miles had done back when they were together.

'Fuck,' said Miles. 'Is that what happened? Book should come with a fucking disclaimer.'

'I think the fact that it was an old Latin book of spells was probably warning enough, Miles.'

'*Still.*'

'Please, Erik,' said Sam, drawing his attention once more. 'Please don't let Logan near her again. He's tried to kill her more than once already.'

Erik held her gaze for a long time before nodding. He didn't even know what he was agreeing to. He just knew he'd do whatever Sam asked.

'Thank you,' she said. 'Really.'

'This is so fucking shit,' he muttered, lighting a cigarette with shaking hands. He smoked with increasing agitation and began to walk aimlessly around.

After a while, Paige fell into step beside him. When they were away from the others, he stopped walking and turned to face her. The image of her flickered in the night beside him, but even still, it was good to see her.

'Why did you do it?' he finally managed. 'I would have torn him apart if you'd told me. I would've –'

'What? Made it better?'

'No,' he allowed. 'But I would've tried so hard to make you see that he doesn't get to win.'

A sad smile playing on her lips, Paige tucked a stray strand of blonde hair behind her ear and shook her head. 'Sometimes you can't make your brain see past the pain.'

He reached out, wondering if he could touch her. When he realised that he could, he wrapped his arms around her. It was like hugging someone who had been in the snow for far too long, but he didn't pull back.

'I know it doesn't help,' he murmured, 'but I would have killed him for you.'

'He didn't win,' she whispered into his ear. 'He died sad and alone.'

'It's not enough.'

'It's enough. And Sael told me I can start over. After isn't an end. It's a place where you can make a choice to either linger for those you left behind or start over. And I think I want to start over.'

'You deserve to,' he choked out. 'I'm sorry I couldn't save you.'

'You saved me the first time. I never forgot that.'

Unable to conjure a response adequate enough, Erik simply held her.

———————

When Eliza woke up, she was a locked in a closet. To her relief, she wasn't tied up or gagged, but there was a lump on the back of her head that was tender to touch and throbbed. The smell of mould and damp filled her nose and she gagged as she sat up. Already queasy, the smells didn't help.

A minute's inspection showed that there wasn't much in the closet. A few buckets, a mop, bottles of chemicals with grime around the rims. Nothing that could help her get out.

'Great,' she muttered. 'Fucking Wyatt.'

She was just contemplating trying to yank the metal handle out of one of the buckets to use as a lockpick when the temperature dropped and her breath came out fog. Despite preparing herself, she still jumped when Paige materialised, soundly bashing her head against the wall.

'Paige,' she greeted through gritted teeth, clutching her skull. 'Nice to see you.'

Paige flickered a few times, but to Eliza's relief, she didn't disappear. 'Are you okay?' she asked, sitting on one of the buckets.

'Fantastic.'

Paige smiled. There was something very kind about her smile. 'Good,' she said. 'Erik's worried.'

'Is he coming?'

'He's sending help.'

Eliza nodded slowly, trying not to panic. 'Do you know where I am?' she asked, waving a circle with her finger.

'A forest,' said Paige. 'In the mountains.'

Eliza knocked her head back against the wall, temporarily forgetting about her previous bump and sending a fresh wave of pain through her skull. '*Ow*,' she moaned, hand going to the throbbing bump.

Paige crossed her legs and looked at the door with a thoughtful expression. 'What do they want?'

'To piss off Erik, I suppose.' Eliza frowned, suddenly curious about something. 'Did you know what Erik's job was when you two were together?'

Paige flickered, disappearing and reappearing, before her image steadied. 'No. Not really. He'd show up covered in bruises or have weird hours, that sort of thing. I was too depressed to notice. I also thought it was cool he was into scary shit. Teenage stupidity and whatnot.'

Her words made Eliza terribly sad. She leaned in and caught Paige's eye. 'I'm sorry,' she said earnestly. 'I'm sorry that all this happened to you.'

'Thanks.'

'Why did you call me that night?'

'I knew Logan was going to hurt you like he hurt me,' she muttered. 'So I tried to get you away. But it's hard for ghosts to get people to listen. It's hard to stay at all. Sam was my first point of contact to you.'

Eliza gazed at her for a minute, the realisation of that settling over her like a blanket. Nothing to do with Erik, really. 'Thank you,' she said at last, a genuine smile on her face.

Paige drew her legs into her chest and rested her chin upon her knees, obscuring the strangulation marks around her throat. 'I made everything worse.'

'No, you didn't.'

They were still smiling at each other when there was a sudden smashing sound and Paige flickered and disappeared.

The door was wrenched open and Eliza found herself looking into familiar coal-black eyes. But it wasn't Erik who blinked back at her.

'My name is Sael,' said the stranger. He held out a hand. 'Would you like to get out of here?'

'Who are you?' she asked, not moving.

Paige suddenly reappeared. 'It's okay,' she said. 'He's with Erik.'

Confused, but trusting Paige's word, Eliza took Sael's hand and let him pull her to her feet. She stepped out of the closet and then dearly wished she hadn't.

The sight which greeted her in the room turned her blood to ice.

Wyatt and two others were dead on the floor, blood still dripping from their mouths.

Eliza glanced at Sael, stunned and frightened. Only the fact that Paige was there kept her from bolting.

Sael cocked his head to the side as he appraised the bodies he had just ripped apart. He seemed wholly unbothered by the gruesome display.

'I don't like those who interfere in my business,' he said mildly. 'The dead have their time. It is never to be hastened by bullies with bullets.'

Eliza didn't know what to say to that, but she managed to walk around the bodies and out of the cabin into the cold and misty night without fainting.

'Where are we going?' she asked, glancing around nervously.

'Erik's meeting us on the road. It's about a ten-minute walk.'

A rush of relief went through her and she followed him quickly away from the cabin and into the trees. Paige seemed to have vanished again.

'Who are you?' she asked as they walked.

'Erik's father.'

She stopped dead. 'What?'

He gestured for her to keep moving and she walked hesitantly after him, spiralling into confusion.

'Are you human?' she prompted. He didn't seem wholly real.

'No.'

'Are you a ghost?'

'I used to be.'

'Are you the reason he's ridiculously strong?'

Sael nodded. 'It is a strength which comes from the After.'

'After?'

'After.'

She felt slightly dizzy and had to focus to keep from stumbling down an incline. 'That tells me less than nothing, you know?'

He paused and waited for her to catch up. 'How can you name something that is given a name by every creature alive? We are the midway.'

'To Heaven?'

'To more.' He gave her a sly smile and continued on through the trees. He didn't seem to need to look where he was going.

'More what?'

'I can't give away the ending, Eliza.'

'Figures.'

A laugh resonated deep in his throat. 'I like you.'

She smiled despite her overwhelming confusion. 'Thanks, I guess.'

'You are welcome.' He looked back at her, thoughtful, and unabashed about it. 'You met him? Logan.'

'I met him,' she said. 'Wish I hadn't.'

'What was your deduction?'

'I don't think Hell deserves him, to be honest.'

Sael nodded, his expression darkening. 'If there was a Hell, I would agree with you.'

That took her pleasantly by surprise. 'There's no Hell?'

'Why do so many humans believe that? It's an awful thing to tell children.'

Eliza couldn't disagree with him there. 'So, what is there?'

'Atonement. Return. More. Linger.'

Her mind went immediately to Sam and Paige. 'What happens if you linger?'

He pushed aside a branch so that it didn't hit her in the face. 'One cannot linger forever without consequences. Not unless you choose to be part of the balance of things. Not a task to be taken lightly; I'm speaking from experience.'

Worry blossomed in her gut. 'What happens to those who linger but don't balance things out?'

'Ghosts,' he said sadly. 'Restless and trapped.'

Her heart sank. 'Can ghosts ever move on?'

'If they let go. But most will drive themselves to madness and have atoning to do for their afterlife sins atop their human sins.'

'And Sam?'

'Sam is tied to Erik,' said Sael. He said it almost academically, as if he were teaching a student. 'As is Logan. As is Paige. None of them were meant to remain on Earth after their deaths, but his spell had lingering effects.'

'The spell he and Miles did?'

'A boyhood error that had unknown consequences.' Sael sighed and brushed his dark hair behind his ears. He did look remarkably like Erik. 'As he had my blood, the spell worked. It bound the spirits to him.'

'Like a weird kind of reverse exorcism?'

'No, but I suppose I follow your point.'

She smirked at his dubious expression. 'Well, this is all new to me.'

'I understand.' With a polite bow of his head, he gestured for her to carry on, and they turned down another hill.

The appearance of lights at the bottom caught her attention and their conversation was put on hold as she darted through the last stretch of trees and ran straight into Erik's arms, her anger at his choice of employment forgotten about as relief drowned out all other thought.

'Are you okay?' he asked, voice muffled in her neck.

'I'm fine,' she promised. 'Wyatt's dead, though.'

'Good,' was all he said.

It was only then that she realised Miles and Roger were also with him. She drew back from Erik. 'What are you two doing here?'

'I found out Wyatt took you,' said Roger. He offered her a tight smile that was hindered somewhat by a nasty looking welt. 'I'm sorry I ever called him.'

She nodded stiffly. 'He's dead, by the way.'

'Good riddance, then.'

'Fucking ditto,' said Miles. He walked over and kissed her cheek. 'You look a bit runover, baby girl.'

'I feel like it, too.' She looked at Erik, whose arms were still around her and leaned against him. 'Ready to go? I could sleep for days.'

His hesitation made her heart sink.

'What?'

Erik sent a look at Miles before taking her hand and leading her away from the others by a good stretch.

They were on a quiet mountain road where no cars ever went unless they knew where the turn off was. Empty and still. Whether that was a good or bad thing, however, remained to be seen. Eliza almost wished for an interruption. Something told her this wasn't a conversation she was going to enjoy.

'Erik, what?'

'I need to tell you something,' he said after a moment's deliberation.

She let out a tremulous breath and nodded several times. 'Wyatt told me there are things I don't know about you — about what you do for him.'

'I never thought you would get involved.'

'What did you do for him?'

He shrugged bitterly and shook his head. 'I'm good with my fists, Elle,' he whispered. 'Wyatt's known that since he found me.'

'You hurt people,' she concluded.

A soft breeze rustled through the trees. The air was crisp and wet. It felt like a night for spirits and frights. A night for endings and heartbreaks, and somehow the night felt far from over.

'Yes.'

'Did you kill anyone?'

His expression became suddenly beseeching, as if he needed her to believe his next words. '*No*. Only Sam. And I will never forgive myself for any of it.'

'I know that,' she said. 'I never thought you took it lightly, Erik. It's okay.'

'It's not,' he rejoined. 'Everything I've ever done has had too much fallout.'

Only then did she realise why she felt a rising sense of trepidation. 'Why do you sound like you're about to tell me something awful?'

His face screwed up and it was clear he was trying not to break down before he got the words out. 'I have to go. With Sael.'

She stared at him. He had to be joking. 'What?'

'I have to go with him,' he repeated. 'It's the only way to keep Logan from hurting anyone else.'

'What are you talking about? Go where?'

He reached out and brushed her hair back from her face. He kissed her once, twice, and then took a shuddering breath. 'It's me,' he whispered. 'I'm the reason the ghosts are here. I'm the reason they can't move on. Ties

– or whatever it is. Ghosts are supposed to move on. I messed it up.' Tears filled his eyes and he looked up at the sky. 'It's almost dawn.'

'So, what?'

'So, time's almost up.'

'Please don't do this,' she begged, only realising then what he was saying. 'Logan doesn't scare me. Paige and Sam can help.'

'He scares me,' said Erik. 'And I won't put you and Miles – or even Roger – at risk because of a mistake I made.'

'When you were a child!'

He shook his head sadly. 'Actions have consequences, Eliza. Even the actions of children.'

He pressed his forehead against hers and her fingers curled in his hair as she pulled him into a rough, bruising kiss.

'Will you wait for me?' he asked when they finally drew apart to take shuddering breaths. 'I'll come back. I'm coming back. Please. Don't forget about me.'

'I won't,' she said. She'd waited so long already, what did it even matter? Distance hadn't changed how much she loved him. Time hadn't either.

'I love you,' he said. 'I love you so much, Eliza.'

She couldn't narrow down the list of all the things she wanted to tell him, so she settled on the only one that didn't burn. 'Will you tell Sam something?'

'Of course.'

She swallowed her sob. 'Tell her Maya said it rained. Just like she said it would.'

'What does that mean?'

'I have no idea,' she said with a strained laugh.

Erik smiled even as tears fell from his dark eyes. 'I'll tell her.'

'Thanks.'

He took her hand and pressed his keys into her palm. 'Keep my car for me? She's a good car. She won't break down on you.'

'Sure.'

'I love you,' he said again.

'I love you, too.'

They were still staring at each other when Sael came up behind him and put a hand on his shoulder. They vanished into thin air as dawn broke across the sky.

Eliza sank to the ground, staring at the spot where he'd vanished.

Miles and Roger sat beside her.

No one said a word.

Torches on the wall illuminated their descent and everything smelled like cold earth and crisp water. It was a tunnel with a packed mud floor and walls of tangled vines. Though rats and spiders would not have surprised Erik, there were butterflies, moths and fireflies instead. All flitting from vine to vine, happy and relaxed.

A world beneath the world. Or parallel to it. Or adjacent. He still wasn't entirely sure. And, according to Sael, he wasn't about to be wholly clued in, either.

'Most of the answers will come after you die,' Sael told him as they descended.

'I'm hoping that means I'm not stuck down here for long,' said Erik, mind going back to Eliza.

The look on her face made him feel ill with worry.

Was she okay? Was she with Miles? How long until she went and got more drugs from either Adrian or Roger?

Erik wanted to vomit.

It made paying attention to the After a little difficult.

Until, that was, Sael said something which distracted him completely.

'Your mother will be thrilled to see you.'

Erik looked at him sharply. All other thought fled. 'I get to see her?'

'Of course,' said Sael. 'She's waiting for you.'

'Did you tell her?'

'I thought I would leave it a surprise. I do not meddle in affairs not my own.'

'Except my life.'

'Your childhood spell work is exactly what landed you in this mess,' said Sael with an air of chastisement that was so fatherly, Erik almost stopped short. 'Had you been at my side from the start, Logan would have gone on to atonement and no one would have been hurt.'

Erik glared at his back before following him. 'How was I supposed to know the spell would work? I was ten years old. And you weren't around to tell me it was a stupid idea.'

'I loved your mother the instant I laid eyes upon her. It was a mistake to fall in love with a human, but such is what happened. Had I known of you, I would have come for you. But the year after you were born, she did not come to the woods. Nor for many years thereafter. It was much later, long after Logan's abuse had taken its toll, that she returned to my woods. It was then that I learned about you. I told her to bring you the next time and I would care for you both. She was killed before that could happen.'

It was impossible to inhale, and for several wretched seconds Erik felt like he was going to choke to death. At last a breath forced its way through and he dragged ragged, wretched gasps into his lungs.

'I wish I had been able to be there for you,' said Sael. 'I wish so many things were different. I hope that we will be able to repair much of what was damaged.'

Erik gave him a tight smile. 'Did you break a rule? By being with my mother?'

'There are no rules,' said Sael. 'But it was unwise and unkind. She should not have been alone.'

'But she's happy now?'

'I try my hardest to ensure it.'

Erik marvelled at the strangeness of a ghost he'd known mere days showing him and his mother more love and devotion than Logan had shown them in all the years they were together.

A few minutes later, they came out in a place that looked like a palace yet was entirely carved out of earth. Natural, homey, serene.

Water fell from great crags in the walls above and flowers and vines and plants grew in abundance all over.

'It's like paradise,' he whispered in awe.

A smile curved Sael's mouth and he bowed his head, clearly proud of his home. 'We can hardly welcome souls in drab gloom,' he said. 'Dying is traumatic. We're here to make everything easier.'

Erik turned in a circle, taking it all in with wide-eyes. 'Or they become ghosts?' he asked after a beat.

'Our hospitality is not that powerful,' said Sael with a laugh. 'It's simple manners to have a welcoming court awaiting the dead. Come on.'

Sael led him to the other side of the great chamber where several figures – none of whom looked quite human, none of whom looked as ethereal as the ghosts he'd seen above – awaited them.

Erik stopped short as he met the gaze of one in particular.

'Ma?' It came out a small sound. Cracked and filled with heartache.

Stacey Stern looked the same as she had the day she died. At least, age wise. Unlike Sam and Paige, she wasn't wearing the clothes she'd died in.

Erik was beyond grateful for that.

There were no bruises on her skin, no tears in her eyes, no fear. She looked healthy and whole, and if he hadn't known her to be dead, he would have thought her reborn.

'Erik,' she said, a broad smile breaking out across her face. 'Welcome home.'

He ran to her and threw his arms around her. She even smelled the same, like lavender and honey, and he was suddenly eight years old and she was going to fix everything. That's what mothers did. They made all the horrors of the world seem conquerable.

'I missed you,' he mumbled, the sobs beginning to tear out of him. 'I missed you so much.'

She ran her hands over his back and said soothing words that he didn't quite register but which still somehow sent certainty and calm through him. Seeing her now was like stepping into a dream.

They broke apart after several minutes, wiping their eyes and smiling around their tears.

'You look so handsome,' she said, cradling his face. 'And so grown up.'

'I haven't changed that much,' he replied. He didn't want her to think she didn't know him. 'Still me.'

'Still perfect,' she said.

It wasn't true, but it was so motherly that something inside him cracked and he threw his arms around her again.

It was a long time before either was calm enough to step away. When he finally glanced at Sael, he saw that his father was no longer alone. Sam and Paige had arrived, and they were watching the reunion with empathetic smiles.

He walked over to them, his mother at his side.

Sam thumbed over her shoulder. 'Got a second?'

Erik nodded. Squeezing his mother's hand and promising to come back, he followed Sam out of the room and into the corridor.

The silence felt so heavy between them; so many years with so many unanswered questions, with so much trauma. It was hard to know where to start.

They stopped by a cascading waterfall and leaned against the railing.

'Are we underground?'

'I have no idea,' she said honestly.

He chuckled. 'Fair enough.'

'This is weird,' she said with an awkward smile. 'I've been wanting to talk to you for years. Properly, you know?'

He mulled that over as he tried to force down the lump in his throat. 'Did you wake up here straight away?'

'No.' Sam crossed her arms as she leaned back against the wall. 'I woke up on the mountains. For a long time, I couldn't leave. I'd sort of ... flicker. I wanted to stay, but I was supposed to leave. Being stubborn upsets the system.'

'You're right,' he said with a low, slightly hysterical laugh. 'This is weird.'

'I'm sorry, Erik.' She put a hand on his shoulder, remorse all over her face. 'I'm sorry I got it wrong.'

He shook his head vehemently. 'No, Sammy. Jesus. I would have thought the same. What I did? I can't ever make that right.'

'It's okay,' she said. 'I know you didn't mean to do it. It's okay.'

Tears filled Erik's eyes. 'Thanks.'

She held out a hand and he took it. 'Know what sucks the most?'

'What?'

'There's no ice cream for ghosts.'

A laugh tore out of him unbidden and he wiped his eyes.

'So,' he said, forcing his throat to clear. 'How's life down here? Any ladies for you?'

She giggled. 'Plenty. Ghostly gals abound. None for me, though.'

'No?'

'Nah. Now, come on,' she said, slinging an arm around his shoulders and steering him back to the hall. 'Let's figure out how to get your ass back upstairs so you can keep an eye on our girls.'

'I have more than one?'

'You've got a direct line to me now, little brother,' she teased. 'I want updates on Maya once you're back up there in the world of the living. I never could get far enough to tell her. And I couldn't master phones like Paige did.'

He nodded, a smile spreading across his face. 'I think I can do that.'

'Promise?'

'I swear.'

And so, Erik and Sam walked arm in arm back to the others, both filled with hope for outcomes they had never thought themselves lucky enough to fathom before.

Hope not just for a life after death, but for a love that was strong enough to endure it.

ONE YEAR LATER

CHAPTER FIFTEEN
Imitations of Dreams

It had been a particularly brisk autumn, and both Eliza and Miles were sneezing by the time the evening rolled in.

They'd been in the forest since the previous night. Miles was convinced he'd contract a disease from the wilderness and kept wiping off his hands with a look of deep disgust. But despite his discomfort, he refused to leave and never actually verbalised his complaints. Instead he was doing his utmost to brighten her mood.

Her bottle of sunshine. Who kept sneezing.

Eliza passed him the joint, hands shaking. She hopped in place to get warm. 'What if he doesn't show?'

'He's gonna show,' said Miles, although he looked equally as fretful. 'Screw this rain, though.'

'At least the snow left.'

'Ah yes, snow in October,' he drawled. 'I don't know what we did to deserve that.'

She couldn't disagree. The heat in the apartment had gone out and they'd slept in three layers for a week.

Before she could reply, something snapped to their left and Eliza and Miles whirled around.

'You two look like you've seen a ghost,' said Erik, a smile spreading across his face. He looked as handsome and bewitching as ever.

Eliza launched herself at him. They collided almost painfully, but she didn't care. For a few seconds, the ache of the year vanished as if it had never been.

It was only the loud cough from Miles that forced them to break apart.

Erik turned and yanked Miles into a fierce embrace. 'It's so good to see you, man.'

'It's good to see you too, brother,' said Miles, leaning back to appraise him properly. 'You look like death.'

A noise of exasperated affection left Erik and he clapped Miles on the cheek. 'That is an *awful* pun.'

'It's beautiful,' said Miles with affected pompousness. 'I'm very proud of that one.'

Erik ruffled his hair and winked. 'Well, you look like crap on toast.'

'*Sexy* crap on toast, man.'

A broad grin on his face, dark eyes bright with delight, Erik clapped him on the cheek before wrapping his arm around Eliza's shoulders and kissing the top of her head.

'So,' he prompted. 'Is there a plan? Or are we just camping? I've got three whole days off work. Aren't I lucky?'

'We thought we could go trick-or-treating.'

Erik stared at him. 'Please tell me you're kidding.'

'We thought you could go as a ghost,' said Miles with a straight face.

It took less than a second for Eliza to burst into giggles and give it all away.

Erik snorted and rolled his eyes. 'So, what is the plan?'

Miles beckoned them to follow him and set off into the darkening wood. 'So many plans, EJ!' he called over his shoulder.

'What did you have in mind?'

'We had an idea ...'

'Oh?' Erik glanced over at Eliza. 'What?'

Miles started walking backwards, drawing their attention once more. His face was alight with more joy and animation than Eliza had seen him display in a year and it was instantly infectious. 'We thought you two could get married,' he announced.

Erik's eyebrows shot up and he looked down at her. 'Really?'

'If you want?' she said with a small smile.

A look of joy spread across his face and he kissed her before replying. 'More than anything.'

'Excellent,' said Miles, clapping his hands together. 'To the ranch!'

'To the ranch!' they echoed.

The drive passed in a haze of loud music, laughter, hugs hampered by seats, and kisses on cheeks. All three more than in the mood to pretend the last year had not been slowly rotting all three from the inside with chronic worry for what was happening to the ones they couldn't reach.

When the trio reached Calico Ranch, Eliza saw that the barn had been decorated in fairy lights and lanterns.

The only ones there were those who knew everything. It felt right. A ceremony without secrets.

Eliza and Miles had considered inviting her parents and Gloria, but as all three thought Erik was away for the time being, it would be too complicated to try explaining everything. And, Eliza reasoned, when Erik was back at home properly, they could always have a second ceremony.

The lone outsider was Henry, who smiled broadly at them both when he concluded the ceremony. He didn't linger for the party and was just heading to his truck when Miles ran after him and presented him with a very old, very frayed looking book.

'Curses?' she guessed, holding tightly to Erik's hand.

'Yep,' he said with a rueful chuckle.

Miles jogged back over, a sheepish grin on his face. He held up both hands. 'No more dead people except you, man,' he said to Erik. 'I'm officially out of the ghost business.'

Erik kicked out at him and Miles danced away with a howl of laughter.

The group stayed awake until the break of day, and then Eliza drove Erik to Willow Lane. She'd been desperate to show him the progress. It wasn't yet liveable, but it was cosy.

'Miles and I have been fixing it up,' she told him as she led him up the steps and into the warm house. 'What do you think?'

'I think it's the best homecoming I could have imagined,' he told her.

She'd made a fort of sorts in the sitting room and they dropped onto the pile of blankets.

'Tell me what's new,' he said, pouring them each a glass of wine as Eliza set about rolling a joint.

She caught him up on the events at the ranch. Mitch was dating Isaac, their new vet, and he seemed overflowing with joy at all times.

'If I didn't love him, I'd punch him,' she added with a laugh. 'They're cute together, though.'

'And Maggie?'

'Off to college soon. She wants to be a lawyer.'

'She's definitely fierce enough.'

'Very true.'

They curled up against the pillows and Eliza tucked her head into the crook of his neck.

Erik's fingers traced absently over her arm. 'I was terrified you'd met someone,' he admitted, kissing the top of her head. 'I think I spent half the year sick with dread.'

'I know the feeling,' she whispered. She heaved a sigh. 'Have you learned to control Logan yet?'

He hesitated before shaking his head. 'It's harder than it looks … Although Paige chose to be reborn, so I'm no longer tied to her. But Sam wants to wait for Maya and your parents, so that one I have to learn. She's helping me, though.'

'She is?'

He nodded. 'We're actually friends. It's nice.'

Eliza grinned even as jealousy burned through her chest. 'I'm glad you guys have each other.'

'She's cool.'

'Yeah.' Eliza's fond smile at the news of Sam was somewhat tapered by her next question. 'And Logan?'

He scowled. 'Sael's helping me. He wants me free of Logan, too.'

'Then how are you here now?'

'Sael is keeping them under control until I return. He thought we could use the break.'

'What sort of atonement is there for someone like him?'

'It's complicated.'

Eliza mulled that over as she sipped at her wine. When she finished, she muttered, 'I suppose your last job came with secrets, too,' and stood, not wanting to look at him.

'Babe —'

'I just need a drink,' she said, trying not to sound upset and failing miserably.

In the kitchen, she set about making tea just to have something to do with her hands, her foot jiggling with mounting anxiety.

'Are you off the hard stuff?' he asked, coming up behind her and wrapping his arms around her stomach. 'I didn't want to bring it up, but I've spent so many nights sick with worry that I can't not ask before I have to go.'

'I'm trying,' she whispered. Trying didn't always mean succeeding, however.

Her dad had been sober and functional for months now and she made sure that whenever she saw her parents, she was smiling and laughing. Showing them how she wanted them to be. It was only when she got home to Miles, or showed up at Roger's, that she let the façade fall away. She tried to wake Miles up when it happened. He'd play cards or watch a movie with her until her thoughts stopped racing and she was able to breathe enough to sleep.

'Some days are harder than others,' she muttered.

He reached out and brushed a strand of hair behind her ear. 'Do you see Roger ever?'

'The odd time,' she admitted. She and Roger were almost friends, much to her amusement. He'd given up asking her out, but from time to time, he asked her how she was, a worried glint in his sly eyes, and she knew he was genuinely concerned.

She was also entirely certain Erik wouldn't find it amusing, but she figured she'd deal with that when he had more than three days out of the year to discuss it with him.

'He's seeing Beth,' she added, hoping it would make him feel slightly better. 'When we do talk, though, it's friendly. He's ... not a friend, but we're not antagonistic or anything.'

The kettle went off and Eliza poured them both cups of tea. The heady peppermint scent was instantly soothing.

He leaned back against the sink and appraised her. 'Will you really wait for me forever?'

She looked at him, slightly thrown. 'I didn't marry you just to change my mind.'

'Then why do you look so unhappy?'

'Because I am,' she replied. 'The two aren't mutually exclusive.'

'I'm getting better,' he said. 'I'll be home soon.'

'Promise?'

'I swear.'

And then he kissed her with unrestrained desperation, turning her in his arms and moving her against the counter. He hoisted her up and she wrapped her legs around his waist.

They spent that night together, unable to let go, unable to stop touching. But by midday the following day, Miles arrived with food and movies, and the three of them whiled away the hours in easy company. None of them brought up the lessening amount of time, none of them wanted to darken the mood. Miles' presence helped with that immensely.

On the third morning, the second day of November, Eliza woke up to see Erik sound asleep beside her. The morning light cast him in a soft glow and he looked as beautiful as always.

She left him in the bed and stepped outside. The morning air kissed her skin and she lit a joint and inhaled before pulling out her phone. There was a cheeky text from Miles and a question from Roger.

Same as always?

She typed, *Yeah*, and sent it with a sigh.

The door squeaked open behind her and a second later Erik sat down on the steps beside her.

'Hi,' he said, voice thick with sleep. He nudged her gently and kissed her shoulder. 'Wife.'

She blushed, only then able to stop dwelling on her unhappiness. 'Hi. Husband.'

They smiled at each other. For that one moment, just two fools in love.

'Tell me about the After,' she said when the silence had dragged on and both had looked away. 'Since you're leaving tonight.'

'What do you want to know?'

'Whatever you can tell me.'

Erik wrapped an arm around her and kissed her temple before speaking. 'Sael's like … like a steward of souls. Ones who have unfinished business remain in there until they're able to move on. Ones who need to atone go somewhere else. Somewhere he says I'm not ready to know about yet.'

'And the rest?'

'The rest go on,' said Erik. 'But it's their choice. Some have chosen to remain in the After. They're able to return to the world on All Hallowtide. Even if only to haunt it.'

Eliza smirked. 'Now I get where the legends come from.'

He nodded.

'And Sael? What is he?'

'He was once a ghost,' said Erik. 'He remained in the After for millennia and when the last overseer decided to move on, he took over. Now he's … I don't even know. He gets annoyed when I call him Reaper, though.'

She giggled. 'Is there more than one? After? Afters, as it were.'

He nodded thoughtfully. 'Dozens? Hundreds? Thousands?'

'You sound so certain,' she teased.

'Sael isn't really forthcoming. He tells me when he thinks I can "handle" it.' Erik made a face. 'He says I won't get most answers until I die.'

'Cheery.'

'That's what I said.'

'Is it weird?'

'What? Having a father?'

'Yeah.'

He let out a long breath. 'It's weird having *parents*. I'm twenty-five and for the first time, I'm answering to two. It's odd.'

'But you like it.' She could tell by the way he spoke. The way he carried himself. There was a light to Erik now that he had never possessed before.

He nodded slowly. 'If you were with me, it would be perfect.'

A heavy silence fell between them as they both felt the weight of the words he didn't say.

'How's Gloria?' he asked, clearly wanting to change the subject.

'She's good,' said Eliza. 'Dating again. Guy named Fred.'

'Is he nice?'

She nodded. 'He's respectful and dedicated. He makes her laugh. He's a doctor, actually. Treats her like a queen.'

A smile of relief spread across his face. 'Good. That's good.' He reached into his coat pocket and produced a letter. 'I wrote this for her. Just so she doesn't think I've abandoned her.'

'Don't worry, I tell her you ask after her when you call. Mostly because I wish you *could* call.'

'What do you say?'

'That you're lying low until things with Wyatt's thugs cool off.'

He scowled. 'She's going to think I'm in deep shit.'

Eliza took the letter. 'Then you'll have to come home soon and tell her.'

'Soon,' he echoed.

She cast about for something light-hearted. 'You know,' she said with a small, forced smile, 'Miles calls you Son of Death.'

A snort tore out of him. 'That's *awful.*'

'He also calls you Death's Bastard and Little Boy Reaper.'

Erik threw his head back in laughter and it was impossible not to giggle. One of the ways Eliza and Miles kept their spirits up was by entertaining themselves with amusing thoughts of what Erik might be up to.

'I miss that boy,' he said when he finally ceased laughing.

'He misses you.'

They spent the rest of the day avoiding the subjects which would cut them too deep to maintain the superficial joy they wanted so badly to last.

Eliza kept asking about Sam, to which Erik remained frustratingly uninformative. Until, that was, they returned to the forest that night.

There, in the clearing, was Sam.

'A belated birthday present,' he said in Eliza's ear. 'I can only hold her here for a couple of minutes before I have to go.'

A couple of minutes was far better than nothing. Eliza ran to her sister without a second thought and they embraced with the same fierceness they'd shown as children.

As cold as snow, Sam was still comforting. She smelled like pine needles and frost, and Eliza clutched her close for several wonderful moments.

When at last they broke apart, the first thing that left Eliza was, 'At least you don't smell dead.'

And then they both began laughing hysterically.

When they finally managed to stop, they sat cross-legged on the grass, their toes touching.

'I'm sorry I couldn't come before,' said Sam, twisting her still-pink hair in a knot. 'It's almost impossible to control. I'm only here now because of Erik.'

'And Roger?'

'Strong emotions make it easier.' Sam smiled tightly. 'They're also a little heightened. I may have been a bit overzealous.'

Eliza chuckled and shrugged. 'It taught him not to grab me.'

'Good.'

They grinned at each other.

'I'm sorry I didn't listen to you about Erik,' said Sam. She reached out and tucked a strand of loose hair back behind Eliza's ear.

Eliza shook her head. 'Don't be. That's what made you a good sister.'

'I tried.'

'You succeeded.'

But it was clear Sam was still upset and Eliza cast about for something else to say.

'Oh!' she cried a second later. 'I spoke to Maya.'

Tears filled Sam's eyes. 'How'd she look?'

'Hot.'

They both laughed.

'Is she okay?'

'I told her you're waiting.' Eliza's throat tightened as the tears fell from her sister's eyes. 'I think she's waiting, too.' She quickly relayed the rest of Maya's messages.

Sam took her hand when she finished and squeezed tightly. 'Thank you.'

'Of course.'

'And the 'rents?'

Eliza had to force her throat to clear before she could answer. 'Better than they were. Dad's been going to meetings and he's working again. I have dinner with them twice a week. It's taken a long time, but they're getting there.'

Sam rubbed her cheek roughly. 'I feel so bad.'

'Yes, I'm sure you meant to die,' said Eliza sardonically. 'It's not your fault.'

'I still feel bad.'

'Yeah. Me too.'

Sam reached out and pulled Eliza close. 'I really miss you, Elle.'

She didn't reply. She closed her eyes and tightened her grip on her sister. It was, without question, the best she had felt in years.

But it wasn't long before Eliza was bidding Sam farewell and walking back over to Erik.

He'd been leaning against a tree, gazing into the night and giving them time together.

When she reached his side and took his hands, the anguish on his dark face made her chest clench painfully.

'I love you,' he told her. 'Wife.'

'I love you, too. Husband.'

They smiled sadly at each other before he vanished into thin air.

'That's so weird,' she muttered.

The wind picked up as if in agreement and she turned towards the car. Even seeing Sam didn't quell the painful twisting in the pit of her stomach. Another year until she'd see him again.

When she was in the car, she turned it on, but didn't move, her fingers tapping with anxious energy on the wheel.

She pulled her phone out of her pocket and checked the notifications. One message from Miles, one from Roger. Both asking the same question.

You coming over?

After a moment's silent debate, she drove down the road.

FOUR YEARS LATER

CHAPTER SIXTEEN
It's Not

Smoke curled off the tip of Eliza's cigarette in delicate grey furls that danced on the air before disappearing. She'd been watching the smoke curl and dip for so long her eyes had started to ache.

Blinking slowly, she ran a hand through her hair and squeezed at the roots.

It was her twenty-ninth birthday and she couldn't feel like celebrating less. Another year, another birthday without Erik.

She tapped off the end and swallowed hard.

There was a knock at the door and she left the cigarette in the ashtray to answer it. To her surprise, her parents stood in the doorway. They both looked good, if a little tired, and their smiles now reached their eyes.

One of the few bright spots in Eliza's life was seeing her parents. Ten years since Sam's death and they finally seemed to have snapped back to themselves. Her father had been sober for almost five years with only two lapses, and he was working consistently. Her mother smiled again, laughed again. They were leaving in a month's time. Travelling to all the places they'd dreamed of seeing. All the places they used to tell Eliza and Sam about.

'We have a surprise,' said her father, holding out his hand. 'Come on, birthday girl.'

She grimaced. 'I'm not —'

'Get your coat, Elle,' said Mira, tone brokering no room for argument.

With a heavy sigh, Eliza grabbed her coat off the hook and followed them out into the blustery night. It was far from spring time and the wind was still biting.

'Where are we going?'

'It's a surprise,' said Ryan again.

'I hate surprises.'

'Get over it.'

She snorted. All she wanted to do was sleep. They had been repainting the barn all week and she was exhausted and in no mood to celebrate. Miles had gone out for pizza and cake and would be back soon. They'd planned to celebrate her birthday the same way they did every year: quietly, without mention of Erik.

Her parents said nothing on the drive and Eliza watched the trees flash past.

A sign caught her eye and she frowned. 'Are we going to Willow Lane?' she asked.

'Possibly,' said Ryan.

Eliza's stomach tightened. 'I really don't want to.'

'Too bad.'

He flashed her a grin before turning back to face the road. After another minute, he drove left down a small path and the house came into view.

There were lights on inside when they pulled up. Leaves had been swept off the porch and someone had put plants by the door.

Eliza glanced at her parents with raised eyebrows. 'Did you guys really deck out the house? Why?'

Ryan turned in his seat and glared at her in exasperation. 'Do you have any concept of a surprise, Elle? Get out and go look.'

'If it's a clown, I'm going to kill you,' she muttered, opening the door and stepping out into the cold night.

She was halfway up the steps when the door opened.

She stopped dead.

Erik's hands were tucked into his pockets, his hair brushed back from his sharp features. He held himself with a calm assuredness she'd never known him to possess.

'Happy birthday,' he said.

She stared at him, immobile. 'It's not Halloween.'

'No,' he agreed with a smile that lit up his entire face. 'It's not.'

finis